From A To Z

CASTRO BOOK 2

From A To Z

Sherryl D. Hancock

P R E S S

Published by Vulpine Press in the United Kingdom in 2024

Cover photo: Sharon and Michele Bettega

ISBN: 978-1-83919-675-1

www.vulpine-press.com

Thank you to Sharon and Michele Bettega for the use of their picture of the Castro theater for this cover. Love you both!

Prologue

February 23, 2006

Sitting amongst her family and friends, Amy Calvert did her best to drink in everything. Her brothers, all six of them were engaged in various antics with several girls. The Calvert boys were flirts, everyone knew that! Looking over to her father, Robert, Amy could see he was chatting with Jenny Slattery. Inside she winced. Their mother had been dead for a year. Was he really ready to move on already? It didn't matter. After tonight nothing would matter, because she'd be gone, and she was betting every last dime of her savings that she'd never be welcome here again. The thought made her sad.

She glanced at the pictures on the walls of her and her brothers throughout the years. A picture from when she was six. There were her five brothers' faces smiling back at her, the twins Bobby and Carl, Danny and Eric, and Frankie but George hadn't been born yet. All of them grouped in their Navy shirts that Dad had gotten them. Amy smiled; they'd been playing battleship with their bikes in the street in front of the house. Mom had found it endearing that the five of them loved playing together so much. Amy remembered those carefree days with affection. She remembered when the boys would strip off their shirts because of the late summer heat in Lewiston, New York and she would do the same. No one said anything, she was a little girl, no one

1

cared then. Nobody noticed that she wanted her hair short, like the boys had theirs. Of course, her cut was a 'cute little pixie cut' but it looked the same as the boys' hair. Amy didn't know the difference. She never knew what a 'tomboy' was, but she knew she could climb trees better than any of the boys and she could hit any baseball thrown toward her in a game.

She'd played, ran, rode bikes, swam in the river down the street from their house, most of the time without a shirt on, other times with a T-shirt with the arms cut off just like her brothers. And then it all changed... When she was just about to turn twelve, she noticed she was starting to ache in her chest area. She complained to her mother about it. Suddenly, her mother, Jean Calvert, who had always encouraged her to have fun and live life her way, was wary. That same night there was a hushed conversation with Robert, and the next day Amy and her mother went to the Kmart in town. Her mother made her try on bras, and then there was 'the talk.' It wasn't a talk about sex, it was a discussion about 'becoming a woman' and no longer being a 'child.'

It scared the living hell out of Amy! It was the strangest day ever.

The next day, Amy and the boys were set to play a game of baseball against the kids down the street. She took extra time that morning to oil her baseball glove, to ensure it was ready for the game where she had every intent

ion of clobbering the other team. When she heard her mom call to her that breakfast was ready, she rushed downstairs in her usual jean shorts and T-shirt. Sitting down at the table, she dug into the pancakes and bacon. It took her by surprise that her mother had made so few, clearly the boys were gonna starve! Too bad, they were slow to come down to breakfast, she was going to eat up while she had the chance. She was surprised when her mother sat down at the table, wiping her hands on her apron. Her mother perched primly with her legs crossed and smoothed out her apron. Jean had watched her daughter eat, and made a mental note to talk to her about eating more delicately, like a lady.

"Where are the boys?" Amy mumbled through a mouthful of food, as she glanced around wondering why it was taking them so long to come to breakfast. Usually, they were ravenous beasts first thing.

"Don't talk with your mouth full, ladybug," Jean admonished. "And your brothers have already left the house."

"What!" Amy exclaimed as she stood up, stuffing the last few bites in her mouth, even as she reached for her glove laying on the chair next to her. "I gotta go, Mom!" she practically shouted.

Jean's hand on her arm stopped her. "Honey, you can't play with the boys like that anymore," Jean told her calmy, her voice soft.

"What?" Amy was dumbfounded. "Why not?"

Jean shifted in her seat, giving Amy a 'we have had this conversation' stare.

"Amy Jean, you are becoming a woman, and women do not play with boys like that…wearing this." Jean gestured to the armless T-shirt and jean shorts, surveying the beat-up tennis shoes Amy wore without socks. "Where is the pretty little bra we bought you?" she added.

Amy looked back at her mother, then looked down at the table, banging her feet together underneath it in agitation. "It is in the bag in my closet," she answered dispassionately. "It's itchy!" She shrugged in annoyance, slouching down in her chair.

"Well, you're going to find that sometimes being a lady is a bit uncomfortable." Jean sighed, having no idea that what she was saying was so alarming to her daughter.

"Then I don't wanna be one!" Amy exclaimed, jumping to her feet and running out of the room. Her legs pumped as she ran back upstairs to her bedroom, slamming the door and throwing her baseball mitt across the room.

It was just the beginning, and 'uncomfortable' didn't even begin to describe the following years. Being banned from playing with the boys was just the tip of the iceberg of womanhood. Dresses, with frilly socks, and patent leather Mary Janes, and that abominable itchy bra, and 'pretty' panties! Some days she refused to leave her room because she absolutely hated her new clothes.

One day she ventured out of her room, hearing that the television was on downstairs. She made her way down and watched the old musical on TV. Her mother was taking one of her rare breaks from housework, and was watching Ginger Rogers and Fred Astaire dancing in what she'd later find out was Swing Time. She was fascinated by the steps, and also by the costumes the characters wore. When her mother noticed her standing in the doorway, she motioned for her to come and join her. They spent a nice afternoon watching the musical and it was in this moment Amy discovered her fascination for old movies, and a love for them was born.

It was through her mother she discovered musicals like Shall We Dance, Singing in the Rain, The Gay Divorcee, and Ginger Rogers...

One weekend, her father was watching old war movies, and she got her first glimpse at Casablanca and not only Humphrey Bogart, *but Ingrid Bergman! Suddenly, she couldn't get enough of old movies and rented every single one she could find from the local video store. She would watch them over and over again. It was her escape, and little did she know, she was falling in love.*

She fell in love with the actions of the characters, like Rhett Butler from Gone with the Wind, *Rick Blaine from* Casablanca *and Captain Mallory from the* Guns of Navarone. *What she didn't realize was that she was also captivated with the leading ladies. Vivien Leigh, Ginger Rogers, and Rita Hayworth all drew her in. She was fascinated by the language and the gentility, the gallant actions of the men, and their simple black-and-white thinking.*

Not long after that first year into puberty, Amy figured out that she wanted to best the boys at everything, including getting the girl. Not that she was able to do anything about that outwardly, of course. Being the daughter of a retired Navy man, even if he'd only been a clerk by the time he retired, there was no way her father would accept his daughter being anything other than the picture of a little lady. So, she faked it, up until her eighteenth birthday.

Amy peered over at her father and brothers, happily eating cake; she knew she was going to break their hearts the very next morning. Her family had no idea that the very next day she'd gone down to the Naval recruiting office and signed up. She had marveled at her luck as she was told she would be shipped out to boot camp later that week.

As she brushed her long dark blonde hair back with one hand, she reached into the pocket of the sweater she wore over her dress with her other hand. She touched the envelope concealed there, knowing she was chickening out by leaving them a note, but she couldn't face them, she just couldn't. She wanted to tell them her other secret, but she had a feeling that her father would let the military know that she'd admitted to being gay. 'With Don't Ask, Don't Tell' in place, she knew she couldn't take that chance.

The note read: *You'll be surprised to know that yesterday I joined the Navy. I leave for boot camp on Friday. I love you all, but I need to be on my own. Amy.*

It was a new beginning.

***

April 3, 2023

The first thing Jaims noticed as Raquel came up the jet way was that her friend looked gaunt, tired, and her eyes were a bit glassy. Jaims smiled and walked to meet her, reaching out to hug her.

"It's good to see you," Jaims said smiling as she hugged Raquel.

"Yeah, yeah, don't get all mushy and stuff," Raquel said gruffly, shoving Jaims back slightly with a grin.

"I see your personality wasn't affected," Jaims said, grinning even as she turned to lead Raquel toward the baggage claim. "Still an ass."

"Fuck you," Raquel replied, a standard comment from her.

"Not today," Jaims shot back.

It was something they always said to each other. Jaims was marveling at the fact that three months after being shot in the head and almost dying, Raquel was back to her old self and finally home!

On the drive back to their apartment, Raquel looked over at Jaims. "So did you take care of that stuff I asked you to?"

Jaims rolled her eyes. "Yes, I did the entire list."

"Including getting my Jeep tuned?" Raquel asked, arching an eyebrow at her friend and roommate.

"I said the entire list, Rock, sheesh!"

Raquel nodded, looking satisfied with that answer. Jaims just shook her head, her roommate could be a pain in the ass sometimes.

It was another couple of minutes and lots of traffic later when Raquel spoke up again.

"You haven't been letting anyone sleep in my bed, have you?"

Jaims laughed. "Well, actually we've been having orgies in there, but don't worry I changed the sheets..."

"Asshole," Raquel replied simply.

"Jerk."

Jaims' phone began ringing then and she answered it on the hands free, grimacing as she did, and seeing that it was Zion.

"Hey Z, what's up?" Jaims asked, trying to sound unconcerned.

There was silence on the other end of the line for a long moment, prompting Jaims to query. "Z?"

"Yeah, hey," Zion said, her voice uncharacteristically quiet.

Jaims grimaced again. "You okay, Z?"

"I...yeah..." Zion stammered. "I guess I just...Where are you?"

Jaims glanced over at Raquel and saw that she was practically glowering.

"I just picked Rock up from the airport."

Again there was silence for a long moment. "That was to-day?"

"Yeah, Z, that was today. Look, do you want me to come by after I get Rock settled?"

"Nah, nah, it's okay," Zion answered far too quickly.

"Okay I'm gonna come by," Jaims replied, as if Zion hadn't just said no.

"Okay," Zion said simply.

A few moments later they hung up.

"What's up with that?" Raquel asked, her tone snide.

"Fancy's back in town, you know how it is," Jaims re-plied, surprised by Raquel's tone.

"So why ain't she callin' D?"

"Because D's out of town for a bit, so I'm kinda helpin' out," Jaims said, hoping that would be the end of it.

"So what, you're like Z's best friend now?" Raquel snapped, sounding really irritated by the idea.

Jaims forced herself to take a deep breath and blow it out to calm her annoyance at Raquel's attitude.

"No," she said calmly. "Like I said, I'm just helping out. You know how Z gets when Fancy's around."

Raquel's lips twitch, and Jaims could tell she wanted to say something else, but she obviously thought better of it and changed the subject.

"So how many girls do you have on the line these days?" Raquel asked, her voice overly bright as if to make up for her previous antagonistic tone.

Jaims grinned. "Some."

"Uh-huh," Raquel murmured, her own grin starting. "Which means at least ten."

Jaims laughed out loud at that, shaking her head. "Nah, I'm just having fun at this point."

"You say fun, I say whoring…" Raquel intoned.

Jaims chuckled again, shaking her head. "Not that bad, geeze!"

They were both silent for a bit. Jaims' music was on and her fingers were tapping to her usual club music.

"Still listen to this shit, huh?" Raquel asked, grinning.

"Yep," Jaims replied, knowing Raquel was trying to get things back on an even keel.

"So where's D?" Raquel asked then, keeping her tone light.

"In Sacramento right now."

"What the fuck for?" Raquel asked, sounding disgusted by the very notion.

"Well, her new girlfriend got a contract there, so D's flying with a Cal Fire team there."

"New girlfriend, huh? Already?"

"Yep, hotter than hell and smart too."

"TJ been strung up yet?" Raquel asked, her tone darkening. Jaims had told her about TJ's betrayal.

Jaims blew her breath out in a snort. "Nah, you know D, she just moved on."

Raquel curled her lips in annoyance. "Yeah, she's better at that kind of thing than I'd be. I would have taken TJ's fucking head off."

Jaims grinned. "Yeah, we wanted to, trust me."

"How's everyone else?"

"BB's dad had a heart attack, but he's okay now. The good thing was that BB went home and actually made nice with her family for a bit."

"She shouldn't have had to," Raquel said her tone annoyed again.

"No, but it is what it is," Jaims said, not wanting to argue with Raquel. She knew it always pissed Raquel off when a family wasn't

9

supportive of their child's life choices. "BB does have a girlfriend now though," she added, hoping to divert Raquel onto better topics.

"How'd that happen? BB trip over the girl or something?" Raquel asked, knowing that Jayden was extremely shy.

Jaims chuckled. "Actually I introduced them. The girl works in the same department as me."

"Is she ugly?"

"No, she's a cute little blonde."

"And why didn't you go after her?" Raquel asked, an odd light in her eyes.

Jaims shrugged. "I like her, don't get me wrong, but she and BB hit it off so well that I figured the kid could use a shot at it, and she's done pretty good for herself."

Raquel gave Jaims a sidelong look. "You're givin' up women to help the kid out now?"

"It's not like that," Jaims said, rolling her eyes. "It worked out good. Better not to date people you work with anyway. Right?"

"If you say so," Raquel said, shaking her head and rolling her eyes.

"Shaddup!" Jaims said, shoving at Raquel's shoulder. She immediately saw Raquel wince. "Shit, I'm sorry, are you okay?"

Raquel closed her eyes for a few moments. "Yeah… I just have a headache from the damned flight. All that pressure and shit."

Raquel reached into her jacket pocket and pulled out a bottle of pills. She popped one into her mouth then put the bottle back.

"What're those?" Jaims asked.

"Just oxy."

"Do they help?"

"They keep me high as a kite, so yeah, they help," Raquel said, an edge to her voice.

Jaims looked over at her friend and saw the closed look on her face. It worried her. Raquel was all about natural stuff going into her body, and now, suddenly, she was being flippant about painkillers? Jaims made a mental note to find out all she could about Oxycodone and its effects. She just hoped that it was the plane ride that had caused the headache, and that it wasn't a problem.

Little did Jaims know, Raquel had popped two pills prior to landing, and a number of them during her sixteen plus hour flight. Raquel knew in the smallest part of her that she didn't want to look at, that she was addicted, but she refused to face that fact. She was home now, everything was going to be okay. She wanted it that way and that's how it was going to be. Period.

Chapter 1

At 3:30 a.m. Zion Calvert crawled into bed. Although she'd had many offers of *company* for the night, she lay in bed alone staring up at the ceiling. Her club, Fancy's, was doing incredible business lately. The new influx of clientele was due to the closing of another club in the Castro, another primarily lesbian bar that had dominated the scene for years. Fancy's had started out as a bar with a small dance floor, and it was named simply Z's. Over the first three years in business, Zion had managed to acquire more space and had expanded into a night club, that was when she'd acquired a *silent partner*. Slowly but surely her business had climbed, even as her personal life had gone to hell, thanks to that same partner.

When The G Bar, the other lesbian bar, had closed three months before, everyone had been surprised. Sadly, everyone knew the couple that owned it had broken up and the bar was sold from the result of their divorce. The new owner had decided to go a different direction wanting to cater more toward gay men in the Castro and had drastically changed the club to reflect the change. It wasn't something the lesbians in the Castro were interested in and had therefore started checking out Fancy's.

Now Zion was facing the need to expand yet again. She'd heard one night that the bookstore next door was closing its doors. It was her intent to talk to the owner about buying him out so she would own the entire building. She was fairly sure she could swing the money, but there was the nagging worry in the back of her mind; would her business partner show up to throw a wrench in the works, like she liked to do on occasion.

Grimacing up at the ceiling, Zion did her best not to think about Fancy. It didn't work, memories of the beautiful blonde slid through her brain like an insidious snake.

"So, you come here often?" the beautiful blonde with the ruby red lips asked coyly.

"Does that line actually work?" Zion asked, giving her a pointed look as she waited for the woman's drink order.

"No," the blonde said laughing, "but I figured I had to say something to get your attention."

"I'm sure you get attention wherever you go," Zion stated flatly. The woman was beyond hot, but she didn't want to be too easy.

"What can I get you?" Zion asked, her cornflower-blue eyes direct.

Jane Farro looked over at the handsome butch bartender, wondering at her lack of interest. Usually, the butches reacted to her overt sexuality, like dogs in heat. Her look oozed sexuality. With her long, tanned, toned legs on full display in the long white dress slit up to almost the top of her thigh, her feet clad in four-inch red stiletto pumps. Her makeup was perfect as always, understated but with enough sparkle to light her sweetheart-shaped face, even in the dim lighting at the bar.

"White wine," Jane answered, her brown eyes framed by long sooty black lashes, watching the bartender move.

The bartender was tall, Jane figured she was at least five ten. She had dark hair. It was short on the sides and worn back from her face. Her hair had a long section at the top that was bleach blonde. It gave her a sexy kind of wild look. Her face was quite handsome with a strong jawline, and a nicely shaped mouth and dark eyebrows. She was also dressed nicely, with a long-sleeved, white button-up shirt, dark navy-blue trousers and a matching vest with a red and navy tie at her throat. She also wore a thick black leather cuff on one arm and a thick silver watch with a navy face on the other. The bartender was definitely stylish in a sexy way that Jane found she couldn't stop watching.

"So, what's your name?" Jane asked as the bartender set the wine glass up on the bar, lifting the bottle of wine and uncorking it. Holding the base of the glass with two fingers, she poured the wine, looking back at Jane.

"Zion," she said simply, setting the glass of wine on a napkin. "That's seven," she said with a wink.

Jane smiled, taking out her credit card. "Can you run a tab for me, Zion?" she asked, her red lips parting in a seductive smile.

"I can," Zion said, inclining her head and picking up Jane's credit card. She ran it and handed it back to her. With that she moved off to help someone else.

Jane continued to watch Zion from her spot at the bar; she saw how she smiled and leaned across the bar to kiss certain women that came in. At one point, a small group of butch women walked up to them, and Jane heard one call the bartender "Z." Zion reached her *hand out, clasping her hands with one of the butches, putting her other hand over their clenched hands as she smiled warmly. It was obvious that Zion knew the group.*

A little while later, Zion was relieved by another bartender and Jane couldn't help but notice that Zion seemed quite popular. A lot of women seemed to hover around her, and all the ones that hung around her were femmes. There were a lot of hugs and kisses exchanged, both on the cheek and lips. Zion seemed to know everyone...

One of the butches that Zion had greeted at the bar approached them, ordering a drink from the bartender now on duty. She was good looking with short dark hair, worn just slightly longer at the top. Her arms were adorned with tattoos that all seemed aviation related. She could distinctly make out a jet and one that said Top Gun.

"Heya Zip," the butch woman said, nodding to the bartender, "can I get a Hefeweizen for Z and a Corona?"

"You got it, D," Zip said, smiling brightly at the woman.

The woman Zip had called "D" glanced at Jane, her lips curling in a grin as she inclined her head acknowledging Jane's presence.

"How's it going?" Jane asked smiling, her tone friendly.

"It's going," the woman responded, nodding. "How's your night?"

"It could be better," Jane replied, sighing, "the cute bartender apparently got off her shift..." Her voice trailed off as she smiled again.

"Who? Z?" the butch woman asked, her lips curling in a more sardonic grin this time. "She is the owner, not the bartender, Zip was late tonight."

Before Jane could respond, Zip appeared with the beers. The woman tossed a twenty on the bar. "Thanks, Zip." She looked at Jane again, nodding as she picked up the beers and walked away.

15

Jane watched her go, thinking it made more sense that Zion was the owner of the bar, with the way she dressed and her smooth way with her customers. This information had Jane watching Zion more closely that night.

Rubbing her face with her hands, Zion did her best to push aside her memories and get some sleep. In the end, she gave up and got up, grabbing her laptop and turning it on. She spent the rest of the night running numbers to calculate her financial needs, versus what she had to spare at the moment. She finally fell asleep as dawn was breaking.

***

Jaims woke to the sound of cabinets being slammed in the kitchen. The noise continued long enough for her to decide to get out of bed and see what was going on. Walking into the kitchen, she saw Raquel opening drawers, shoving things aside looking for something, then slamming the drawer when it became apparent she didn't find whatever she was looking for.

"Dude! What are you looking for?" Jaims had to practically shout over the sound of items falling out of the drawers and hitting the floor.

"My fucking keys!" Raquel exclaimed.

Jaims closed her eyes slowly as she shook her head. Turning around she went into her room, picking up a set of keys from her dresser. Walking back into the kitchen, she leaned against the doorjamb, and whistled to get her roommate's attention, holding the keys dangling from her finger.

Raquel snapped her head around, her eyes widening, then narrowing when she saw the keys.

"What the fuck, man!" Rock snapped as she snatched the keys away from Jaims.

"How else was I going to get all the shit done on your Jeep?" Jaims glowered.

Raquel grumbled as she sat down, tossing the keys on the table in front of her. Jaims watched her friend for a long moment, then shook her head, turning to go back to bed. She had no idea what was up Rock's ass this morning, but she was in no mood to deal with it.

In the kitchen, Raquel got up to make coffee, she had to tamper down her irritation that her roommate had kept her keys. As she put coffee in the machine, her subconscious told her she was being unreasonable; after all Jaims had taken care of things for her, in order for her to come home. Her lips twitched as she did her best to let go of the anger, her head hurt, damn it! Why were her meds not working like they were supposed to?

As her coffee brewed, she took out her pill bottle and popped another. *This one had better work!* she thought angrily.

***

The heat was so oppressive, Jack felt it sticking to everything, his clothes, his rifle, his hair! The cool water of the river was so inviting, but they were marching, no time to stop for a dip.

The lieutenant said they were looking for a way to cross. The Confederate troops were certainly nearby, Jack could hear the sounds of cannon fire in the distance. He shuddered inwardly, is that how he'd die? By cannon fire? He thought that volunteering to fight the Confederates would bring him glory, but so far it had only brought him heartache and exhaustion. His friend Will had died at the Battle of South Mountain a couple of days before. Now they were marching to claim a bridge, and Jack was certain it was his turn. He'd had a feeling for days now.

"Watch your flank!" screamed one man to his left, as bullets started to fly.

They were at the bridge, the one General Burnside had sent them to protect, but the Confederates were everywhere! Even so, they were charging down the hill, trying to take the bridge. Men were falling in front of him, Jack did his best to skirt around them. He was fast approaching the bridge with members of his brigade. There were screams and yelling as men were hit and went down. Jack slipped in blood on the hill at the bottom, but then ran headlong toward the bridge, doing his best to keep his head down.

He was surprised when a bullet struck him in the chest. Feeling a burning heat and pain. He felt himself stumble, grabbing at his chest, as if to take the bullet out. He realized that it was too late, that he was now on the bridge. Jack felt himself falling into the water. I'll drown, *he thought, just as his body hit the water. The water cooled the pain in his chest for a moment, then it returned, and he felt himself sinking further into the water. He struggled to swim up to breach the surface.* I'm running out of air! *came the panicked thought,* I can't breathe!

***

Morgan Collins woke with a start. Rubbing her eyes she sat up, trying desperately to catch her breath. *I can't breathe!* The thought screamed through her head. She felt the searing pain in her chest, still feeling the panic he felt. She sat rocking back and forth on the couch, trying her best to calm herself.

"I don't like this," she told the therapist with a shake of her head, her long red curls bouncing around her shoulders.

The woman sitting across from her nodded her head, looking circumspect. "But you did just see something, didn't you?"

Morgan looked over at her therapist, knowing that the woman already knew the answer, but nodding anyway. Closing her eyes, she could see the tall grass in the meadow, and smell the acrid smell of gun powder mixed with blood. She could hear the echoes of screams from men as they fell, likely to their death, the sound of gunfire bouncing off the trees. It was awful!

"Tell me what you saw," Charlotte Thompson prompted, her pen poised to take notes.

Morgan recounted what she'd seen and felt, and Charlotte dutifully wrote down notes. It was a long day.

At home, Morgan sat down with a glass of wine, her laptop in front of her. She did her best to work on her latest novel, but the words just wouldn't come. She sighed, picking up her wine, walking out onto the small terrace of her condo. She stood staring out at the ocean, letting the ocean breeze calm her mind.

Her writer's block was becoming a concern; if she couldn't write anymore, what would she do? It wasn't that she made millions writing her romance novels, but she did make enough to afford this nice condo in Pacifica, just south of San Francisco. How long would that last if she couldn't write? She felt like she was at a dead end, and it was terrifying.

***

"What's going on with Rock?" Zion asked Jaims.

Raquel had just snapped at one of the bartenders for giving her the wrong beer. Usually everyone on the crew was very respectful of the staff at Fancy's.

Jaims shook her head, shrugging. "She says she has a headache."

Zion shrugged. "Makes sense."

"Yeah..." Jaims nodded, thinking of the scene in the apartment earlier that evening.

Once again Raquel had been angry and throwing things.

"What the fuck, dude?" Jaims had asked, walking into the living room, in complete disarray.

"Can't find my fucking keys again!" Raquel raged.

Jaims had blown out a breath, shaking her head as she pitched in to search. It had taken another ten minutes before Jaims finally walked into Raquel's room, finding the keys sitting on the other woman's dresser, plain as day. Raquel had accused her of fucking with her, and had stayed mad all the way to the bar. It seemed to be Raquel's new normal. Jaims wondered if the bullet that had struck her friend in the head months before had altered her personality permanently.

* * *

As he awoke, the room came into focus; it was unfamiliar. Moving to sit up, the pain in his chest screamed through him, making him lay back with a wince. That is when he remembered, he had been shot! He remembered falling into the river, being breathless...he remembered nothing after everything went black.

Hearing a door open behind him, Jack tried to look, but it sent another ripple of pain through his chest. He smelled the scent of lavender.

"Hello?" he croaked, his voice barely a whisper.

"You're awake!" a woman's voice exclaimed, sounding shocked.

"Yes, ma'am," Jack replied.

From his right, a woman came into view and he looked up. He was surprised by her bright blue eyes; they reminded him of the cornflowers he'd seen in a vast field in Maine once. Her hair was dark and pulled back from her sweetheart-shaped face. She was probably the prettiest woman he'd ever seen, and for a moment he was dumbstruck. Even when she sat down in the chair next to where he lay, her eyes sweeping over him as she did, he couldn't seem to find his tongue.

"How are you feeling?" the woman asked solicitously.

"I...um, I think I'm okay," Jack stammered.

She nodded, smiling at him. "You will need to lie still for a bit, the doctor had a hard time getting that bullet out. I'm afraid you're going to have a scar."

"A scar?" he squeaked in surprise. "How am I even alive?"

The woman pressed her lips together, as her eyes sparkled in subdued pride. "I was picking flowers along the riverbank, I found you. My pa helped me bring you to the doctor."

Jack blinked a few times, unable to believe his good fortune. "I was sure I was a gonner."

"Nope." She shook her head. "I'm Amelia, by the by."

"I'm Jack."

"Where are you from, Jack?" Amelia's tone was casual, but Jack read more into it.

"I'm with the Union," he told her proudly.

Her smile was patient this time. "Your uniform gave that away."

"Oh." He blushed. "I'm from New York."

"Well, I am pleased to meet you, Jack from New York." She put her delicate hand out to pat his hand gently. "You rest now. I'll bring you some food soon."

"Thank you, Amelia," Jack said softly. After she left the room, Jack wondered at his luck. To not only be saved, but to be saved by such a beauty!" He sighed, smelling the lingering scent of lavender that seemed to hang in the room, it comforted him.

Morgan woke from the hypnosis with the scent of lavender still in her nostrils. She shook her head, to try and clear it of the visions that still swam through her mind.

Once again Charlotte waited for her to tell her all about what she'd seen. Morgan blew out a breath and began to tell the other woman about the experience. When she was finished, she made a face as she got up off the couch.

"I'm not sure this is worth the trouble," she grouched.

Charlotte made a clicking sound with her tongue. "You said you wanted to get in touch with the faces that were haunting you."

"I know," Morgan snapped. "But it's moving so slowly, I don't know that it is doing any good."

"You have to trust in the process!" Charlotte told her. "If it's moving slow, it's probably because you need to learn something."

Morgan twitched her lips, feeling uncertain she believed that. The fact of the matter was, she had initiated this process, so she needed to try and see it through. It had all started when she had begun having dreams, but the dreams weren't about her, they were about different people, and different times, times she knew very little about.

She had contacted Charlotte who was a renowned hypnotist that claimed she could get her in touch with her past lives. Well, it had worked so far, but she hadn't figured out why these past lives were surfacing in her dreams. It was driving her a little stir crazy!

Chapter 2

"What are you doing?" Jessie asked.

Morgan jumped, not realizing that her longtime friend had let herself into the condo. "Jesus! Don't do that!" she yelled.

Jessie shrugged, leaning her hips on the kitchen counter, gesturing to the mess all around them. Containers, vegetables, pans, packages of food lay strewn on every available surface in the small kitchen.

Morgan sighed from her spot on the floor in front of the refrigerator. "I was making some tea."

Jessie blinked a couple of times, then snorted. "I'm sure that made sense to you, but to those of us not stuck in your head…"

Morgan blew out her breath in exasperation again. "I was making tea, and when I went into the cabinet to get the teabag, I saw that my pantry was a mess, so I started pulling stuff out. Which lead to rearranging the pots, thinking I needed to order a nice pot rack for the island. But then I got into the fridge to get out the cream for my tea that was now cold and I noticed that I'd spilled cream on the shelf, so I started cleaning that…and that led to cleaning out the fridge…" Morgan's voice trailed off as she sat back on her heels, blowing a stray red curl of hair her face.

Jessie pressed her lips together, widening her eyes. "Let me guess, you were trying to work on your latest book."

Morgan curled up her lips in self-disgust. "Yes!"

"And you're still blocked."

"You know…" Morgan said threateningly.

Jessie held up her hands in immediate surrender. "I'm just pointing out the obvious."

Morgan shook her head mournfully. "I suck! I'm never going to be able to write again!" She took off the gloves she'd been wearing to scrub the refrigerator shelves, tossing them aside and scrubbed at her face.

"Well, that's going to depress your publisher," Jessie quipped.

Morgan narrowed her eyes. "You're not helping."

Jessie smiled brightly. "Hey, I hooked you up with that therapist, that was me helping. How's that going, by the way?"

"Hand me those vegetables," Morgan told her.

"Is that how it's going?"

"No smart arse, but I need to put my kitchen back together, and you just volunteered to help me!"

An hour later, the kitchen was back together, and Jessie and Morgan were sipping tea on the couch.

"It's going alright," Morgan was telling her friend. "It seems that I was a soldier at the battle of Antietam."

"Wow, really?" Jessie exclaimed.

Morgan nodded. "He was shot."

"He?"

"Yes, I was a boy," Morgan mused.

"Did you die?" Jessie asked in subdued voice.

"I was rescued by a woman. She had the most beautiful eyes…" Morgan remembered.

Jessie grinned. "Did ya make whoopie with her?"

"For goodness' sake!" Morgan rolled her eyes, but then grimaced out of embarrassment.

He breathed in the lovely scent of lavender; she was so close as she gave him a sponge bath. His healing had been slow, but steady. Amelia had been taking excellent care of him. They talked while she tended to his needs.

"You were telling me why you volunteered," Amelia reminded him.

Jack shrugged, grimacing as the gesture tugged at a stich in his chest. "We had slaves, my father was against the war, he thought people should be free to own slaves." Jack curled his mouth in disgust at the idea. "I didn't like seeing people treated like that, so I snuck off and joined the Union Army."

Amelia looked impressed. "That was very brave of you."

"I had to do something."

"How long have you been with the Union?"

"Almost a year now," Jack replied. "I guess I will need to join back up with my unit after I get better."

Amelia gasped, turning to look at him. "You are going back?" The shock in her voice made Jack realize that he hadn't mentioned going back before.

"I ain't no deserter."

"You were shot!" Amelia exclaimed, her voice becoming shrill in concern.

Jack blinked a couple of times, trying to reconcile what he would need to do in order to not be considered a deserter. He heard what they did to deserters. Some were sent to work camps, others were marked with a tattoo or brand, and others were shot.

"You cannot go back there," Amelia insisted, her blue eyes started to glaze with unshed tears.

"I have to find my unit, I have to…" Jack began. Amelia's tears began in earnest, and he was so struck by them he couldn't think past trying to comfort her.

He shifted in the bed, taking her into his arms, to do his best to make her feel better. He was surprised when she leaned into him willingly.

Stroking her hair, he shushed her. "It will be okay."

"No!" Amelia exclaimed. "What if you are shot again? What if…" Her voice trailed off as she sniffed in an effort to get her emotions under control, reaching up to wipe at her tears almost angrily. She sat back, shaking her head and averting her eyes.

Jack could see her fighting the urge to say something else. "What is it?"

Cornflower-blue eyes pinned him with a searching look, but she shook her head again, and stood up. "I have work to do, I will come back later." With that she left the room.

Jack sat trying to figure out what he'd done wrong. Certainly, she wouldn't want a coward living in her home. It just made no sense at all. Now he was worried that she was angry at him, and he wanted so much to change her heart. Slowly he moved to the side of the bed.

His chest burned, but he needed to talk to Amelia, and he did not want to wait until she came back. As he stood up, he felt unstable on his feet, he'd been in bed for weeks. His heart felt like it was going to beat out of his chest, but he could rest when he had talked to his care-taker.

Forcing his feet to move, he took a bit longer. Slowly but surely, he made his way across the small room. At the door, he leaned against the cool surface, breathing heavily and feeling light-headed. There was a definite burning in his chest, but there was also an ache that he knew felt far more important.

Opening the door to the room, he peered out into the kitchen. Amelia was standing at the stove, stirring a large steaming pot. Jack noticed that she was sniffling, and he wondered why, but before he could change his mind, he called her name. Amelia turned to look at him, her blue eyes widening with shock seeing him standing in the doorway.

"Jack!" she exclaimed, moving immediately to him, afraid he would fall and hurt himself.

As she moved toward him, Jack pushed off the doorjamb and opened his arms to her. Amelia looked taken aback temporarily, but stepped into his arms all the same, wanting to support his body weight, lest he reverse the healing he'd done in the past few weeks. She was surprised when his hand touched her face, tilting her chin up to look up at him. The look in his eyes made her breath catch in her throat.

"Please don't be afraid for me," he told her, his breath uneven. Amelia blinked a couple of times, but then gestured to guide him back to bed. He refused to budge, which made her look up at him more

intently. He shook his head, then pinned her with a serious look. "I
love you, and if I have to leave, I will always come back to you."

"Wow!" Jessie exclaimed, her stunned look backing up her statement. "So in your past life you loved her, huh?"

Morgan nodded looking bemused. She could see that her
friend was doing her best to understand the idea of *past lives*. Even
Morgan knew that it probably all sounded crazy.

***

"What the hell are you watching?" Raquel asked, horrified. The
noise of screaming had brought her out of her room and into the
living room.

Jaims glanced over her shoulder, worried that her roommate
was in a bad mood again...she'd been moody a lot lately. But
Raquel didn't look mad, just comically dismayed. "It's *Shaun of
the Dead*, have you never seen it?"

Raquel stepped around to peer at the TV screen. "Can't say I
have..." she muttered. She stood for a long moment watching the
movie, then she slowly backed up toward the couch. "Scootch!"
she ordered. Jaims did as she was told, happy that her friend finally seemed like she wanted to hang out again.

Raquel had been one of those people that Jaims had always
had a connection with. They'd met at Zion's club years before,
and they had just clicked. Raquel had been a cop, and was looking
for a new place to blow off steam after work. Jaims had been helping out behind the bar that night, and had found herself attracted

to the dark-haired, dark-eyed, no-nonsense cop. They'd swiftly become friends, and later roommates, so Jaims had stashed that attraction for her further down in her soul.

They'd always gotten along well, and Jaims had been the one person, besides her brothers, that Raquel had emailed on a regular basis when her reserve unit had been called up to go to Iraq. There had even been late-night phone calls, while Raquel tried to maintain her sanity during many a lonely night. Even daytime phone calls, when things were quiet on base. But then she'd been shot, and things had changed dramatically, even after she came home.

"Oh, that's such a hideous waste of beer!" Raquel complained.

"Right?" Jaims agreed.

"You know what we need…"

"Popcorn!" Jaims yelled, jumping up to make some.

Suddenly, it was just like the good old days and Jaims was thrilled. Maybe the *real* Raquel was coming back.

"Ouch, damn it," Raquel hissed as she took an unopened kernel out of her mouth and tossed it on the coffee table. "I hate it when those suckers don't pop!"

"Losers," Jaims mumbled with a mouthful of popcorn.

"Under achievers."

"Failures."

"Bums!" Raquel laughed, enjoying the game.

It was a nice afternoon.

"What's the haps?" Jaims answered her phone, seeing that it was Raquel.

"Same shit, more sand," was her acerbic reply.

"Bleh! How hot is it there right now?" Jaims asked, looking at her watch. It was 2 a.m. in San Francisco, so it was noon in Iraq at that point.

"A hundred and fucking nine already!" Raquel complained. "Supposed to get up to about a hundred and fifteen today."

"Dude…" Jaims commiserated.

"You just get back from Z's?" Raquel queried, anxious to be back home in the cool San Francisco weather.

"Yeah, it was hopping tonight."

"Hopping?" Raquel repeated with disdain. "You're starting to talk like Z."

Jaims laughed. "Yeah, I know, gotta knock that off or I'll be old before my time!"

"As your elder," Raquel, who was only two years older, pronounced, "I'm telling ya, it doesn't slow down once you start sliding!"

"Oh shut up!" Jaims laughed. "So what's really going on there?"

Raquel grew quiet. Jaims knew her well enough to know if she was calling in the middle of the day it was probably because something happened.

"We lost Jimmy today," Raquel said solemnly.

"Damn…"

Jimmy had been a gunner and had been hurt in the field the week before. There had been some hope of recovery, but clearly, with this news, it didn't happen.

"You okay?"

Raquel sniffed, trying to be brave and hold back tears. "No," she said simply. "Distract me."

Jaims nodded. "So you know that L word's been talking up Stacy, right? Well, tonight Stacy showed up with someone new! So, L word made a point of seducing the someone!"

"Holy shit!" Raquel exclaimed, laughing. "I swear that one can get 'em all!*

Jaims smiled at her end, glad she could offer her friend a way out of her sadness. It was one of the few things she was able to do for Raquel.

***

"Are you okay?" Garrett asked Raquel, not for the first time during the visit.

"What?" Raquel queried, looking distracted. "Yeah, yeah, I'm good."

They were sitting in the quad at the college Raquel's brothers, Garrett and Jackson, were attending in Santa Clara. They'd both been able to use Raquel's GI bill to go to college. Fortunately, it also included onsite student housing for both boys.

"How is school going?" Raquel asked, trying to look engaged in the conversation, even though her mind was having trouble paying attention.

"It's good," Jackson said with a smile. "You look good, sis."

"Yeah, yeah," Raquel murmured, grinning back. "I'm sorry I couldn't get out here to see you two sooner, things have just been crazy lately."

"Are you back on the PD?" Garrett asked.

Raquel had been a police officer with the San Francisco Police Department when her Army Reserve unit had been called up.

"Nah, not yet, they want medical clearance, so I'm workin' on that."

Both boys nodded. They detected their sister wasn't really there with them, but did their best to enjoy the time with her. Their lives had been so disturbed by her being shot, they'd worried that she would die. The relief of her recovery had been absolute. Even if she didn't seem the same, they loved their sister dearly.

***

"And there she goes again…" Raquel observed as Shayne 'L Word' walked away with yet another woman, a different one from the night before.

"What?" Jaims asked, as she sat down with their beers, seeing Raquel's expression as she approached.

"Good old L Word." Raquel shook her head, picking up her beer and taking a swig.

"Aw." Jaims nodded. She was used to their friend's ease with women. "You could score if you tried."

Raquel shrugged. "Too much work."

Jaims chuckled, shaking her head. "Seriously!"

"Dude, these girls are so materialistic these days, they won't even look at ya if you don't drive a Jag or something."

Jaims ran her tongue along her teeth. Reminding Raquel that Shayne didn't have a Jag wouldn't be wise.

"Maybe we should just get together," Raquel said, her tone casual.

Jaims glanced over at her friend, wondering how drunk she was. Raquel had been there for an hour before Jaims had joined her. She rolled her eyes and chuckled. "Uh-huh."

Before Raquel could say anything further, Zion walked over to them, nudging Jaims on the shoulder. "Could you go down and grab some Corona for me? Ziggy hurt her wrist and you know Amelia won't lift anything." The words were said with an eyeroll.

"Well, she's a delicate flower," Jaims replied, sighing as she stood up.

When Jaims returned a little while later, Raquel looked annoyed. "What?" she queried.

Raquel shook her head, leaning back in her chair, her legs splayed out in front of her in an exaggerated but relaxed pose. Jaims didn't trust it for a minute, but sat down all the same. Raquel tilted her head in a sidelong look. "What's up with that anyway?" Jaims blinked a couple of times, trying to figure out what her friend was referring to, before she attempted to answer.

"With Z," Raquel clarified.

"With Z," Jaims repeated, "what? She needed help."

"And you're the only one that can help her these days?" Raquel said accusingly.

Jaims' mouth hung open for a long moment. It almost sounded like her friend was jealous, but *jealousy* didn't really make sense.

"No," she began carefully, not wanting to piss Raquel off. She was so volatile these days. "But like I told you, Dax asked me to keep an eye on Z while she was out of town, and that's what I'm doing."

Jaims continued, "Ya know, helping her out and stuff." She shrugged indicating that it was no big deal.

"That's right. D is off with her hot new girl…"

Raquel rolled her eyes, her annoyance radiated in waves.

Jaims shook her head and walked away, lest they get into a fight at the club. The last thing Jaims wanted was for the rest of the bois to see how things with Raquel could get at times.

***

Jane walked into the bar, immediately scanning the room for Zion. She located the owner quickly; she was standing near the bar. Making her way in that direction, Jane noticed all the heads turning to look at her. After all, she was stunning, her lithe body draped in red silk, her platinum blonde hair swept up in a fancy chignon. With supreme confidence, born of getting her way consistently in life, Jane strolled straight up to Zion, smiling enticingly.

"I need to speak to your manager," Jane drawled sexily.

Zion's lips quirked in a slight grin. "I'm the owner, but I know you know that."

Jane's eyes gave nothing away, as she smirked. "Is there somewhere private we can talk?"

Zion stared back at the blonde, as if trying to discern what her intentions were. Finally, she nodded and lead Jane to her office behind the bar. No sooner had Zion closed the door, Jane slid her arms around the owner's neck and leaned in for a kiss. Zion's hands shot out to the side, in a gesture of both alarm and caution, she had no idea what this woman's motivations were.

Zion was no fool, she knew a predator when she saw one, but damn the woman was just too beautiful to be believed. With her platinum blonde hair, sultry eyes, and the clothes she wore, she emanated the classic blonde bombshell image, which only further attracted the bar owner.

Before long, Zion gave into her desire to take the woman fully into her arms. Jane exalted in the surrender and pressed closer. Zion had the presence of mind to reach behind her and lock the door. She could then give her full attention to the woman pressing against her.

The next morning, they were in Zion's bed.

"How much do you need?" Jane asked as they lay in Zion's bed catching their breath.

"For what?" Zion's eyebrows knitted together in confusion.

"To expand the bar."

"I…it's a lot." Zion sighed. "But I'm working on it, I'll probably just sell a few properties."

"But then you'll lose monthly income," Jane pointed out, smoothing her hand down Zion's chest, her nails sliding over immediately taut nipples. It made Zion suck in her breath at the sensation.

Zion shrugged, trying to concentrate on the conversation. "Once I finish the expansion, I'll make that money up in revenue from the bar."

"That's going to take time, sweetie…" Jane's voice trailed off as she nipped at Zion's neck. "Just let me give you the money."

Zion's eyes closed, reactive to Jane's touch, her body betraying her. "I can't...um...I can't let you do that."

Jane sat back, looking like Zion had slapped her. "You don't trust me?"

It took Zion an extra couple of seconds to catch up to the change in Jane's direction. "I never said that."

"Then why don't you want me to invest in your bar?" Jane asked petulantly.

"I just..." Zion searched for the right words, she didn't want to say she wanted to keep business and pleasure separate. The fact of the matter was, no...she didn't trust Jane, for reasons she couldn't quite put her finger on. "I can do this."

Jane recoiled away. She stood up, picking up her discarded dress and under garments as she went and headed for the bathroom. The door to the bathroom slammed and Zion knew she'd just pissed her off. Laying back in her bed, Zion sighed, she never seemed to know exactly how to deal with the hellcat she was dating.

***

The headache was back; Raquel ignored that her hands were shaking as she reached for the pill bottle. Opening the bottle, she was surprised when she noticed that there were only two left.

"Fuck," she muttered to herself.

She grunted as she popped both remaining pills. She was unable to recall the last time she refilled the prescription. She dialed the number on the bottle to order a refill. Punching in the numbers from the pharmacy prompt, she waited for the automated voice to tell her when to pick up prescription. It was a shock to hear a voice on the end of the line say, *There are no refills remaining on this prescription, please contact your doctor for a new prescription.*

"Son of a fucking bitch!" Raquel yelled, throwing her phone across the room, narrowly missing Jaims who'd just walked in.

"Whoa!" Jaims exclaimed, ducking to avoid the latest missile. Raquel was always throwing things these days.

"What happened?"

"They say I don't have any refills on my meds," Raquel hissed.

Jaims leaned down to pick up Raquel's phone.

"Just leave it!" Raquel snapped.

Picking up the offending device, Jaims set it next to Raquel on the couch. "You'll miss it soon enough," she joked good naturedly.

"I said," Raquel gritted out, as she picked up the phone and hurled it at Jaims' face, "fucking leave it!"

Jaims didn't duck fast enough this time, and the phone caught her near her eye.

"What the fuck, man!" she cried, as she reached up to touch the spot the phone had hit.

Raquel just stared back at Jaims, her lips twitching in annoyance. Jaims made a quick exit, wanting to get away from the storm she could see brewing.

Leaving the apartment, Jaims went out to her car: her neon blue, BRZ that made her happy. Getting inside the low-slung vehicle she started the ignition and let the house music that could be heard from the speakers surround her. The latest from Laidback Luke, Flexin' played as she drove off down the street.

Her thoughts were in turmoil as she accelerated down the street, heading for the water, her lifelong refuge. The relationship with Raquel that had once been easy and comfortable was quickly becoming a constant tiptoe through the landmines! On one hand, she knew that Raquel was going through a lot, trying to get back on with the PD, and still healing from the gunshot, and on the other, Jaims was aware of the PTSD she must be going through.

That thought had her wondering, was that what this was? Was Raquel experiencing PTSD and that is what had her lashing out so often?

Parking at her favorite spot at Heron's Head Park, Jaims pulled out her phone and decided to look up PTSD symptoms.

"Changes in physical and emotional reactions," Jaims read out loud to herself. "Irritability, angry outbursts or aggressive behavior…check, check, check!"

A feeling of guilt settled around Jaims. Had she been ignoring her friend's distress? Raquel hadn't said anything, but it didn't mean she wasn't feeling things.

Getting out of her car, Jaims walked toward the water. She made her way out the dirt path and took out a cigarette and lit it. She'd been cutting back lately, but this situation was too stressful to forego the vice.

Once at the water she sat down, smoking and looking out over the bay, her mind turning to the events of the last couple of months. She thought of all the screaming fits, and the throwing things and the mood swings. The guilt compounded more and more. Jaims cursed herself for not being a better friend.

Finally, she stood up, intent on going back home to apologize and ask how she could help Raquel get through what she was dealing with. When she walked into the apartment however, Raquel was nowhere to be found.

***

"You don't like her?" Zion asked Dax, her best friend, as her eyes tracked Jane making her way to the bar, a slow sexy stroll, as always.

Dax's lips twitched, as she leaned back, crossing her arms over her chest, knowing that Zion was smitten, and not wanting to torpedo her friend's mood.

"She's…just…so fancy."

Zion looked surprised but pleased. "Fancy," she tried out the word. "Yeah, that's definitely her."

Dax relaxed, glad she hadn't offended Zion. They'd been friends since the Navy, and the last thing she ever wanted was to upset her. Zion was the closest thing she had to family.

Dax had fought her way through getting her aeronautics degree and attending the Navy's Officer Candidate School. She had just about had it with attitude from men in the Navy. There were constant comments about her short haircut; did she think she was a man? They criticized how she dressed off duty was off-putting to some of her fellow pilots. It also seemed to really annoy her fellow pilots that she was a great pilot; she couldn't win. Now being assigned to an aircraft carrier, it put Dax in a whole new environment. At least at her previous post she'd found a small group of friends that she could trust and hang out with. This was all new.

Stepping onto the Carl Vinson, Dax got her bunk assignment, and headed off toward the flight deck.

The aviation wing was always located under the flight deck, her previous crew had already told her that. She also knew she was likely to get stuck rooming with some guy, since the Navy didn't really have room to segregate men and women on an aircraft carrier. She steeled herself for that conversation.

At the door to her assigned cabin, Dax paused, she could hear someone moving around inside. Getting settled quietly and on her own wasn't happening. Taking a slow, deep breath, she reached for the handle. When she opened the door, she wasn't at all surprised to encounter a man. He had the classic short hair, shaved at the back, and a little longer on the top. To her shock, the person who she had mistaken for a man, turned around, and it was not a man at all, but another woman!

"Holy shit!" was the first thing out of Dax's mouth.

"Hiya to you too," the stranger said with a grin.

Dax shook her head, smiling widely. "I just really expected to get stuck with a guy."

"Well, you're stuck with me instead. I'm Zion." Zion extended her hand, her blue eyes twinkling with humor.

Dax grasped Zion's hand, shaking it firmly. "Great to meet you, I'm Dax."

Zion nodded her head. "Pilot?"

Dax grinned. "Is it obvious?"

"Yeah, ya got that cocky, useless look about ya." Zion laughed.

Dax guffawed, winking. "Then that must make you deck crew."

"Only if you want your shit to work."

"Avionics then?"

"You got it."

"We might just get along then." Dax chuckled.

"Keep your drift factor low and the dolly count high and we'll be alright." Zion winked.

Dax felt a sense of relief flood her veins. Zion had just confirmed what she'd suspected. That she was gay too. What were the odds? It didn't matter, Dax was just happy to have found a new ally. They'd been fast friends after that first meeting.

The fact was that Dax didn't like Jane, neither did many of their friends. It was obvious to everyone that Jane 'Fancy', as she quickly became known, wasn't interested in anything but controlling Zion, and that didn't sit well with Dax at all. Zion was the unofficial head of their small group, no one wanted to be the one to say anything about Jane to Zion. The problem was, Dax knew it was going to fall on her and she was dreading that.

Things stepped up a few days later when Zion was delayed getting to the bar. Dax opened up for Zion. She was helping with the back bar when Jane strolled up. As usual, Jane was dressed in a long, provocative silk dress with high heels. Today's color was a sapphire blue.

"Dax, right?" Jane announced with a sexy smile.

"Yup," Dax replied, pouring Jane a glass of white wine and placing it in front of her. White wine was all she ever drank.

Before Dax could pull back, Jane ran a red fingernail along Dax's jawline. "So sweet," she purred. "Thank you."

Dax simply gave Jane a curt nod, then went to help someone else. The last thing she wanted was to have her best friend's girlfriend flirting with her. Jane watched her closely for long time.

Dax made a point of staying away from her. It bothered Dax to the point that she was very relieved when Zion finally got to the bar.

***

Two days passed before Raquel reappeared at the apartment.

She walked in while Jaims was watching a movie in the living room. Glancing up, Jaims immediately turned down the volume. She was watching *Avengers: Endgame*, and she'd read that loud noises could trigger someone with PTSD.

"Hey." Jaims nodded.

Raquel said nothing. She instead surprised Jaims by siting down at the other end of the couch. She took a pillow, putting it in Jaims' lap and laid her head on top of it with an extended sigh. At first, Jaims wasn't sure how to react, but then Raquel picked up the remote and turned the movie volume up.

"I love this one," Raquel finally said.

"Me too, except…"

"The end, when Tony Stark dies," Raquel finished.

"It sucks!"

"You are such a marshmallow." Raquel laughed.

"Yeah, yeah." Jaims chuckled, making a face.

Raquel surprised her again by reaching up to touch the spot next to Jaims' eye; it was still slightly bruised. The light touch surprised Jaims. "I'm sorry about that," Raquel said.

Jaims chewed on the inside of her cheek contemplating. On the one hand, she did not want to say it was *okay*, because it wasn't, but she also wanted to open up the conversation about the PTSD.

"You know…if you want to talk about what happened over there," she began.

"Pfft!" Raquel dismissed, with a wave of her hand. "I don't want to even think about that shit."

"But…" Jaims was about to protest but saw the annoyance flash in Raquel's eyes. Instead, she just shut up and turned her attention back to the movie.

Raquel felt a pang of guilt, she knew that Jaims was only trying to help, but she didn't need help. People were pushing her, telling her she should probably *talk to someone* about her PTSD. As far as she was concerned, she didn't frigging have PTSD, she just had an injury that made her damned head hurt all the time. Why would it be PTSD? Couldn't it just be a headache from getting shot in the damned head? Why was everything about PTSD now-adays?

She just wanted to get back to living her life. Not that it was working out that way, the PD wasn't ready to let her come back—they kept telling her she needed a medical clearance. The fucking army kept telling her she needed to get counseling before they'd clear her. It was a catch-22 and she was sick of thinking about it.

It helped that she'd scored some more meds from a friend, so her head was swimming with that onboard. She didn't want to think, so she sat back and lost herself in the movie, that had always been hers and Jaims' thing, *movies*.

"April twenty-third!" Jaims crowed as she walked into Fancy's that night.

"What's April twenty-third?" L Word looked perplexed.

"Only the coolest thing ever!" Jaims replied happily.

"And that would be…" Flynn moved her hand in a 'come on' gesture.

"Infinity Wars comes out," Raquel commented as she joined her new friends.

Jaims opened her mouth in shock, but smiled as she did. "Yeah! Dude!" Her exclamation was made along with a high five gesture, which Raquel answered with a grin.

Raquel had never felt more included in a group before in her life.

Growing up in Los Angeles, she'd always had looks going for her, but her aggressive nature coupled with the knowledge that she was 'different' had pushed people away quickly.

It had taken her years to come out to her Latino family, and it had ended in disaster. At eighteen she'd bravely told them. They'd immediately kicked her out of the house and disowned her. It had been a horrible scene. She'd ended up joining the Army, because she had nowhere else to go, and at least the Army would clothe and feed her and give her a place to live. Fortunately, Don't Ask, Don't Tell had been repealed the year before and she was able to be herself in the

Army. Still, it wasn't what she wanted to be, so after four years, she was honorably discharged and went for what she really wanted.

With the money she'd saved during her time in the Army, she had moved to San Francisco, a place she was sure she could be her real self. She applied to join the San Francisco police department. Becoming a police officer had been a dream of hers since she'd seen one of her cousins gunned down in the street many years before. Being the one to arrest bad people who committed crimes seemed the best thing to do with her life. Her military experience meant she would be a shoo-in for the PD. So at the age of twenty-two she'd started her career in law enforcement.

Even as a police officer, she never really felt like she fit in much. She never found her niche, until she'd walked into a bar called Fancy's on its grand reopening. She recalled it was four years ago. That's when she'd met Jaims, and later her friends. That is when she knew she found her tribe. They'd become even more important the following year because Raquel's parents had been killed in a car crash, leaving her two little brothers, they were only fifteen and sixteen at the time. Raquel and Jaims had been living together to save rent money. Zion had offered them a place to rent, a place that had three bedrooms, at a very reasonable rent for San Francisco. The Castro Bois Crew had become family to Garrett and Jackson also. Raquel could never repay them for the comfort they provided for not only her, but for her brothers too.

Chapter 3

The weather was surprisingly warm for San Francisco that morning, and Maureen Prescott was surprised. She was used to the cold wind blowing through the buildings in the Financial District where she worked. This warm morning was certainly welcome, she looked forward to a lovely day. She was making her way to work—her boss wanted her in early that day. She'd promised him that she would be there by 6 a.m. She liked her boss, he was kind, and paid her well.

She was just stepping off the curb when she felt the rumble underground, and a low hum in the air. Suddenly, everything was shaking. As she looked around her, she did her best to keep her balance. There was a crashing sound as glass shattered in the windows near her. Looking around, she could start to see shards of glass hit the ground. She immediately covered her head, and tried to make a quick decision to move to safety, but where?

Looking up and down Clay Street she remembered there was a park about two blocks away, she'd go there!

She started to run. As the street beneath her rolled and shook, she headed toward the park, and tried to watch for falling glass on the way.

She never saw the car that clipped her from behind, nor did she see the man who was desperately trying to control the vehicle's movement. All she felt was something heavy shove her forward. She tumbled, and felt herself falling. She didn't know she'd fallen down an open basement doorway, but she felt the debris that tumbled in after her, pinning her to the ground. A scream escaped her throat right before everything went black.

Tom Palmer was doing his best to extricate the older gentleman from his car. He doubted the man was alive, since the car was partially buried in bricks, crushing the windshield and part of the vehicle, but he knew he had to try. Chaos reigned everywhere, but as a volunteer firefighter, Tom had learned that he needed to block out everything but the job at hand. He was sure that it was for that reason alone that he hadn't heard the feeble cries five feet away. He was certain the cries were coming from below ground.

Once he'd helped the man out of the car, Tom sat down on the ground for a moment to catch his breath. His feet were planted on the ground, his arms draped over bent knees as he did his best to calm his breathing. In that moment he started to hear something. At first, he thought it was a cat trapped somewhere, it was such a high-pitched cry. Not actual words but muffled sounds. Then there was very definite "Help!" The word came out as a gasp.

Tom got to his feet and moved to the open basement door a few feet from where he sat moments before. He did his best to peer into the darkness, but he couldn't see anything.

"Hello!" he called. There was no reply. "Is there someone down there!"

There was no reply, but he was sure that this was where he'd heard the cry for help. He listened intently, even descending a couple of stairs. His flashlight had long since gone out, so he had no way of seeing what was down in the hole.

"Hello!" he called again, ready to give up, thinking his ears were playing tricks on him.

"Help," came the smallest of sound again.

"I'm here! I'm going to help you!" he declared, as he made his way further down into the hole.

He did his best to gaze through the darkness around him, but he couldn't see any movement. Now he knew there was someone down in this hole, he knew he needed to help. "Can you please make some more noise, so I can find you?"

There was silence for a moment, but then he heard a brick shift to his right. He carefully moved in that direction, running into a pile of debris. "Are you here?" he asked into the darkness.

"Here," came a soft reply.

Tom bent down and began to check the debris carefully. He cursed under his breath for not having any light, but he needed to figure out where the person was. He was cautious as he dug, so he didn't cause the person more injury when he started to shift the surrounding debris. He patted gingerly along the outline of the pile, feeling sharp objects almost penetrating his gloves. Suddenly he felt a hand, and when he reached for it, it grabbed his in response.

"There you are." He smiled, glad that the person was still conscious. "I'm going to try to get you out. Just hold on for a little bit longer, okay?"

The hand clutched his a couple of times, in what he assumed was relief. He began to shift debris from the pile and moved it to an area behind him. It took some time, but he finally uncovered a person.

"Are you hurt?"

"I…I yes, a little bit," came the soft reply.

"Where are you hurting?"

"My leg, and my head hurts."

"How about your back or your neck? Any pain there?" Tom asked gently.

A couple moments of silence passed between them, then he heard, "No. No pain there."

"Okay, I'm going to pick you up, so I can get you upstairs into the light. I can assess your injuries then." With that he moved to slide his hands under the person's body. He was fairly sure it was a woman— she weighed very little as he lifted her. It was then he realized, she might be a child.

Maureen was so relieved she had been found! She breathed a sigh of relief as she was carried upstairs and out into the daylight. As they came up out of the basement, she looked up into the man's face, and found that he was looking down at her. She was surprised by the bright blue hue of his eyes; they were particularly emphasized because of the soot and dirt covering his face.

"Thank you," she told him.

He smiled. "Glad I heard you."

He began to set her down, but that was when they both heard it: there was an explosion in the distance, not too far from them. Turning toward the commotion, Tom saw that many of the buildings were burning.

"I think we should get farther away from here."

Maureen nodded, looking around for what she assumed would be a fire truck, since he was wearing a fireman's uniform, but she saw no truck.

"Where's your fire truck?"

Tom grinned, as he began to hurry farther down the road toward the park she'd been headed for when the earthquake had struck.

"No truck."

"But, why?" she asked, dumbfounded.

"I'm a volunteer, we don't get trucks." He chuckled.

Maureen blinked a couple of times, surprised by his statement. "You volunteer to do this?"

"Yes ma'am." He smiled.

"You are braver than me."

"Bravery is just a state of mind, ma'am."

Morgan came to, sighing as she did.

"Oh my, what is that sigh about?" Charolotte asked, grinning.

"I was just rescued by a handsome volunteer firefighter," Morgan answered wistfully.

"Okay, where did you end up this time? I'm guessing this wasn't in the civil war."

"I was in San Francisco, there was an earthquake," Morgan told her, proceeding to tell her everything she'd seen.

Charlotte nodded. "Maybe the big one in 1906?"

Morgan thought about it, comparing the clothes and cars of the day, finally nodding. "It might just be."

"So, we're in the 1900s, that's moving forward." Charlotte smiled.

"And then there were the blue eyes again."

"The cornflower-blue colored eyes?" Charlotte quizzed.

"Yes! It's such an odd color, I wonder why it keeps appearing," Morgan mused.

Charolotte shrugged. She wasn't sure what the eye color meant, she wondered if Morgan was imposing the color on various people in her hypnotic dreams.

Driving home along Highway 1, Morgan reflected on the fireman and Maureen. She wondered if Maureen ever saw him again. She remembered the way the fireman's arms wrapped around her and how it had felt so comforting. She smiled. That surely wasn't the end to their story?

It occurred to Morgan that she should be writing down the information she was getting from her past lives. She located a parking area with a view of the beautiful Pacific Ocean. Opening the center console of her vehicle, she pulled out a notebook and began writing everything. Her visions, her impressions, her feelings, it was a very cathartic experience. As she closed the notebook, she realized the sun was starting to set. She started her car again, not wanting to drive in the dark on the two-lane highway. She knew that there were perilous drops on every corner on these coastal roads.

That night, after a couple of glasses of wine, she fell asleep and dreamed of a handsome, blue-eyed firefighter who morphed into a beautiful blue-eyed, dark-haired woman.

***

"How many has she had?" Zion asked Jaims, as she watched Raquel dance wildly on the dance floor.

"Too many," Jaims replied.

"She has been drinking a lot since she got home," Case added.

"Yeah," Jaims confirmed. Not mentioning the number of pills her roommate/best friend was taking lately as well. She knew Rock thought she was hiding it well, but since Jaims knew her so well, that wasn't the case.

"Just keep an eye on her, J," Zion said, patting her on the shoulder. Zion saw one of the bartenders holding up her hand to get Zion's attention, so she headed toward the bar.

"I'm tryin'..." Jaims said, her voice trailing off as her eyes tracked Zion's movements.

There was a man in a suit waiting for Zion. Zion shook the man's hand and they headed back to Zion's office.

"What do you think that's about?" Jaims asked Case, who noticed the man too.

"Dunno," Case replied. "Doesn't look bloody good as far as I can see."

"Hopefully it doesn't have anything to do with Fancy," Jaims said.

"Too right," Case agreed, in a clear British accent.

Zion paced in her office.

"She's been getting the payments, right?" Zion practically snapped.

"Yes," the man replied calmly, "but she wants in on your next expansion."

"How did she hear about that?"

The man smiled evenly. "She hears about everything."

"Well, maybe she should send her spies to watch someone else." Zion's mouth curled in derision. Leave it to Jane to hear about the bookstore going up for sale and knowing that it would be the perfect opportunity to expand the bar again, she thought.

"She's willing to fund the entire expansion," the man, who'd introduced himself as Mr. Brown, *an associate* of Jane's, said.

Zion shook her head. "No, I'm not doing any more business with her. Once I pay her off from that first expansion, we're done, for good."

"That's just not going to work for my client," Mr. Brown said.

"Tough shit," Zion snapped. "You can leave my club now." She gestured toward the office door and the exit that lay beyond it.

Mr. Brown drew in a deep breath, blowing it out slowly as he stood up. "You'll be hearing from us again."

"Yada, yada, yada," Zion scoffed, as she motioned for the man to precede her.

Mr. Brown left, looking far from pleased. Zion was less pleased. Jane's claws were apparently still trying to hold on to something. Not that Zion understood why.

Driving in Zion's Cadillac, Jane looked over at the bar owner. They were working on a deal for Jane to buy into the club. She really liked that Zion wanted to name the club after her new nickname 'Fancy'. The nickname amused Jane. Zion had told her that it had been how Dax had described her. The idea that Dax was even thinking about her, excited Jane a bit—the hot pilot definitely had a sexy streak a mile wide.

Sitting next to Zion, Jane was evaluating her current lover. Zion was certainly one hot-looking butch lesbian, but some things about the woman just didn't jibe. It bothered Jane no end, especially when yet another weepy, whiney song came on the stereo. What the actual hell?

"Why do you listen to this crap?" Jane asked sourly.

Zion, who'd been lost in her own thoughts, blinked a couple of times, always shocked at the changes in Jane lately. In previous months, she'd been sweet, complimentary, and extremely affectionate. Recently, however, she'd developed a habit at picking at things and being rather acerbic.

Perplexed, Zion raised a hand off the steering wheel and gestured to the stereo. "I didn't realize it was classified as crap." Her voice held no anger, it was its usual cordial tone, the same tone that also annoyed Jane.

Making an irritated noise in the back of her throat, Jane threw her hands up in anger. "You just don't…match!" she blurted out.

Zion needed a moment to take in what Jane had just said. Her brows furrowed, even as she mouthed the word 'match'. Finally, she shook her head. "You're going to have to explain that one to me."

Jane gestured to Zion as a whole, then pointed to the stereo and the surroundings inside the car. She twirled her finger as she said, "This! All of this!"

Zion nodded slowly, her blue eyes tainted with confusion.

Jane blew her breath hastily. "You are this hot-looking dyke, with the nice clothes, the cool hair, the right look, hell, even the badass sleeve tattoos! Not that anyone ever freaking sees them, 'cause you always wear damned long sleeved shirts!" She reached over, yanking at

Zion's sleeves that were turned up at the cuff, revealing only the slightest glimpse of the tattoos that adorned her arms.

"You've got a rock star look, and a damned folk singer heart!" Jane snapped.

Zion pressed her lips together, inclining her head. "And I'm guessing folk singer hearts aren't acceptable?"

Jane stared back at Zion in obvious exasperation.

"I just don't get it." Jane shook her head. "I thought you'd be so...exciting."

"I'm sorry I don't meet your expectations," Zion said colorlessly. She refused to show how much Jane's words were hurting her. She'd learned years ago to keep her feelings to herself.

"Pfft!" Jane snickered. "Don't play the poor hurt creature now." She shrugged. "I'm still here, right?"

Zion licked her lips, nodding slowly, turning her attention back to the road. It was the beginning of a long weekend of complaints and more character critique.

What was meant to be a nice trip to the Napa Valley, turned into the longest weekend of Zion's life. By the time Zion got back to the bar on Sunday night after dropping Jane at her condo, she grabbed a bottle of Jack Daniel's from the bar stock and headed up to the apartment to get quietly drunk.

Chapter 4

"Don't you got work?" Raquel said rousing Jaims, who was still in bed at 8:30. She usually left for work at 7:30.

"Not goin' in," Jaims mumbled, doing her best to block the light from the hallway behind Raquel.

"Hung over?" Raquel grinned.

"No," Jaims said. "Could you shut off the hall light please?"

Raquel did as she asked. "What's wrong with you?"

"Migraine," Jaims muttered.

"Frigging headache?" Raquel questioned incredulously. "You don't know what a headache feels like…" Her tone was snide.

"Maybe you should give me some of what you have been taking…" Jaims replied laconically. She heard Raquel's sharp intake of breath and knew in that moment she'd pissed off her roommate.

"Fuck you!" Raquel snapped, then kicked the foot of Jaims' bed. She stomped out of the room and slammed the door a minute later.

Jaims grimaced, not only for the jostling, but for the pain that ripped through her head at the sound of the slammed door.

She slept most of the afternoon, and when she finally came out of her room, Raquel was not home.

Jaims made herself some soup from a can and sat eating it with the TV on. She'd had migraines before but hadn't had one for a long time. They usually started again when she was stressed. The situation with Raquel was certainly stress inducing. She never knew which version of her roommate she was going to get.

At Fancy's that night, the Crew was hanging around their usual tables.

"Where's Jaims tonight?" Ari asked Raquel, garnering a nasty look.

"Why do you care? Aren't you with BB?" Raquel snapped.

Ari's eyes widened, she nodded. "I was just wondering…" She stepped back, looking around for Jayden.

"Well, don't wonder," Raquel sneered. "She's none of your business."

"Hey…" Jayden announced as she walked up, hearing Raquel's nasty tone. She could see Ari doing her best to hold back tears.

"So, what's your problem!" Raquel yelled.

"Whoa, what's goin' on here?" Zion asked, having heard Raquel's raised voice.

"Nothing," Raquel commented, her eyes on Ari. "Princess was wondering about Jaims."

Zion remained calm, but her eyebrows arched. Raquel had been nasty with everyone lately. "I'm wondering too," the bar owner stated, "is she okay?"

Raquel looked flabbergasted, blowing her breath out in a huff. "She's fine, Jesus! She just had a headache, that's all."

"So simple enough to tell us." Zion nodded, her voice placating.

Raquel curled her lips in disdain. She shrugged, as if dismissing the entire incident.

Zion, Jayden, Case, and Flynn all exchanged a look of surprise. Raquel's personality had indeed changed a great deal since she'd been back. She acted much more aggressively than she previously had.

In her office, Zion sat down to call Jaims, to check on her.

"You alright?" she asked when Jaims answered her cell phone wearily.

"Yeah, Z, just a migraine," Jaims told her.

"You're getting those again?" Zion queried worryingly.

"Yeah, this is the worst one in a while." Jaims sighed. "It's better tonight though."

"Good." Zion nodded at her end. "Well, I'll leave you alone, just let me know if you need anything."

Jaims smiled. "Thanks Z."

Later that evening, Jaims was sleeping on the couch, having fallen asleep watching TV, when Raquel entered the apartment. Jaims sat up and rubbed her eyes. She glanced at the clock, it was 2:30 a.m. When she looked back at Raquel, she noticed her eyes narrow.

"You watching what time I get home now?" Raquel asked moodily.

"Uh, no," Jaims said, stretching as she stood up. "I fell asleep and I was just wondering what time it was."

"Bullshit."

"Seriously? Get over yourself," Jaims commented, as she moved past Raquel to head to her room. She was caught completely off guard when Raquel grabbed her up by the shoulders and slammed her into the wall.

"What the fuck do you mean by that!" Raquel growled at Jaims, their faces close.

Jaims refused to show any of fear she was suddenly feeling, and didn't balk. "I mean you've been a royal pain in the ass lately, and I'm fucking sick of it!"

Shock registered on Raquel's face; her grip loosened on Jaims' shoulders. Jaims used the opportunity to shove Raquel away and escape to her room.

As she shut the door, Jaims felt herself shaking. She locked the door with trembling fingers. There was definitely something going on with Raquel and ignoring it wasn't making it go away.

Sitting on her bed, Jaims dialed Zion's number.

"'Lo?" Zion answered, sounding distracted.

Jaims could hear the sounds of glasses clinking together and the banter of people in the background. She realized Zion was probably cleaning up for the night at the bar.

"Z, we need to get the crew together."

"What's up?" Zion asked, setting bar glasses down on the counter for cleaning.

"It's Rock, we need to figure something out to help her."

Zion nodded. "She seemed pretty agitated tonight."

"She's agitated all the damned time."

"I'll get the crew together," Zion said, "come down to the bar at two tomorrow."

"Got it, thanks Z."

"Of course," Zion answered.

The next day, Jaims slipped out of the apartment before Raquel came out of her room. It was still too early to head to the bar, so she stopped by her parents' bakery.

"Mom?" Jaims queried as she poked her head in the back office, away from the bustling front counter.

"Jaimie, honey!" Her mother looked over from her computer, her computer glasses perched on her nose. "What are you doing here? Did you get a pastry?"

"No, Ma, I just stopped by." Jaims smiled, her mother was always trying to feed her.

Celeste Carpenter stood up, walking over to hug her daughter tightly. "Come get a pastry," she prompted, as she took Jaims by the arm, guiding her back to the front counter. "You love my pistachio cannoli!"

"I do," Jaims agreed, as her mother pulled out two for Jaims, putting them on a plate, and adding powdered sugar. "Come, come, sit with me." Celeste motioned to the break room.

Jaims enjoyed the pastries, knowing she wasn't getting out of eating every bite. Celeste looked on, smiling brightly. "Such a good girl..." she observed.

"Because I eat when I'm told?" Jaims chuckled.

"Of course! So, what is wrong?" her mother asked seriously.

Jaims sighed, knowing there was never any point in keeping things from her mother. "Just a problem with my friend."

"Which of your friends? You have so many." Celeste smiled proudly.

"Rock, Mama."

"Oh…" Celeste grimaced. "How is that poor child?" She of course knew about Raquel being shot in the Middle East. Jaims shared everything with her family; she loved that they were always supportive of her and her lifestyle. It was a great source of comfort to her.

"She's struggling, Ma, so we are getting together to try to figure out how we can help."

Celeste nodded. "You are good girls, all of you."

"I heard my baby is here!" came a booming voice from behind her. Jaims was immediately grabbed in a bear hug.

"Hi Dad!" Jaims laughed.

It was a nice visit.

"Aww, always a good reason to come to a family meeting…" Steel 'SJ' said, as she dug into the box of pastries Jaims had brought from the bakery.

"My mom said none of you eat enough." Jaims laughed, rolling her eyes.

"Your mother is a bloomin' angel!" Case reached for a filled donut.

"I really do love her," Shayne sighed contently, grabbing two cannoli.

"Hey, L Word, leave some for everyone else!" Flynn called, as she got herself a soda from the fountain at the bar. "Anyone else need something?"

"Coke for me, Errol!" Jayden raised her hand.

"Is it too early for a shot?" Steel asked.

Zion made a face. "With your danish, SJ?"

"Yeah, I guess you're right." Steel rolled her eyes. "Coke for me too!"

"Is Dax comin'?" Shayne asked.

"She'll be here, she was having an issue earlier at the Martinez Bridge," Zion said.

"Driving from Sacramento is dedication," Jaims added.

"Family is family," Dax said from the doorway.

All the bois greeted Dax, smiling and shaking hands.

"How is Sacramento, Dax?" Jaims asked.

"Eh." Dax shrugged, "It's a job."

"How's the hot red head?" Shayne raised her eyebrows a couple of times with a knowing grin on her face.

"Kenzi is fine, thank you." Dax smirked.

Flynn handed out drinks from the tray she was holding. "Kenzi is *definitely* fine."

"Watch it…" Dax murmured, even as she grinned.

Everyone settled in, chatting for a few minutes, and catching up with each other and Dax.

"So, what's going on with Rock?" Zion finally got to the point of the meeting.

Jaims took a deep breath, blowing it out in a long sigh. "Well, you've seen how she is lately, moody as fuck, snapping at everyone."

"Right…" Zion prompted, waiting for the rest of what Jaims had to say.

"At home she throws shit all the time, she doesn't sleep for days, and then she crashes for like two days at a time. And then there's the pain pills."

"Pain pills?" Dax queried.

"Yeah, whatever they gave her in the hospital in Germany, she ran out, and they won't refill her prescription."

Zion grimaced. "So you think she's getting them somewhere else?"

"I know she's still poppin' 'em, like fuckin' M&M's," Jaims replied.

"Damn…" Steel breathed.

The others shook their heads, not sure what to say. They'd all been completely freaked out when they had heard that Raquel had been shot in the head. There had been relief when they'd learnt that she was coming home. Zion and Dax had even put together money to send her brothers to see her in Germany.

"Have you talked to the boys?" Dax asked Jaims.

Jaims shook her head. "I didn't want to worry them."

"So, what do we do?" Steel asked.

"Stage some kind of intervention?" Case asked, looking like she didn't relish the idea.

"Maybe?" Jaims looked to Dax and Zion.

As the two oldest members of the crew, Dax and Zion were the unofficial heads of their little family.

Flynn shifted. "She ain't gonna take it well."

"Hell no," Shayne agreed, grimacing.

Dax and Zion exchanged a look. Zion's lips twitched. "I think we have to at this point."

"We can't just let her keep on, if it's that bad…" Dax said.

"Oh, it's that bad," Jaims assured them.

"Then that's what we'll do," Zion decided.

"When?" Dax questioned.

"The sooner the better," Zion said.

"Maybe tomorrow?" Jaims suggested. "It's park day."

"Yeah…" Zion nodded, her voice trailing off.

"I'll call Kenzi, let her know I'm staying here tonight." Dax sighed.

"You can stay with me, if your place isn't available," Zion told Dax.

"It's not," Dax sighed. "I've sublet it to a couple while I'm in Sacramento."

Zion nodded. "Figured."

The group discussed a few details about how they would handle things, and once they'd finalized a plan they broke up for the afternoon.

The next day the crew showed up at the park a bit earlier than normal, finding a more secluded section of the Mission Dolores Park so they could talk to Raquel in privacy.

Zion and Dax stood together, watching the others mill about, they were not sure what to do, to look *casual*.

"Nervous as cats…" Zion commented.

Dax chuckled. "Yeah, this really isn't our area of expertise."

"Not hardly," Zion agreed. "Gotta do what we gotta do, though."

Dax nodded then she saw Raquel's Jeep pull up to the park. "Look natural you idiots!" she called to the group.

Shayne and Flynn started tossing the football back and forth. Case and Jayden joined in, by the time Raquel walked up, they were picking teams.

"You joining the game, Rock?" Dax called.

"What are you doin' here?" Raquel asked.

Dax shrugged. "Came for a visit."

In the end, they split into teams and played a game until everyone was tired. They sat as a group on the grass, enjoying the warmth of the sun on their faces.

"How are you doin', Rock?" Dax asked, glancing at her friend.

"Alright," Raquel answered, she was laying on her back, her longish dark hair in two braids. "How's the valley?" she said, her tone joking.

"Hot most of the time," Dax grumbled.

"Sucks to be you," Raquel retorted. "Is the little woman ever gonna let you come back?" This time there was a bit of a bite to Raquel's tone. Everyone heard it.

Dax's eyes narrowed behind her mirrored shades. "Kenzi's contract is done in about two months, then we'll be headed back this way."

"Good, you can get back to having Z's back, so Jaims doesn't have to handle your shit all the time," Raquel remarked jeeringly.

Dax glanced over at Zion and saw her lips twitch, which usually meant she was irritated.

"I tend to handle my own shit," Zion barked.

Raquel sat up and guffawed. "Funny, Jaims seems to be havin' to help out a lot these days."

"Excuse me, I'm right here," Jaims commented dryly.

"What's the real problem here?" Zion questioned, looking directly at Raquel.

Raquel didn't respond, she simply laid back on the grass.

"Rock you've been kind of a bitch to everyone lately," Steel put in finally.

"Yeah, and it's gettin' old," Shayne added.

"Like moldy old," Flynn said.

Raquel sat up slowly, looking around at the group. "So you all got a problem with me suddenly?"

"It ain't sudden," Case uttered.

"You too?" Raquel snapped. She turned her head to look over at Jayden. "What about you? You got something to say too?"

Jayden looked terrified.

"Lay off BB," Jaims said. "You know you haven't been the same since you got back. We've all noticed it, and we want to talk to you about it, okay?"

Raquel's lips curled derisively. "Oh I see, it's fuckin' gang up on me day, right?"

"No," Zion retorted calmly. "We wanted to know what's happening with you, and what we can do to help."

"Well, right now you're all up on my jock, and it's startin' to piss me the fuck off!" Raquel got to her feet, her body looked tense. "You can *help* by knockin' it off."

"Is it the drugs you've been taking?" Jaims asked. "Are they making you act like this?"

Raquel whipped her head around to look at Jaims. "I've been taking pain pills for my fucking head, you'd take pain pills too if someone had tried to blow your fuckin head off!"

Jaims nodded slowly. "I get that, but I think they're messing with your head right now."

Raquel let out a short angry bark of laughter. "My fuckin' friends… thanks for the support! I don't fuckin' need this shit."

"Rock wait!" Zion called, as Raquel started to walk away.

Jaims jumped up and went after her. "Will you just wait a second!"

Jaims positioned herself in front of Raquel. She held up her hands to try and get the woman to stop walking.

"I can't fucking believe you did this!" Raquel accused. "You let them attack me like that!"

"They weren't attacking you Rock, you're worrying us and we wanted to try to tell you that," Jaims said, feeling desperate to get through to her friend.

"Fuck 'em!" Raquel spat.

"And fuck me too?"

Raquel looked at her for a long moment, an ugly sneer appeared on her face. "Fuck all of ya." With that she shoved Jaims hard, knocking her to the ground and walked away.

"Woah!" Dax exclaimed, rising to her feet, as did the others, to go to Jaims' aid.

"You okay?" Zion asked, as they helped Jaims to her feet.

"Yeah," Jaims said, not wanting to show the rest of the group how hurt she was feeling. "I guess this didn't work."

Dax shook her head. "She isn't ready to hear anyone yet."

"I don't think we handled it well either," Zion added.

Case's eyebrows knit together, disapprovingly. "I'm no bloody therapist."

"None of us are." Steel sighed.

Chapter 5

"I see you found the safe place to be," a voice spoke into her ear.

Maureen turned around; it was Tom. "Oh, yes, Red Cross station." Maureen gestured behind her. "Always the best place to be."

Tom grinned, his bright blue eyes twinkling. "I'm glad to see you're playing it safe."

"Safe is my state of mind," Maureen quipped, making Tom chuckle. "Are you finally done volunteering for the day?"

"I am just on a break," Tom told her. "Too many people need help right now."

Maureen sighed, nodding. "You're right, I should be helping too, since I was lucky enough to be rescued by a wonderful knight."

"I'm not sure about all of that." Tom blushed. "I am glad to see that you got checked out." He pointed to the bandage on her head. "How is your leg?"

"It's better." Maureen smiled. "Did I thank you for saving me?"

"You did," Tom confirmed, smiling.

Maureen nodded, feeling silly in the moment, but this man made her feel nervous and fluttery. He was so handsome, and obviously a good person—he volunteered to rescue people after all.

"Have you eaten?" she suddenly thought to ask.

"I, well, no, but I should probably get back," he answered, feeling like a complete oaf at that moment, standing with this pretty young woman.

"Nonsense!" Maureen shook her head. "You need to eat something," she exclaimed, taking his hand in hers and leading him back into the Red Cross tent.

Tom smiled softly, finding the bossy side of this young woman quite enchanting.

Maureen proceeded to procure a sandwich and a bottle of juice for him, and then made him sit at one of the tables in the tent to eat and drink under her watchful eye.

"There, isn't that better?" Maureen asked, sounding very much like his mother used to.

"Yes, ma'am," he answered obediently.

"Ma'am? Oh my, I don't think I'm old enough to be a ma'am, just yet."

Tom pressed his lips together. "I don't know your name…"

"Oh my! That's true, isn't it? I'm Maureen. Maureen Prescott."

"My name is Tom Palmer."

Maureen stuck her hand out to him; he took her hand in his, his hand was twice as big. Maureen couldn't help but notice how large his hand was, but also how gentle his hands felt against hers.

"I think we're going to be friends, Tom Palmer," she stated.

"I'd like that, Maureen Prescott."

Morgan woke, sighing again. Charlotte smiled. "Who was it this time?"

"His name was Tom Prescott…" Morgan said dreamily. "So handsome, brave and those eyes!"

"The blue eyes," Charlotte nodded. "So, where was this?"

"He found her in the park, at the Red Cross tent."

"On purpose?" Charlotte asked.

Morgan considered the question, then shrugged. "I don't know." She went on to tell Charlotte the story of what happened.

Later, as she left the therapist's office, she felt a little melancholy. It was obvious that Maureen and Tom liked each other—she could feel Maureen's heartbeat increase and trip when he'd taken her hand. She missed that feeling. That rush of excitement upon meeting someone new and just knowing that they were the one. Not that she'd ever found the one. She'd found a lot of *not the one*, but still, the feeling of something new, someone new. That giddy feeling of wanting to know everything about someone, and excited about them wanting to know more about her in return. Wondering what that someone special was doing at that moment in time, hoping they were wondering that about her too.

Driving home, Morgan sighed loudly, feeling sad, suddenly. Reaching out she turned on the music from her phone on the car stereo. She found one of her favorite standbys; Fleetwood Mac, the song 'Everywhere' flowed through the speakers. It seemed to echo what she was feeling: Christine McVie sang about being with someone everywhere. She listened to Fleetwood Mac all the way home.

* * *

"Hey, I know we just moved in here," Raquel began as she and Jaims set down the couch they'd just dragged up the stairs to their new apartment, "but would it be okay if my brothers came to visit?"

Jaims dropped down on the couch, still breathing heavy. "You have brothers?"

Raquel laughed, nodding. "Yeah, two, they're younger."

"How young?" Jaims asked warily, she really wasn't up to dealing with little kids.

"They're like fourteen and fifteen."

Jaims shrugged. "Where do they live?"

"In LA with my parents, I'm lucky they're letting them come."

"Why lucky?"

"My parents don't approve of my 'lifestyle.'" Raquel used air quotes on the word lifestyle.

"Aw, they are those kind of parents," Jaims said, nodding.

Raquel canted her head. "What are your parents like?"

Jaims shrugged. "They're totally cool with who I am."

"Wow, lucky you." Raquel sighed.

"You'll get to meet them, trust me." Jaims chuckled. "They've already invited you to Saturday night dinner."

"Uh…" Raquel looked quizzical.

"They host dinner for our family and any random misfits that need every Saturday."

"Oh, and I'm invited?"

"Yep, anytime you wanna go." Jaims grinned. "My mom is Italian, so she likes to feed people."

"You're Italian?" Raquel was shocked, they had really only been friends for a few months. They'd never really discussed family before. Mostly just movies and current events.

"Half," Jaims told her. "My dad is like German and English, so I'm a mishmash."

"Aww, one hundred percent Latino." Raquel grinned. "Well, I dunno, could be some juera in there somewhere."

Raquel laughed, so did Jaims.

"So, if your parents don't approve of you, how come they're letting your brothers come visit?" Jaims asked.

Raquel gave a snort of annoyance. "'Cause my aunt won a cruise, and she's taking my mom and dad with her. They got no one else to watch the boys."

"Aw, so necessity," Jaims surmised.

"Yup." Raquel curled her lips. "Whatever. I get to see them; it's been a couple of years now."

"Cool." Jaims nodded. "Well, let's go get the rest of our crap," she said, standing up from the couch.

"Yeah, sooner we're done, the sooner it's—"

"Beer thirty!" Jaims crowed.

"Damned straight!"

Raquel disappeared for a full week. Jaims was beside herself with worry. She was worried that their aborted intervention attempt had driven Raquel to more desperate acts. On Monday morning, when she left her room to go to work, Jaims noticed Raquel's bedroom door was closed, whereas it had previously been open.

Nodding to herself, Jaims made her coffee and left for the day. When she got home that night, Raquel was gone again. Jaims peaked into Raquel's room to see if she'd done anything drastic like move out. Her possessions were still there. It took Jaims a couple of minutes to talk herself out of going through her friend's dresser and bathroom to see if there were any drugs in evidence. She knew that would be a complete invasion of privacy. Even if it was only with Raquel's well-being in mind, it wasn't her place.

Later Jaims met up with Shayne, Flynn, and Jayden for dinner.

"So she is back?" Jayden queried.

Jaims shrugged. "I guess…she didn't make a sound when she came in, so I'm figuring she's still all-time pissed at me."

"Hey, she's the one being uber-bitch," Shayne commented sourly.

"Right?" Flynn replied, her lips curled in derision.

"She's my best friend," Jaims offered sadly.

The other three nodded in agreement, realizing that Dax or Zion would knock their heads together for making Jaims feel bad.

"She needs to get help," Jayden offered.

"I know, but I've heard over and over again that people won't accept help until they're ready." Jaims let out a sigh.

"I hope she gets ready soon," Jayden said, feeling bad for Jaims.

Jaims was the one in the group that was always trying to help everyone. She helped Jayden when Ariana had been interested; she had also accompanied Jayden back to her childhood home when her father had a heart attack. She was helping Dax keep an eye on Zion while Dax was out of town. Whenever anyone needed help, Jaims was the first to step up. It sucked that no one seemed to be able to help Jaims with the problem she had.

Jaims smiled softly, she knew Jayden was trying to help and she appreciated it. To avoid making her friends feel worse, she changed the subject. The rest of the meal proceeded happily.

***

"Any word on Rock?" Dax asked Zion on the phone that same night.

"L Word texted me to tell me that Jaims said Raquel came home, but avoided her," Zion told her.

"Great, so now she's going to start that?" Dax grimaced in response. "Jaims is gonna be wrung out, you know that."

"I know, she takes everything to heart."

"Who she is, dude…" Dax replied.

"Yeah." Zion shook her head. "I'll try to keep an eye on her, since *apparently* she's been doing that for you when it came to me…"

Dax chuckled unapologetically. "Hey, that started when Fancy breezed into town and I was out of town."

"Well, Fancy ain't here now, is she?" Zion commented dryly.

Dax muttered under her breath. "Not today."

"Can it." Zion grinned.

"Yeah, yeah…" Dax quipped.

It was their way of communicating, it worked for them, it had for years. It was their way of showing each other that they cared. It was a comfort.

"I got Jaims' six," Zion confirmed.

Dax blew her breath out. "Roger that."

"So, this is the famous Raquel?" Celeste exclaimed, as she held Raquel's face in her hands. "Bellisima!"

Raquel almost blushed at the compliment. "It's good to meet you."

"Welcome to our home!" Daniel, Jaims' father put his hand out to Raquel, remembering that Jaims had told him that Raquel was more of a handshake than a hug kind of girl.

Raquel shook Daniel's hand, looking him square in the eye. "Thank you, sir."

"No sir here," Daniel replied with a quick smile. "Just call me Danny, or Dan, or Daniel, or Dad...whatever works for you!"

Raquel smiled, nodding. Jaims' family was definitely friendly.

"Rock, this is my sister Teresa, she's three years older than me." Jaims introduced Raquel to a woman who resembled Jaims in coloring only. Teresa was dressed to the nines and had long flowing hair that curled attractively at the ends. She also wore just enough makeup to enhance her looks, but not too much.

"It's lovely to meet you." Teresa smiled warmly at Raquel.

"You too..." Raquel covered Teresa's hand in hers, smiling her sexiest smile.

"Don't even think about it," Jaims murmured to her friend as they walked into the living room. Raquel simply laughed. "This is my

brother, Carlo, he works at the bakery with my parents, one of the best pastry chefs in the city." Jaims smiled.

Carlo was a nice mix of Celeste, with his dark brown eyes, and had the same sandy brown hair as Daniel, that had just a bit of a wave to it. He clasped Raquel's hand, smiling at her.

"Good to meet a friend of Jaims," he told her.

"Good to meet a guy who makes great desserts!"

Daniel leaned in close. "I'm also an excellent cook," he said, grinning. "But don't tell my parents, they'll start a restaurant next!"

There were laughs all around.

Dinner was a loud, but entertaining affair. Raquel sat watching the interaction and felt sad. Her family had once been close, but when she'd come out, things had just gone up in smoke overnight. She missed having a family.

It was another week before Jaims actually ran into Raquel late at night in the kitchen of their apartment. She'd gotten up to get a bottle of water. Raquel was in the kitchen heating up a can of soup.

"That's where all the soup is going…" Jaims observed lightly, grinning.

Raquel didn't respond initially and Jaims worried she'd sounded like she was accusing her roommate of stealing.

Finally, Raquel shrugged. "It's easy."

"I can pick more up next time I hit the store, if there's something specific you like," Jaims offered.

"That would be cool, my mom used to make me tomato soup and grilled cheese when it got cold like this."

"Tomato soup, bread, cheese," Jaims listed with a nod and a quick smile. "Check!"

"American cheese?" Raquel queried, giving Jaims a sideways look.

"Is there any other cheese?" Jaims arched an eyebrow.

"Some other yucky kinds." Raquel laughed softly.

"Right?" Jaims countered, feeling relief that her friend seemed to be back for the moment. "Just a waste of cooler space at the grocery store."

"Yeah, they could use that space for important stuff, like pickles and deli meat."

"Pickles?" Jaims queried, making a horrified face.

Raquel shrugged. "Their juice is good in chicken salad."

Jaims looked like she was weighing that reasoning, and finally nodded. "Accepted."

Raquel chuckled, then glanced down at the bottle of water in Jaims' hand. "What's up with that?" Her tone was serious.

Jaims shrugged and let out a deep sigh. "Getting another migraine, trying to head it off. Need the water to take my pills."

"You're getting them a lot?" Raquel sounded concerned.

"Lately, yeah."

Raquel grimaced. "That sucks."

"It is what it is," Jaims replied. "I'm gonna go take the meds."

Raquel nodded, watching Jaims leave the room. In her heart of hearts, she knew that she was probably to blame for Jaims getting migraines again. She knew that things were all messed up at the moment, and she knew it was her fault, but she just couldn't seem to stop the fury when it came over her. When she got mad, things just came out of her mouth, or she threw, hit or destroyed things. Unfortunately, those things seem to be prevalent most in her relationships lately.

Half an hour or so later, Jaims was lying in bed, staring out her window at the clouds moving past the moon. There came a light knock on the door.

"Yeah?" Jaims called softly, not wanting to make her head hurt more by being loud.

The door opened. "How's your head?" Raquel asked, her voice equally soft.

"Hurts," Jaims replied.

Raquel stood halfway in the room, still holding the doorknob. Then she stepped inside, closing the door behind her and walking over to the other side of Jaims' bed. Getting in behind Jaims, laying down, she reached out, putting her thumbs to the base of Jaims head.

"Here?" Raquel asked.

"Mmmhmm," Jaims murmured, indicating that her fingers were placed in the right location of where the pain was.

Raquel began massaging with her thumbs, moving over the back of Jaims' skull and neck. Jaims sighed. "That feels so good."

"Good," Raquel whispered softly.

"Thank you," murmured Jaims.

Raquel put her hand to Jaims' cheek, it was her way of apologizing for the turmoil of the past few weeks. Then she went back to massaging Jaims' head, until Jaims dropped off to sleep.

Later when Jaims got up to go to the bathroom, she noticed that Raquel had fallen asleep on the bed next to her. She smiled in the semi-darkness of the room. Even if it was temporary, it was times like this that she remembered exactly why they were friends.

***

"It is so nice of you to help me with this," Maureen told Tom.

"It didn't sound like you had any other help," Tom replied, as he continued to mud the drywall in her apartment.

When she'd finally been able to go home, she'd been happy to find that her apartment building was still standing. Her apartment, however, had a few minor cracks and a couple of pipes leaking. After a few chance encounters, which Maureen was hoping had nothing to do with chance, Tom had asked for her phone number and she happily gave it to him.

He called just as she was discovering the water leaks under her kitchen sink. He'd walked her through turning off the water to the sink, and offered to come by to check things for her. Naturally, she had offered to make him dinner. When he'd seen the cracks in her drywall, he offered to help her fix everything that needed fixing.

Today was his third time at her apartment. They'd been taking things very slowly. He hadn't even made an honest pass at her yet. Maureen appreciated that he was a gentleman. Pushy men always made her nervous.

"My family is back east," Maureen told him, gesturing to the picture of her parents and brother on the wall near where he was working.

"Where abouts?" he asked.

"New York."

"Way over there?" Tom marveled. "What brought you here?"

"Well, certainly not the earthquakes," Maureen teased. "I wanted an adventure."

"This is definitely an adventure," Tom quipped.

"My mother never ventured past the borders of Lewiston, I wanted more than that," Maureen said, her gaze melancholic. "What about you? Do you have family here?"

"My family is in the mid-west, in Kansas. I left there to join the Navy."

"And ended up here?"

"This was my last port. I liked it, so I stayed." He shrugged.

"And started saving damsels in distress?" Maureen smiled.

"Yes, ma'am." Tom inclined his head.

Over dinner later that evening, they talked about her job and what he did when he wasn't rescuing people after an earthquake. "I work in construction," he told her.

"It sounds like you're going to be busy here soon."

He grinned. "I definitely am."

It was a nice evening, he even built her a fire in her small fire-place, after assuring himself that the chimney was in good shape. They sat on her small couch and chatted long into the evening.

"This is nice," Tom mused, his eyes sparkling in the firelight.

Maureen smiled. "I was just thinking the same thing." Glancing up at him, she canted her head. "I'm not usually this comfortable with men."

"Why?"

Maureen sighed softly. "I just never have been, I've had some bad experiences before."

Tom looked back at her; concern written all over his face. Slowly he put his arm around her shoulders, hugging her gently. "Stick with me, you won't have any more of those," he told her confidently.

Looking up into his blue eyes, Maureen believed him completely.

Morgan woke with a sigh once again.

"Man, this Tom guy must be amazing!" Charlotte said enthusiastically.

"He is, he really is." Morgan smiled, remembering the feeling of his strong arm around Maureen's shoulders. "He was helping her repair her apartment after the quake."

"Helpful and macho, I love it," Charlotte marveled.

* * *

"She used the term macho?" Jessie pulled a face. "How old is this woman?"

"She's not old!" Morgan laughed, taking a bite of her pasta. "Oh this is good…"

"Gimme a bite," Jessie insisted, using her fork to take a taste of Morgan's pasta Primavera. "Maybe that's what you need…"

"More pasta?" Morgan replied wryly.

"No, a macho man," Jessie raised her eyebrows in quick succession.

Morgan rolled her eyes. "Uh, no, thank you. No man, no how, right now, thank you."

"Gonna switch sides again?" Jessie asked, her eyes sparkling with humor.

Morgan gave her friend a narrow-eyed look. "I just don't think I need any more distractions right now."

"Morgan, you're a romance writer!" Jessie exclaimed.

"Right, and *those* romances are the ones I need to concentrate on right now," Morgan insisted emphatically.

Jessie sighed, then put her elbow on the table, and rested her chin on her hand. "Maybe that's your problem right now."

"My what?" Morgan practically snapped.

"Your problem," Jessie repeated unapologetically. "The reason you're blocked. No romance."

Morgan made a sour face, pressing her lips together. "Let's just have our lunch, okay? I'll get my head shrunk some other time."

Jessie chuckled. "Fine, fine." She raised her hands and surrendered.

Regardless of her blasé response to Jessie's suggestions, Morgan thought about what Jessie had said on her drive home. She'd meant it when she said she didn't want any relationship at this point. Trying to write was her main focus; it was, after all, her job. She did wonder, though, if Jessie had a point about life basically imitating art. She couldn't write romance, because she had no romance. It was something that would sit like a kernel in her heart for days to come.

***

"You look nice…" Zion commented to Jane that evening at the bar. "Fancier than usual."

84

"Do I usually look like some kind of slouch?" Jane asked acerbically.

"No," Zion assured with a smile, "but your hair all done up, and all the jewels, kinda makes you look more extravagant."

"Well, I had a thing tonight, that's why," Jane told her, waving her hand dismissively.

"What kind of thing?" Zion asked. Jane never seemed to share much about her life.

"Nothing." Jane shrugged. "Just business a thing, you wouldn't understand."

Zion looked back at Jane, wanting to point out that she ran a fairly successful business, so she must understand something about business. But knowing it would just start a fight, she kept silent.

"Speaking of business," Jane continued, not paying any attention to the annoyed look on Zion's face. "Did the contractor get back to you about the expansion plans?"

"I have a meeting with him next week."

"Well, that's not going to work," Jane snapped. "I'm on my trip next week."

Zion had to bite her tongue to keep from replying with equal fervor. Taking a deep breath, she blew it out slowly, before she answered. "I am fully capable of meeting with a contractor on my own."

Jane rolled her eyes. "Don't be silly, just reschedule it."

With a great deal of control, Zion shook her head. "I will handle it."

"Good. Try for the fifth, that's a good day for me."

"I meant I will handle the meeting," Zion told her.

"This is my money too," Jane commented. "I should have input on the project."

Zion blew her breath out in a rush. "Yes, and you said you were going to be a silent partner, but that doesn't seem to be happening now, does it?"

Jane's jaw dropped in shock, and Zion could see the fiery reply forming in her head, but then suddenly, the blistering look turned to tears as Jane's pursed lips started to tremble.

"You don't consider me a partner?" she mumbled, moving to stand. "I think I'm going to just go."

Zion felt guilt flood her instantly. "I'm sorry!" She reached her hand out to stop Jane from leaving. "Please don't go."

Jane shook her head. "I don't understand why you don't just trust that I only want the best for you." Turning, she left the bar quickly.

Zion stared after her dumbfounded, trying to process what had just happened between them.

"She's a vampire, dude!" Steel commented later as Zion lamented and retold the incident.

Dax grimaced at the term, but didn't disagree with Steel's estimation. "Z, how did it go from you doing this, to the two of you doing this?"

Zion sighed. "She wanted to help with the money, she didn't want me to sell properties that are income, to pay for the expansion."

"Why does she give a shit about your income? You two getting married or something?" Steel snapped. She had never liked Jane; she'd always seen her as a user. High-maintenance femmes had never been her thing, so Jane's glamour didn't impress her at all.

Shrugging, Zion shook her head. "I don't know, but she got really mad when I said I could handle it."

Dax and Steel exchanged a knowing look. They both felt that Jane was looking to control Zion, and having a 'business partnership' with her would certainly accomplish that goal.

"Why don't you tell her that you don't want to put this kind of stress on the relationship? Tell her that you just want to keep things with you two on the intimate level," Dax offered, hoping that Zion would be able to extricate herself from Jane's financial clutches at the very least. Zion contemplated what Dax was suggesting, nodding, thinking it might be a good tack to take.

Boy was she wrong. Jane had come to the bar the following night just before closing. Zion had taken her upstairs to have a conversation. Saying what Dax had suggested. Jane's reaction was instant and truculent.

"You wanted my help!" Jane screeched, making Zion wince at the sheer volume of her voice.

"I told you I was able to handle it myself…" Zion interjected.

"But you'd lose income, and you couldn't afford that. I offered to help you and now you want to push me out?" The accusation was sharp.

"It's just causing problems; I would rather we just remain—"

"I know! You want to fuck me, but you don't want me in your life otherwise," Jane accused.

"I never said that," Zion uttered quietly, refusing to raise her voice.

"You didn't have to," Jane sneered, "I can see what's going on."

Zion exhaled sharply, shaking her head sadly. "Nothing is going on."

"I'm just a toy to you, something to play with!"

"That's not true," Zion insisted, walking over to where Jane stood by the windows that looked out all the way down to the water. "I love you," she told her, touching her cheek gently.

Jane looked back at Zion, her eyes widening with surprise. "You do?" she breathed, eyes widening with wonder.

"Yes," Zion repeated, knowing in the back of her mind that she wasn't completely sure, but she was willing to do anything to stop the fight at this point. Jane gave a small cry, and then wrapped her arms around Zion, kissing her passionately. They melted into a passionate embrace, and made love for hours.

Later, as they lay together naked, their bodies still entwined, Jane's body over Zion's, Jane levered herself up, looking down at her partner.

"So, when is our meeting with the contractor?" she asked, her eyes triumphant. Zion felt defeated. After a few moments, she shrugged. "Whenever you want."

Zion crumpled up the letter from Jane's 'associate' reiterating her desire to be part of the current expansion project. Zion had already lined up the money for the project, and was moving ahead. The purchase of the bookstore was already in escrow, and the contractor was finishing up the blueprints for the expansion. The last thing Zion wanted was to deal with Jane and her need to control things.

"Not this time, sister," Zion commented as she tossed the letter into her waste basket.

In the bar, everyone was having a good time. Zion was a bartender short, so Jaims stepped in until Zion could call someone in to help, so the crew was testing Jaims' drink knowledge.

"I need an Alabama Slamma," Steel ordered.

"A what!" Jaims laughed. "Do *you* even know what's in that?" she asked as she looked down at the bartender's guide.

"Sure!" Steel laughed.

"Didn't you almost die once when you overdid it on Southern Comfort?" Jaims queried, raising an eyebrow.

Steel made a gagging face at the mention of the memory. "Yeah."

"So, I'll add extra Southern Comfort to your Alabama Slammer, huh?" Jaims smirked.

"Uh, no, never mind." Steel shook her head, holding up her hands as if to ward off that particular alcohol.

"How about a White Russian?" Jayden suggested.

"Easy!" Jaims laughed, as she mixed vodka, Kahlua, and cream, and handed the drink over to Jayden.

"This is pretty good!" Jayden exclaimed, after one sip.

"Let me try." Shayne nudged.

"How about a slow comfortable screw against a wall?" Flynn asked with a wicked grin.

Jaims sighed, shaking her head. "With friends like you, I really don't need any enemies."

"Aw, but we love ya!" Raquel said, as she slipped behind the bar. "Can I help?"

"Sure!" Jaims readily agreed, stepping aside.

Raquel winked as she mixed Flynn's drink. "I learned a lot of random skills in the Army."

The crew all *ooh'd* and *aww'd* at Raquel's flare, as she poured the various ingredients in the drink, drizzling the sloe gin on the surface and even making easy work of *floating* the Galliano L'Auntentico on top. She handed it to Flynn with another wink.

The crew and even a few bystanders clapped in appreciation.

"What's goin' on here?" Zion asked with a smile, as she approached them all.

"Rock is demonstrating her mad skills." Shayne laughed.

"I see." Zion nodded. "Well, I'll need all the help I can get tonight, Zip can't make it in, and Sherry is starting to feel sick now too."

"Dayum…" Jaims murmured. "You know we got you, Z," she said, looking around the crew and receiving affirming nods.

The crew took turns tending to the bar as best they could.

"Hey handsome." Sarah, one of the regular patrons, winked at Shayne. "Will you put my purse behind the bar?"

"You got it, babe." Shayne smiled.

"Always on the make," Raquel commented to Jaims, as they watched the exchange.

"Disgusting," Jaims replied, grinning.

By 2 o'clock in the morning everyone had taken their turn behind the bar. They were all tired, but they'd made it through.

"I really appreciate all of you pitching in, it helped me out a lot," Zion told them as she wiped down the bar.

"No problem," Jaims said.

"It was fun," Flynn added.

Shayne grinned unrepentantly. "I got numbers."

"Of course you did!" Steel rolled her eyes.

"Glad I could help." Zion winked at Shayne.

The group laughed.

The next morning Zion was surprised to get a message from four different regular patrons saying that there was money missing from their purses. She contacted the crew, asking if they'd seen anyone behind the bar that wasn't supposed to be there. Everyone messaged back that they had not seen anyone.

Jaims messaged Zion separately and asked if the till had been missing any money. Zion told her it hadn't been counted out at that point.

"Why?" Zion messaged.

Jaims grimaced. She had seen Raquel around the area where the purses were set behind the bar. She'd even seen her squatting down in that area. When she'd asked Raquel what she was looking for, Raquel had said something like napkins. Jaims hadn't wanted to believe that it had been anything but what Raquel stated.

Jaims called Zion and told her about her suspicions.

"I don't want to be that friend, you know? That suspects her friend of doing shit like this, but…" Jaims' voice trailed off, as she contemplated what they'd do about Raquel.

Zion blew her breath out at the other end of the line. "This blows."

"I know, Z, I'm sorry." Jaims winced.

"It's not your fault, J," Zion assured her. "I just don't know what we can do about this."

"Still…I saw her, and I just hoped she wasn't doing anything she shouldn't be.

"Saw what?" Raquel asked from Jaims' doorway.

Jaims looked over at her roommate and saw that she looked irritated. "I gotta go," Jaims said into the phone. "I'll talk to you later."

Jaims hung up, looking over at Raquel. "What's up?" she asked, hoping to avoid the question Raquel had asked.

"You were talking about me," Raquel questioned.

Jaims had no idea how to get out of the conversation, she figured she better just *deny, deny, deny.*

"I don't know what you mean," Jaims said, as she stood up from her bed and pocketed her phone. "I'm hungry, did you eat yet?" she asked, moving toward her doorway, which Raquel stood inside.

"What the fuck were you saying about me?" Raquel snapped, adopting an aggressive stance.

"Dude, why are you so paranoid?" Jaims asked, refusing to lie, but not willing to get into an argument with her ever so-volatile roommate either.

Without warning, Raquel shoved her shoulder into Jaims' chest, pushing her back, then using her hands to shove Jaims to the floor. She then proceeded to kick Jaims over and over while Jaims did everything she could to cover herself. Raquel finally stepped back, and Jaims used every ounce of energy and rage she had left to get up off the floor. With a banshee yell of anger, Jaims shoved Raquel out of her room and slammed the door, locking it.

"Get the fuck out!" Jaims screamed through the door. "Get out and don't fucking come back, until you get your fucking ass dried completely out! Get out now, or I'm calling SF PD and you can kiss your fucking career goodbye when I'm done!"

The last threat seemed to get through to Raquel. Jaims heard her slam out of the apartment moments later. Jaims moved to the window in her bedroom, and saw Raquel get into her Jeep and drive off. She slowly made her way to her bathroom. Lifting up her shirt in front of the mirror, she could see bruises already starting to form on her ribs. Her head was aching wildly—one of Raquel's kicks had caught her in the head. When she reached out to turn on the water, she noticed her hands were shaking badly; the adrenaline was beginning to wear off. Splashing water on her face, she felt tears start to sting the corner of her eyes.

She felt undecided in what to do, should she call someone? What would she say? Jaims just couldn't face it at the moment. She lay down on her bed, sighing, tears coming released now, which only made her head hurt more.

Raquel drove aimlessly, her mind reeling between anger that Jaims was ratting her out to Zion, and shame when she remembered what she'd done in retaliation. All she'd been able to think about was the betrayal and the fact that it was Zion that Jaims had confided in. Zion! Why was it always Zion these days? Getting on a freeway on ramp, Raquel pushed the gas pedal down as she did her best to escape the demons inside her head.

Yeah, she'd stolen some money from the purses behind the back bar. It had been easy, since hardly anyone frequented the area. She'd been able to score some pills from the chick that dealt behind the bar. They helped her sleep for a little while. But then she'd been in the kitchen trying to make coffee, when she heard Jaims on the phone.

Wincing, Raquel shook her head, refusing to think about what she'd done. Jaims shouldn't have betrayed her like that. They were best friends…they were like family, damn it!

"They're dead," were the first words out of Garrett's mouth when Raquel answered her phone.

"Who? What are you talking about?" Raquel asked, glancing over at Jaims who had paused the movie they'd been watching.

"Mom and Dad, they're dead," Garrett explained, his voice shaking as he said the words.

"Oh my gawd…what happened?" Raquel paled as she understood what Garrett was saying.

Jaims moved to sit next to where Raquel stood. She extended her hand, and took Raquel's free hand, seeing that something was definitely wrong. Raquel held Jaims' hand, squeezing it as she listened to her brother.

"They were out getting last minute things for their cruise, there was a pile up on the 405. The cops just came to tell us. They're gone."

Raquel nodded her head, as her mind raced. "Okay, okay, I'm coming down, okay? I'll be on the next flight."

"Okay…" Garrett said, his voice trailing off as the doorbell rang. "I gotta get the door."

"I'll be there Garrett, I promise. I'll be there as fast as I can," Raquel assured her little brother.

Garrett hung up without another word. Raquel stood staring off into space for a long moment.

"What happened?" Jaims asked, pulling Raquel down onto the couch, afraid she'd pass out. She looked so pale.

"My parents are dead," Raquel replied, her voice flat.

"Holy shit, okay," Jaims exclaimed, pulling out her phone.

Raquel sat like a statue, still staring into space, blinking every so often, but it was obvious that she was reeling, her mind whirling with the news.

"Okay, there's a flight to LA in two hours, I got us on that," Jaims said.

"Us?" Raquel echoed softly.

"Hell, yes, you don't think I'm going to let you go deal with this alone, do you?"

Raquel blinked a couple times, then looked at Jaims. "I…I don't know what to do."

Jaims nodded, putting her hands on Raquel's shoulders. "That's why I'm going, I'll help you, okay? We will get through this."

Two hours later they were on a flight to Los Angeles. And another two and a half hours later they were pulling up in front of Raquel's childhood home.

The next two weeks passed in a blur for Raquel. Jaims worked with Raquel's Aunt Rosa to arrange the funeral. She also stayed in contact with Zion and the rest of the crew. During that time, Raquel had only asserted herself one time, it was regarding where her brothers would live.

"They're coming back to San Francisco with me," she'd told her aunt, who'd been talking about foster care, since she had three children of her own.

"I do not think that is wise," Rosa dismissed.

Raquel's face had hardened into stone at the thought. "I don't fucking care what you think."

Her aunt had exploded into a barrage of Spanish, most of which Jaims didn't understand, but it was obvious from Rosa's expressions, and Raquel's defiant look, that they weren't nice words.

"They are my family," Raquel countered, "and they are going to live with me. That's all there is to it...."

The next evening, Raquel and Jaims sat at the kitchen table. Jaims made Raquel sit down and eat a sandwich, since she hadn't eaten all day.

"How am I going to do this?" Raquel blurted out loud.

"With help."

Raquel shook her head, looking lost. "I'll never get a chance to make up with them now."

Jaims frowned. "No, but you can honor them by taking care of your brothers."

Raquel nodded, taking a bite of the sandwich and chewing it, looking like she was trying to reconcile what Jaims was saying. Setting down the sandwich, Raquel scrubbed her face with her hands. "I don't even know where we'll live..."

Jaims' phone pinged, disrupting the moment, and she looked at the message, grinning as she did.

"I do," Jaims told her. "Z and the rest of our friends have just finished moving all of our stuff into a three-bedroom apartment."

"What?" Raquel asked. "How?"

Jaims shrugged. "When you told your aunt you wanted the boys with you, I messaged Zion. She has a three-bedroom place that we are now moved into. The boys will have to share a room, but it's the master, so it'll have room for two beds." Jaims looked at her phone again as another message popped up. "Which Dax and Steel just put together and put into the room."

"Wow." Raquel looked amazed. "I…I don't even know what to say."

"You can thank them when we get back." Jaims smiled. "We're family, dude, that's what we do."

Raquel shook her head, unable to believe the generosity of the crew.

Two days after the funeral, Jaims, Raquel, Garrett, and Jackson lugged suitcases and a couple of boxes to the airport and flew back to San Francisco. Raquel had petitioned the family court to request custody of her brothers. According to the court officer, the petition had every chance of being approved, since Raquel was a responsible adult and had proven means and ability to care for the two teenage boys.

Upon arrival in San Francisco, they rented a van to drive the four of them and the boys' possessions to the new apartment. Zion, Dax, Steel, Case, Shayne, Flynn, and their newest member Jayden were there to greet them. They ordered pizza as the boys set themselves up in their new room.

"I'll never been able to thank you guys enough," Raquel told the crew.

"You don't have to thank us," Zion told her. "This is what we do for our family. Jackson and Garrett are ours now too."

Raquel reached out and hugged Zion in a rare show of affection. The rest of the crew piled into the hug, making everyone laugh. The action relieved the emotional moment and bonded the crew closer.

Remembering that moment, Raquel found herself crying as she drove down the freeway; she wasn't entirely sure where she was going. Reaching into her pocket, she clutched the small bag of pills she had left. Making a quick decision, she pulled off on the next exit and found a motel. Checking herself in, she went up to the room that smelled like stale pizza and mildew. She sat on the bed and took the pills out of her pocket. She pulled them out of the bag, and started swallowing them one by one.

*Maybe I'll just die and I won't have to deal with this shit anymore…*was her last thought before everything went black.

Chapter 6

Zion and Steel strode down the hallway of the hospital. At the nurses' station for the ER they spoke with the nurse on duty.

"Our friend was brought here," Zion told the woman. "It was a car accident."

"I'm sorry, if you're only friends, we can't tell you anything. Patient confidentiality," the dark-haired nurse said.

"You can't just tell us if she's, okay?" Steel insisted.

The nurse shook her head. "Patient—"

"Confidentiality," Steel snapped, "I know."

They walked away from the desk, looking at each other. "This is bullshit," Steel growled.

"Indeed," Zion agreed.

It was another hour before Celeste and Daniel arrived. They walked over to the waiting area to talk to Steel and Zion, who had been joined by Shayne and Flynn.

"Have they told you anything?" Celeste asked.

"They wouldn't tell us squat." Zion shook her head.

"They're waiting for you," Steel added.

"For God's sake," Daniel growled, striding over to the nurse's station. "Our daughter, Jaims Carpenter was brought in, she had a car accident."

The same dark-haired nurse looked at her computer. "She's still in the ER. You can go back and see her," she told them. "Here, put these visitor badges on, she is in bed nine."

"I'll tell the bois," Daniel told his wife. "You go ahead."

Celeste walked through the double doors, buzzed in by the nurse. At bed nine, she steeled herself, then poked her head behind the curtain. Jaims lay in the hospital bed with her eyes closed. There was a bandage wrapped around her head, and her arm. Celeste moved to sit down next to the bed, her eyes fixed on her daughter.

Jaims came to, looking around her, realizing she was in the hospital. Glancing over she saw her mother sitting in the chair by her side.

"Mom?" Jaims queried.

"Oh baby!" Celeste exclaimed, leaning forward to touch Jaims on the face gently. "What happened, honey?"

Jaims looked confused for a moment, trying to remember how she ended up where she was. "I...I had another migraine...My pills weren't working...I needed a shot." Jaims hesitated, still trying to remember what had happened.

"Why were you driving, honey? Couldn't Raquel take you?"

At the mention of her roommate, Jaims grimaced. "She, um, she wasn't there."

"Oh honey, you should have waited for her, or called one of us," Celeste soothed.

Jaims nodded, but didn't answer. She remembered just lying in bed for the entire day after Raquel had left. Getting up to go to the bathroom had been excruciating, but she'd done it when she had no choice. The headache had gotten worse. The truth was she had been afraid it was something other than a migraine. The thought had pushed her to drive to the ER in the early hours the next morning. She knew that it was risky, but she'd been afraid to call 911, in case they saw the bruises on her body. In hindsight, the ER staff would have seen them anyway, but she hadn't thought that far, hoping she could keep the focus on her head.

What she hadn't accounted for was the bright headlights of approaching cars in the early hours of dawn, before the sun fully rose. They had blinded her, and she hit a parked car, then careened into oncoming traffic. Afterwards everything went black.

The doctor came into the curtained area then, helping Jaims avoid having to talk about the accident with her mother any further.

"Ah, I see you're awake," the doctor, a middle-aged man with kind brown eyes, said. "And you must be Mom."

Celeste smiled, nodding. "How is she, doctor?"

"Well, she took a nasty blow to her head, I've ordered some scans to check for internal bleeding. I've also ordered a CAT scan." He looked at Jaims then. "You were complaining about a severe headache when you were brought in."

Jaims eyes widened in surprise. "I was?" Jaims replied. She didn't even realize she'd been conscious. "Did I say anything else?" she worried out loud.

"Not that I know of." The doctor grinned. "We'll get you in for those scans as soon as we can, it has been a busy day already this morning."

The doctor left the room, and Jaims did her best to relax. It was hours before they followed through with the scans and many more hours passed until someone finally came to talk to them about the results.

This time, it was a different doctor who came to address the family. Daniel had joined Celeste a little while after the first doctor had been in. He was relaying information to the crew as they were informed of news from the medical staff.

"It looks like we're going to need to admit you," the female doctor announced with a bright but serious smile. "You've got some bleeding in your head we need to watch, and do some more tests for."

"Is it serious?" Celeste asked, her voice laced with worry.

"We won't know until we get those tests run, that's why we want to keep her here until we know what's happening," the doctor told them.

"I understand you have some friends outside that have been waiting to see you," she said with a smile. "As soon as we can get you upstairs to a room, they can come and see you."

"Thanks, doc," Jaims said, nodding and wondering if Raquel was one of those friends.

"Is she okay?" Garrett said anxiously, as they drove to the hospital.

"Is she going to die?" Jackson asked, staring wide-eyed at Jaims, tears in his eyes.

"She's not going to die," Jaims assured the boys. "They said it was a minor gunshot wound."

"But..." Garrett began, his voice trembled.

"Stop!" Jaims told him. "She's going to be fine, okay? She was shot in the arm, okay? It's not fatal."

Both boys nodded somberly.

Jaims exhaled heavily. It was the last thing the boys needed to hear six months after their parents died. Their sister was their world now, and she'd been shot on the job.

At the hospital, Jaims had escorted the boys to the ER, and talked to the nurse there. The pretty redhead had been happy to help. The three of them had been taken back to the ER area Raquel was in, where she was sitting on a gurney as the doctor stitched up her arm.

"Oh Jesus!" Raquel said, seeing the worried look on the boys' faces. "I'm fine! It's just a damned scratch!"

"We thought..." Jackson began.

"I know what you thought," Raquel countered, grinning at her brother. "Gonna take more than some gangster with a gun to take me out."

"That's what Jaims said, but we didn't know."

"Well, you're idiots, so..." Raquel teased.

Relief flooded both boys' faces, as Jaims and Raquel exchanged a look of empathy. Thank you, Raquel mouthed to Jaims. She knew that Jaims had done her best to calm the boys' fears and she appreciated it.

They'd settled into the new apartment as a family unit, with their extended family always on call. Between Jaims and Raquel, things like rides to school and homework were covered. School projects had been split between the rest of the crew, depending on the subject. Jobs like building a mission for school had been turned over to Steel since she was in construction.

"I'm not into tiny construction!" Steel had complained jovially.

Artistic projects had fallen on Flynn and Shayne, who both had artistic flair. Home economic projects were Jayden's area, and anything pertaining to computers fell on Case. Finances were handled between Raquel, Dax, and Zion. It worked well for all of them. They raised the boys together.

"Can we get outta here now?" Raquel asked the doctor. "I need a pizza and a beer."

"Pizza sounds good," Garrett said with a smile.

"I gotta finish my science project!" Jackson interjected.

"Got Dax comin' for that one." Jaims grinned. "Aeronautics degree and all." She waved as if dismissing the degree that Dax held, making the other three laugh.

They left the ER together; another disaster had been avoided.

"Anyone heard from Rock?" Steel asked, glancing around at the rest of the crew gathered in the waiting room.

"Nope," Shayne commented.

"Uh-uh," Flynn remarked.

Jayden shook her head and Case shrugged.

"I texted both Rock and Dax," Zion declared.

"Weird…" Steel murmured.

***

A loud sound outside made Raquel bolt awake. She looked around, not remembering where she was. Slowly it came to her and she realized that she hadn't died as she'd figured she would from taking so many pain pills. Turning over, however, her body decided it wanted whatever was left of those pills out. Jumping out of bed, she ran to the bathroom and threw up into the toilet over and over. Finally, she lay on the floor, exhausted.

Sometime later, she moved to sit up and looked down at her watch. It was 4:00 p.m. She was surprised the manager hadn't banged on the door to tell her to get out yet. She only paid for one day. Getting up off the floor, she moved back into the main part of the room. Sitting down on the bed, she felt tired and hungry. She debated her options; she knew she couldn't go home yet. With that in mind, she went back downstairs and paid the manager for the next two days. Then she walked down to the corner taqueria and bought herself a burrito and a Coke and took it back up to the room.

Turning on the TV, she lost herself in some random show, doing her best to avoid thinking about Jaims. She successfully avoided thinking of Jaims for a while, but eventually she was consumed with wanting to apologize to her best friend and make amends for her ridiculous outburst. She got in her Jeep and drove home.

At the apartment she walked around, noting that Jaims was gone and hoping she'd left a note or something. She did everything she could to kill time. At one point her phone pinged, a text message come through. Hoping it was Jaims she opened the text and saw that the message notification was from Zion. A ripple of fear went through her. Had Jaims gone to Zion and told her what she had done? Steeling herself, she opened the message. It read: *Jaims is in ER, where are you? Come soon!* This set off alarm bells further for Raquel. If Jaims was in the ER, had she really hurt her? She couldn't remember exactly what she'd done. She knew she had been furious, but the rest was a bit of a blur.

If she was in the ER, there might actually be cops waiting there to arrest her. The thought sent a whole new wave of panic through her. The idea that Jaims could really be hurt kept gnawing at her. Had she told their friends? The thought sent a sick feeling shooting through her stomach. She contemplated what their friends would say, what they would be thinking about her. Did they hate her? Of course they hated her now. How could they not? If she was honest with herself, she hated herself too.

She walked to the bathroom and looked in the medicine cabinet. She found nighttime cold medicine; it was brand new. Without bothering to think, she picked up the bottle, opened it and drank the entire contents. Back in her bedroom, she kicked off her tennis shoes and crawled under the covers. As she felt herself growing sleepy. The thought of not waking up occurred again but she just shrugged to herself and closed her eyes.

***

"You scared us!" Zion told Jaims.

"I'm sorry," Jaims replied.

"We're just glad you're probably okay. I mean, except for like your dented skull and all," Flynn teased.

"It's pretty oddly shaped anyway," Shayne added. "So maybe you can wear hats now."

The crew laughed, including Jaims, who immediately regretted it. "Ow."

"Laughing is bad, stop it," Steel told her.

Jaims grinned. "Take the funny twins away then."

"Ya just can't take kids anywhere these days." Case sighed, winking at Jaims.

"You're gonna be okay, right?" Jayden worried, her tone slightly tremulous.

"I think I will."

"Okay, we should get out of here and let Jaims rest," Zion told the group. "Dax said she would be here sometime tomorrow, they're in the middle of some kind of mandatory training."

"Thanks," Jaims told Zion, "I really appreciate all of you."

"We got you," Zion told her, reaching down to squeeze Jaims' hand gently.

No one had mentioned Raquel, where she was, or why she hadn't shown up at the hospital. Jaims wanted to ask if they'd heard from her, but didn't want to start a conversation that could lead to questions she didn't want to answer yet.

The second night in the hospital, Jaims turned over in the bed, trying to get comfortable. She hated sleeping on her back, and because of that, she woke up frequently at night. As she adjusted her pillow, she opened her eyes and almost jumped out of her skin. Raquel was sitting huddled in a chair next to her bed, staring at her.

"Jesus!" Jaims exclaimed, then she scowled. "What are you doing here?"

Raquel didn't answer for a long moment, looking hesitant, like she wasn't sure why she was there. Finally, she answered, "I needed to see if you were okay."

"That's yet to be determined," Jaims replied acerbically.

Raquel visibly flinched. "It's my fault."

Jaims didn't answer, waiting to see what Raquel said next. She wasn't willing to say it was *okay* because it wasn't. What Raquel had done, attacking her the way she did, was far from okay.

Raquel moved to the edge of the chair, grabbing the rail on the hospital bed, her look pained. "I'm so sorry, Jaims!" she whispered desperately. "I don't know what got into me."

Jaims looked back at her friend of years, her eyes searching Raquel's face. "You're in too deep with the painkillers." Raquel sat back, her face falling as she lowered her eyes. Slowly she nodded her head. "You gotta stop."

Raquel sniffed loudly, shaking her head. "I don't know how."

"You need help," Jaims told her.

Raquel seemed to shrink into herself, wrapping her arms around herself. "I can't do it, Jaims."

"Why the hell not?" Jaims asked. Raquel shrugged, shaking her head. "You're one of the strongest women I've ever met, Rock, if you can't do this, then no one can."

Raquel drew a deep breath in through her nose, pressing her lips together. It was obvious she was trying to gather her strength. She bit her lip, contemplating the idea of quitting and what it would take.

"So, like rehab," Raquel commented.

"Yeah, like rehab."

Raquel sighed heavily. "You know I hate talking to strangers about shit."

Jaims let out a short burst of laughter. "Just strangers?"

Raquel scrunched up her face in a humorous mask. "I know, I'm not the proper lesbo, I don't like to talk about my fuckin' feelings."

Jaims couldn't help but chuckle. It was definitely true; Raquel was the last person to talk about feelings. She would just as soon chuck you on the chin and tell you to suck it up. "Maybe talking about things with strangers would be easier."

Raquel slid her tongue over her front teeth. "Maybe having a root canal with no Novocain would be easier."

Jaims didn't reply, waiting for Raquel to come to grips with what she would need to do to get off the drugs.

After some minutes passed between them, Raquel nodded her head, looking resigned. "I'll look into getting into rehab through the Army."

"That's the badass I know and love." Jaims smiled.

Raquel reached out to take Jaims' hand, careful not to bump the IV taped there. "I really am sorry, Jaims, can you forgive me?"

"You're my best friend, Rock, of course I can forgive you," Jaims told her. "But I need you to know that you're not welcome back at the apartment till you're really clean, okay?"

Raquel's eyes widened, but Jaims' words told her that she'd definitely gone over the line. Jaims was the most easy-going person she knew, and if she managed to do this to their friendship, then she was in worse shape than she even realized.

Chapter 7

The night was chilly, but he felt warm. He was in love. Wasn't that what love did to a person? Make them feel all warm and happy. Davis was the first man he'd ever been completely in love with and things were going so well! Sam pulled his coat around him closer and quickened his steps. They were having a nice meal in tonight, and he was anxious to get home with the groceries so he could start cooking!

At their apartment, Sam stopped to pet the calico cat that always sat on the brickwork next to the stairs. She purred and rubbed up against him, begging for more attention.

"I can't today, Sassy." He smiled at the cat. "I gotta make my man some dinner!"

He made his way upstairs, his mind already churning over what he needed to start first. It was such a giddy feeling to know he was cooking for someone who would really appreciate it!

Two hours later, Davis burst through the front door, flowers in hand, and greeted Sam with a huge smile, his bright blue eyes sparkling. They hugged, while the delectable scent of dinner swirled the room.

After a sweet kiss, Davis put his hand to Sam's face. "How was your day?"

Sam smiled, once again feeling warm and content. "It was good. How was yours?"

"Alright. Did Jenny in Accounting get back to you about that account you were worried about?"

Sam pressed his lips together, his green eyes glistened with subdued joy.

"What?" Davis asked as he took his jacket off and hung it up in the closet, perplexed by the look on Sam's face.

Sam bit his lip, trying to keep himself from crying. "I just…" he began, as a tear spilled over.

"Aww, what's this?" Davis moved to take Sam in his arms, hugging him.

Sam snuggled against Davis's broad chest, inhaling the scent of lavender and Old Spice. "What's wrong?" Davis queried gently when Sam sniffled again.

"I'm just not used to someone who actually listens to me about work and stuff," Sam admitted.

Davis grimaced, shaking his head slightly. "Well, you have me now, so that's not going to be a problem anymore." He hugged Sam tighter. "Now, let's eat, I'm starving and dinner smells wonderful!"

It was another great night, in a series of great nights.

Morgan emerged from her hypnotic state with a smile still on her face.

"And what's that about?" Charlotte asked pointedly.

"This is someone new," Morgan intimated. "He's so in love, I can still feel it buzzing in my head."

"Where is this one located?" Charlotte asked as she started her notes.

"San Francisco, I think." Morgan searched her memory, remembering her impressions.

"And when?"

"Seemed much more recent…" Morgan murmured, her mind going back over the experience.

"How recent?' Charlotte queried.

Morgan blinked a couple of times, then shrugged. "They don't come with time stamps, you know."

"Any clues?"

Morgan concentrated harder, trying to look for anything that would give her an idea or indication of the time period, finally shaking her head again. "Nope, nothing really."

"And no more about the girl and the firefighter during the earthquake?" Charlotte asked hopefully.

Morgan grunted in exasperation. "No, it's not like some kind of preview, what comes, comes."

Charlotte nodded, looking disappointed.

Morgan left the office feeling annoyed; suddenly she had to please the hypnotherapist too? It was bad enough her publisher was starting to push her for the next set of pages for her new book, and Morgan had nothing to give them. It became a constant knot in her stomach every time she wasn't writing. And every time she sat down to write, the words just wouldn't come. Previously, the words had flown out of her like water, she couldn't type fast enough. Now…nothing, nothing was flowing. It was beyond frustrating!

Walking out of the office building, Morgan turned right, needing to walk, to clear her head. As she walked, she thought again about Sam and Davis, they seemed so happy, the warm feelings just reverberated through her body. It made her miss having someone to count on, someone to curl up with at the end of the day. Her last relationship had been short and unsatisfying. She identified herself as bi-sexual, and she hadn't really been with a woman in many years, but there had never been anyone who had made her feel the way that she had felt Sam did in her memory. It made her ache at her core, at the remembrance.

She didn't know if it was coincidence or just happenstance that she was walking toward the Castro District of town. She passed the Pink Triangle, the memorial for gay and lesbian Holocaust victims. The thought disturbed her, what so many LGBT members had been through at the hands of the Nazis, and many others for that matter. So many men and women had and were still being targeted for their sexuality, something Morgan felt no one could control.

A block later she saw Orphan Andy's, a local café, with a rainbow flag hanging prominently on the light post outside its doors. She walked into the café, taking in the colorful Tiffany style lamps hung over the tables and diner-style counter. The young man at the counter told her to take a seat anywhere. She sat in a booth at the far end of the restaurant, facing the door. She wanted to do some people watching.

A young man wearing a rainbow tank, long sleeved shirt, impossibly skinny jeans, dangling rhinestone earrings, and makeup bounced up to the table. Morgan saw that his name tag read *Jerry.*

"What can I get ya, sweetie?" he asked cheerily.

"Coffee please?" Morgan answered.

"Anything to eat?"

Morgan smiled brightly. "I'll look at the menu, thanks."

Jerry winked, and sauntered off, returning with coffee, cream, and sugar a minute later.

Fixing her coffee, Morgan checked out the clientele. There was a couple of older men sitting and arguing amiably over coffee. There was a younger woman sitting alone, playing with her phone while sipping her drink and absent-mindedly eating a pancake. Then there was the heated discussion going on behind the counter between two waiters and the cook; they seemed to be debating whether or not George Michael was hotter than Boy George.

Morgan was still grinning about the spicy remarks flying back and forth when Jerry returned. He glanced over his shoulder at his co-workers, then rolled his eyes at them, looking back at Morgan. "They can never solve the mystery of the Georges."

"They do seem to have rather strong opinions," Morgan observed.

"Personally, I prefer Jon Bon Jovi." Jerry chuckled.

"Oh, me too," Morgan agreed.

"So did you decide on food?"

"I did. I think I'll take the stuffed French toast."

"Good choice!" Jerry enthused.

Morgan sat enjoying the atmosphere, watching people come and go. As her food arrived, she heard the bell jingle at the front door, and she glanced up to notice a woman with short blonde hair with dark roots. She was dressed in sweat pants and a dark blue sweatshirt that read Navy on it. Morgan watched as the woman interacted with the staff, it was obvious she was a regular customer as they knew her order, and joked with her as she waited.

At one point, the woman walked down the aisle toward Morgan. Their eyes connected for a long moment. The woman nodded to her politely and Morgan was stunned to notice that the woman had bright cornflower blue eyes. The woman continued on by, as Morgan did her best to catch her breath. She'd never seen eyes that color before, except in the memories of her past lives. The idea shocked her, what were the odds? Desperately trying to think of something to say when the woman returned, Morgan found herself completely tongue tied. The woman walked with long, purposeful strides. She picked up her order from the counter and before Morgan could blink, she was out the door.

Morgan stilled, feeling completely flabbergasted. Maybe it meant nothing, maybe she'd just never noticed other people with the same color eyes. Maybe it was because she was still under the effects and feeling dazed from being hypnotized. After a while, Morgan managed to convince herself that was the reason for her reaction. But then she felt foolish, imagining something was probably just a coincidence.

Regardless, she couldn't help but ask Jerry when he returned with her check a bit later.

"Who was that woman that came in earlier?"

"Who?" Jerry asked.

"The one in the Navy sweatshirt."

"Oh, her? That was Zion, she owns a place down the street," Jerry commented.

Morgan nodded, not wanting to ask too many questions, and appear too stalkerish.

"What do you think it means?" Jessie asked a couple of days later when they had lunch. Morgan had told her about the encounter with the blue-eyed "Zion."

Morgan shrugged. "Probably nothing."

Jessie made a sound in the back of her throat. "Right, that's why you had to tell me about it."

"You're my best friend, who else am I supposed to talk with about this kind of stuff?"

Jessie grinned impishly, taking a bite of her sandwich. "Do you think you were just still floating from the whole Sam and Davis thing?"

Morgan contemplated the question. "I guess that's possible. I mean, the feeling of being in love was really like a drug," Morgan smiled sadly. "It was really nice."

"See?" Jessie gestured with her glass of iced tea. "You need to find a new love interest!"

Morgan rolled her eyes, shaking her head.

"I need to find the will to write again, is what I need," Morgan huffed.

Her writing not going anywhere was like a constant weight on her, and she couldn't get rid of it. She'd been hoping that the hypnotherapy sessions would help, but they didn't seem to be doing anything other than make her feel more depressed about her love life.

"Maybe one leads to the other," Jessie told her.

Morgan simply sighed.

***

"Where is Rock?" Zion asked Jaims when she came to visit her in the hospital, alone for once.

Jaims had been kept in the hospital an extra couple of days, due to a concussion they wanted to monitor. It had been noticed amongst her friends that Raquel had seemingly never appeared to visit.

"Right about now," Jaims said, glancing at the clock on the wall, "she is entering rehab."

Zion's eyes went wide. "Woah," was all she uttered. She then canted her head. "How and when did that happen?"

"She came to see me," Jaims told her. "We talked and I told her that she needed to go into rehab."

"Okay…" Zion nodded, knowing that Jaims wasn't giving her all the details.

"Trust me, she's going," Jaims said. "I told her she wasn't welcome back to our apartment until she was clean."

Zion nodded, still looking shocked. "And she agreed?"

"Yep."

Zion scratched her eyebrow, a sign that she wanted to ask more questions, but was forcing herself not to do so.

Jaims grinned, thinking she was likely driving Zion crazy, but not wanting to talk about what happened to compel Raquel to go to rehabilitation.

Later that night, Jaims's cell phone rang; she knew without looking that it was Raquel.

"Hey," she answered.

"Rehab sucks," Raquel replied.

Jaims grinned to herself. "You thought it was gonna be fun?"

"I figured there would at least be caffeine."

"No caffeine?" Jaims grimaced. "That's gotta be against the Geneva Convention."

"Right?" Raquel said. Jaims could hear the humor in her voice. "Still in the hospital?"

"Yeah," Jaims replied, "no caffeine here either."

"We should stage a rebellion," Raquel mused.

"Indeed," Jaims agreed. They were both silent for a long moment. "You okay?" Jaims asked gently.

"Yeah…" Raquel sighed, "withdrawals will be starting up soon."

"You're strong enough to do this, Rock," Jaims assured.

Raquel blew her breath out. "You better be right."

"I always am."

"Yeah, yeah, I'll call ya when the siege is over."

Jaims drew in a deep breath, wincing at her end, because she knew that withdrawals were likely to be brutal, and she knew she couldn't do anything to help. "Just take good care."

"Got it."

"You do," Jaims told her. "You have got this, Rock. I'm here if you need me."

Raquel smiled sadly at Jaims's words, thinking she was lucky to have a friend that put up with everything that she put through Jaims through, and still, despite it all, was willing to be her friend. "Thank you."

"Thank me after rehab," Jaims joked.

"I will," Raquel answered, her tone serious.

Chapter 8

The heat was oppressive, even at night! It was 102 degrees! Raquel was sure she was baking inside her uniform. The helmets they wore only made it worse. Even though she wore a bandana over her hair, she just sweated through the fabric. Reaching up she loosened the strap; it was making her itch under her chin. Damned heat rash again!

She was lying in the dirt; they'd been told to get down and wait for a signal. Unfortunately, the slight breeze wasn't helping keep the sand out of her eyes. She wished she'd brought her goggles. Turning her head to the right, she checked their line; her team was spread out, they were tasked with checking out a warehouse, but there had been some insurgent activity, and their sergeant was being extra careful tonight. They had lost a guy a few weeks back, and she was sure that had made the sergeant a little more paranoid.

"Clear!" came the radio call.

Raquel was climbing to her feet when there was sudden burst of gunfire from the left. Someone yelled hit the deck, and Raquel did, but her helmet dropped and skittered across the sand. Regardless, she dropped to her knee and brought up her rifle, looking through her night sites to see if she could see movement from where the firing had occurred. There was yelling and firing, and Raquel identified a person moving from the side of the warehouse.

"I have contact!" she called to her sergeant.

"Do not fire!" the sergeant ordered back. There were radio calls trying to figure out who their opponent was. The last thing they needed was a friendly fire incident. They were not sure the firing was meant for them, or if it was between two other combatants.

Raquel settled her finger on the trigger guard, awaiting an order. Things grew quiet again, but the radio chatter continued. Glancing over at her helmet laying six feet away, Raquel wondered if she should try to retrieve it. She debated, thinking about the ass chewing she would get for it not being on her head, but not wanting to move, in case she needed to fire.

After five minutes, she finally decided to grab her helmet. Just as she moved to crouch, there was gun fire. She never felt the bullet hit her...things just went black.

"Hey," Jaims answered like she always did when she knew it was Raquel, which made Raquel smile, inordinately happy that their friendship still seemed intact.

"Home now?" Raquel asked.

"Yep, they decided the dent in my head was fine," Jaims joked. She heard Raquel's swift intake of breath and hurried on. "I'm good, Rock, I really am. They said the migraines were probably due to a small bleed I already had and the accident just really pissed it off."

"I'm sure what I did, didn't help either," Raquel put in seriously.

"Maybe not," Jaims allowed, "but the important thing is that I'm fine. Okay?"

"Okay," Raquel said, not sounding convinced, but obviously not in the mood to argue.

"How are you doing?" Jaims asked.

"Withdrawals were fun," Raquel commented. "But I lived."

"That's good."

"Yeah." Raquel nodded. "I'm just glad that part is over."

"So, what's happening now?"

"A lot of talking, like a lot." Raquel curled her lips in disgust. "They want me to talk about my feelings about being shot."

"That's probably a good thing, right?"

Raquel blew out her breath. "I hate it."

"Do you want to talk to me about it?" Jaims offered, moving to sit up in bed. Raquel was silent for a long moment. "Do you want to tell me about how it happened?" Jaims encouraged.

"It was dark out," Raquel began. "We were on patrol. I was a dumbass and loosened my chin strap, 'cause it was so fuckin' hot and it fell off when I hit the deck…"

"Oh geeze…" Jaims breathed.

"Yup," Raquel said, "that's when it happened."

Jaims grimaced. "Would it of made a difference if you had the helmet on, though?"

Raquel was quiet again; she'd never actually thought about that. "Maybe not…I mean it was a damned sniper…maybe not."

"Those are high velocity rounds, aren't they?" Jaims asked, surprising herself with what she'd remembered from all their talks about weapons.

Raquel let out a short laugh. "Damn, J, you remember everything I tell ya, don't you?"

Jaims laughed. "Yeah I just shocked myself with that one too."

"But you might be right," Raquel commented. "Never once thought about that."

"Well, think about it."

"I will," Raquel said, shaking her head at her end of the line. "So, what's up with the crew?"

It was a shift away from the serious talk, and Jaims knew that Raquel needed to chew on what they'd been talking about, so she indulged her.

They talked for another hour, Jaims regaling her with the happenings of the bar, and with their friends. By the time they were ready to hang up, Raquel was smiling.

"Hey, they have a family day here coming up like next week, would you come?" Raquel asked.

"You bet," Jaims answered. "Are the boys coming?"

"I'm gonna ask them, I wanted to ask you first."

"Just text me the deets and I'll be there," Jaims told her.

"Roger that."

They both hung up feeling better.

***

"What's happening? Where are you going?" Sam's tone was panicked.

"I have to get down there!" Davis told him, his voice raised for the first time since they'd met.

"Why?" Sam said pleadingly.

Davis turned to him as he pulled on his jacket, his face etched with disbelief. "How can you ask me that?"

Sam sat down on the chair in the foyer, looking defeated. "I don't know, I just…" His voice trailed off as he raised his hand in a gesture of futility. "I thought you loved me," he offered quietly.

Davis blinked a couple of times as he digested what Sam had just said. He went down on one knee in front of his partner, taking Sam's hands in his. "I do love you!"

Sam raised his eyes to Davis, his look reflected both hope and confusion. "Then why do you have to go to him?"

Davis blew his breath out, shaking his head. "Because he's in a dangerous place right now, baby. I loved him once; I need to make sure he's okay. He's at the store right now, I need to get down there." Davis squeezed his hands gently. "Do you understand?"

"But what if he hurts you?" Sam asked, his true concern coming to light.

"He won't," Davis stated as he stood up. "I have to go." He leaned down and kissed Sam on the lips, then turned and left the apartment. A loud crack of thunder shook the apartment, Sam shuddered.

The early winter storm raged outside; lightning lit up the therapy room. Regardless, Charlotte went on with the session she was having with Morgan. Glancing down at her watch, Charlotte hoped she could get through the rain to the train station. Why hadn't she driven today? she pondered idly.

Pacing the floor, Sam did his best to calm himself. Davis would be fine, he told himself over and over again. He just couldn't get himself to believe it. Jake, Davis's ex-boyfriend, was a manic depressive and could be very volatile, it was the reason Davis had left Jake. The more Sam thought about Davis going down to the bookstore that Jake owned, the more pictures flashed through his head. Sam knew that Jake had a gun, he kept it in the store for protection, and the idea that Jake would use it either on himself or Davis was the thought that kept rolling around in Sam's head.

It had been a half an hour, and Sam just couldn't take any more. Grabbing his jacket, he left the apartment, running down the stairs instead of waiting for the elevator. He ran out into the rainy night, getting instantly drenched by the downpour. Lightning still flashed, followed by loud claps of thunder as he ran the ten blocks to the store. As he rounded the corner, he could see the lights were on in the bookstore. The bar next door was lit up as well, with music pumping out of the open double doors. It was a gay bar, what else was there in The Castro? Men hung around under the small awning. Sam and Davis had gone there a few times, but tonight was different, and Sam couldn't think about the good times they had there until he knew Davis was safe.

Before he could get to the door of the store, Sam heard a sound that terrified him. It was a gunshot! Sliding as he skidded to a stop at the door, Sam threw open the door, screaming Davis's name!

Suddenly there was a sound like a small explosion right outside the window of the therapy room. Charlotte all but fell out of her chair. It was the sound of the transformer blowing with a shower of sparks, and then the lights went out. Charlotte got up and ran out to the outer office looking out the windows there, seeing that the sparks were still coming off the transformer. She grabbed the phone to try and call the fire department, not sure what else to do.

Morgan jerked upright, looking around the room in a panic. Her heart was racing and she was breathing heavily. She was overwhelmed with dread and it drove her to her feet. Before she could gather her thoughts clearly, she was running out of the room through the open door and out of the office. It was dark so she felt her way down the hallway, toward the glass doors that she could make out because of the lightning firing off. *I have to get there; I have to get there!* Was the thought occupying her head.

Outside the double doors, she made a right and began to run. Her heels caused her to slide a few times so she kicked them off and continued on her headlong flight down the wet streets. She had to get there, she needed to make it!

***

"Oy, it's pissing rain out there!" Case complained as she pulled her beanie off, shaking the rain from the material as they walked into Fancy's.

"Yeah, it's bad." Steel curled up her lips in disgust. "Means the site will be a mud pit tomorrow. That's gonna suck."

"Who's going to suck, what?" Flynn leered next to them.

"Alright, none of that," Zion told the younger woman, giving her a narrowed look. She shook her head, a grin forming on her lips. "BB and Errol are at the table, get outta my doorway." Zion gestured with the bar towel she was holding.

As the small group walked away, a woman burst through the doors to the bar. Zion turned to greet her, but the woman's disheveled appearance and the fact that she looked nearly hysterical had Zion immediately calling to her friends. Despite the commotion, the bar owner couldn't help but notice the striking red hair, as wet as it was, and the bright green eyes.

"Where is he!" Morgan screamed; her eyes were wide with terror.

Zion moved to her side. "Ma'am, who are you looking for?"

"He's here, I know he's here!" Morgan's head swiveled from side to side, her eyes scanning the crowd. "The bookstore, the bookstore! It's gone!"

Zion nodded. "Yes, it closed last year..." Her voice trailed off as she steered Morgan over to a chair. She gestured to Case. "Run upstairs to my apartment, grab me some towels."

"He has to be here..." Morgan said, her tone dazed.

Zion knelt next to Morgan, taking her hand, looking up at her. "Ma'am, who has to be here?" Her tone was soothing. "I can help you, if you'll tell me who you're looking for."

"Davis!" Morgan cried. "I heard a gunshot!"

Zion took a deep breath, exhaling slowly. "Okay, you think that Davis was shot?"

"Oh God no...not my Davis..." Morgan began crying uncontrollably.

"We don't know that he was shot," Zion told Morgan, realizing that this woman might be in the middle of some terrible trauma, and wanting to be as gentle as possible with her state of mind.

Suddenly Morgan focused on Zion's face. Her bright green eyes flicked from haunted to terrified and then recognition finally dawned on her. "Your eyes…" Morgan said, "they're like his."

Zion didn't know what to make of the statement, so she nodded slowly. "Okay."

Morgan blinked a couple of times, like she was trying to come out of a trance. She shook her head. "Where am I?"

Zion stared intently at the woman for a long moment. "You're at a bar called Fancy's. Can you tell me your name?"

Morgan opened her mouth to answer, but her eyebrows knit in confusion. She shook her head, looking down at her hands.

"Okay." Zion nodded, as Case approached them with towels. Zion stood up, taking the towels and giving Case a pointed look.

"Let's get you dried off and warm, maybe we can talk in a little bit, okay?" They draped one of the towels around Morgan's shoulders.

Morgan gave Zion a wonderous look, but then blinked again, and nodded.

"Take her up to my apartment and stay with her, okay?" Zion instructed Case. "I'll be up in a bit."

"Got it." Case nodded, pulling her beanie onto her head and then helped Morgan out of the chair and carefully lead her to the back of the bar, and up the back stairs.

Upstairs in Zion's apartment, Case tried to get Morgan to sit down, but Morgan shook her head and wandered around. Case helplessly followed her. Morgan entered the bathroom and sat down on the side of the large soaking tub, looking wistful for a moment. Then she got up and wandered again.

"Ma'am?" Case queried gently, her British accent evident. Morgan's eyes turned to her. She didn't really see the beanie cap, or the dark-rimmed glasses Case wore.

"Are you alright? Is there anything I can get you?" Case asked hopefully. "A cup of tea maybe?"

Morgan blinked a couple of times, and nodded her head. Case let out a sigh of relief, grateful she could do something useful.

"Aces! Why don't you sit right here..." Case guided Morgan to a chair at Zion's small kitchen table, within sight of the galley kitchen. She knew Zion would kill her if she let this lady out of her sight. "I'll make the tea."

Morgan sat obediently in the chair, her look still very dazed and confused.

As Case made tea, she glanced repeatedly at Morgan trying to assess the woman's state of mind. When the tea was finished, she brought it to the table, and offered her cream and sugar. Morgan shook her head and took a sip of the warm drink. Case sat at the table with her, hoping that Zion got upstairs soon.

"You're from England?" Morgan asked softly.

"Yes ma'am." Case smiled.

"What brought you here?" Morgan queried.

"Trouble." Case grinned laconically.

Morgan smiled, wistfully. "A boy?"

Case raised an eyebrow, obviously this woman had no idea what kind of bar she'd stumbled into this night. "Not bloody likely!"

When Morgan looked back at her in confusion, Case shook her head. "I got into a bit of a pinch with my habit of hacking things."

"Oh, on the computer?"

"Yes."

"So, you're a hacker." Morgan nodded.

"I'm a white hat, not a black hat," Case clarified.

Morgan looked perplexed. "I'm sorry?"

"Never mind." Case waved away the conversation. "How's your tea?"

"It's perfect, thank you."

It was another hour before Zion could break away from the bar and come upstairs.

"Where is she?" Zion asked, glancing around as she walked into the living room.

Case, who was now lounging on Zion's couch with long jean clad legs crossed, her foot bouncing as she played with her phone, grinned and hooked her thumb toward Zion's bedroom.

"The lady got tired, so I figured you'd be okay with her crashing in your bed."

Zion stared at her friend, her mouth agape. Case looked unconcerned, knowing that Zion was always the gallant type, and would have offered Morgan her bed anyway. "Oh, and I gave her a pair of your sweats and shirt so she could get dry."

Zion sighed nodding. "Okay, I'll take it from here."

"I'll bet." Case chuckled as she rose from the couch.

"Watch it…" Zion warned.

Case put her hands up, even as a devilish smile curved her lips. "I'm going, I'm going."

Zion did her best to be quiet as she creeped into her bedroom to grab a pair of sweats and a shirt.

Glancing over at the bed, Morgan was sleeping peacefully, the covers tucked up under her chin. It was impossible not to notice how beautiful this woman was. She reminded Zion of Ginger Rogers, with her fiery red hair and sweetheart-shaped face. Sighing quietly, Zion made her way back out into the living room and quickly changed her clothes. After doing some work on her laptop, she finally stretched and made herself comfortable on the couch, listening to the rain outside.

Morgan sat cross legged on the floor in front of Zion, her green eyes surveyed the woman asleep on the couch. She took in the dark blue sweatpants with the Navy emblem on them, and the white Henley style long sleeved shirt. The woman was indeed handsome, with her white-blonde hair cut short; the blonde hair covered dark hair underneath. She noticed she had chiseled cheek bones and a strong jaw.

Morgan remembered some of what had happened the night before, but she was hoping this woman could fill in the blanks.

As Zion opened her eyes, she saw that she was being stared at.

"Well, good morning." Zion grinned. "How are you feeling this morning?"

Morgan pressed her lips together, watching as Zion sat up and stretched. Her eyes widening slightly when Zion looked back down at her, meeting her eyes.

"I…" Morgan stammered, a bit entranced by the cornflower-blue eyes she'd seen so many times in her hypnotized state. "It's you…" she whispered.

"Me?" Zion's eyebrows arched. "Me, how?"

Morgan laughed softly, shaking her head, knowing she sounded like a crazy person.

"Never mind." Morgan waved away her comment. "I was wondering if you could fill me in on what happened last night?"

Zion stifled a yawn, and nodded. "But can we get some coffee going first?"

"Oh, I'm sorry!" Morgan shook her head, looking somewhat aghast. "You need to wake up, I can just sit quietly while you do that."

Zion stood up, holding her hand out to Morgan. "Come have coffee with me."

Morgan smiled at the gesture, and took Zion's hand, allowing herself to be pulled gently up to her feet. As they made their way to the kitchen, Zion glanced at Morgan with an odd smile on her face.

"By the way, I'm Zion."

"Oh!" Morgan chuckled, realizing how odd their situation really was. "I'm Morgan."

Morgan watched Zion boil water in a kettle, grind coffee beans and put them into a glass pitcher looking contraption. It was fascinating to watch her pour the water over the grounds and then replace the lid of the pitcher.

"Now what happens?" Morgan asked.

"Gotta let it steep for a bit." At Morgan's quizzical look, she continued, "You've never used a French press before?"

"Oh! Is that what that is? I've heard of them, but I've never seen or used one. Is it really better?"

Zion shrugged. "I like it, but you can be the judge."

Morgan couldn't help but admire Zion from behind as the other woman got down coffee mugs. She had a long lean look about her, and a rather nice behind, even in sweatpants. Morgan felt herself blush and looked away when Zion turned around.

A comfortable silence passed between them before Morgan spoke. "I think you're right about the French press, this tastes better than normal coffee."

Zion smiled, and nodded in agreement. "So about last night, what do you remember?"

Morgan closed her eyes for a moment. "I remember being completely terrified about something, and I remember it was raining cats and dogs outside..." As her voice trailed off she shrugged, shaking her head.

Zion blinked a couple of times, surprised at the information Morgan remembered. That was all she remembered? She proceeded to explain to Morgan what had happened the night before.

"Wow!" Morgan exclaimed, stunned by what all she'd apparently mentally missed.

"You can say that again," Zion agreed warmly.

"I was at my appointment with the hypnotherapist and—"

"Say what?" Zion interrupted.

Morgan pressed her lips together, knowing how weird it probably sounded to the woman before her. "I know, it sounds crazy…"

"No, no." Zion shook her head. "It's just not something you hear very often, or ever."

Morgan nodded. "I know, but I started having these dreams that seemed so real, but they were always from another time and place. I had to find out why it kept happening. A friend of mine suggested this therapist that was trained in hypnosis, so I've been giving it a try."

Zion sat back in her chair, a curious look on her face. "And what have you found out?"

Morgan hesitated. Maybe this woman would think she was insane, but then again, this woman had just allowed her to stay in her home overnight, not knowing anything about her. Zion obviously was someone put in her path for a reason, and Morgan really did want to investigate that too. Deciding that it wouldn't hurt to tell Zion everything, Morgan continued.

"So last night…" Zion prompted at the end of Morgan's explanation.

"Last night I was experiencing Sam and Davis, and Davis had gone to check on his manic-depressive ex that owned the bookstore."

"The bookstore that I bought and am working on incorporating into the club," Zion added, nodding. "You were asking about the bookstore, that's why."

Morgan blinked a couple of times, then nodded. "I guess so. I was probably still experiencing Sam and did what he may have done."

"That is wild." Zion sounded amazed.

"Do you want to hear the really crazy part?" Morgan asked.

"What's that?"

"In every scenario I experienced, there was a person with the exact same color of eyes as yours," Morgan told her, wondering if she should have said anything.

Zion's reaction of complete shock and disbelief answered that question for.

"I'm sorry," Morgan offered immediately, "I shouldn't have…I mean, that's just not…" Morgan moved to stand, thinking she needed to get out of there before Zion threw her out for being a nut. Zion's hand on her arm stopped her.

"Morgan, it's okay," Zion told her. "It's just kind of an odd experience to hear about all of this."

"I understand." Morgan nodded. "I'm sorry if it's too much."

"It's not too much," Zion assured, gesturing to the chair Morgan had been sitting. "Please, finish your coffee and let me ponder on this a bit."

Morgan did as she bade, quietly trying to read Zion's thoughts.

Zion's thoughts were racing, marveling over what she'd just heard, and contemplating what it all meant. For whatever reason, she believed everything that Morgan had said. She knew that it was probably strange to trust a random stranger, but she felt a kind of pull toward the woman, and she didn't know what to make of it all.

Zion's cell phone broke the silence, interrupting her thoughts.

"Excuse me," Zion said as she got up to pick up her cell phone lying on the kitchen counter. "Hello?"

Morgan watched as Zion's visage darkened, her lips twitching in agitation.

"No," Zion said, making a cutting gesture with her hand, "I don't have to listen, I'm already finished with this conversation." Zion stood holding her phone away from her face, as the person on the other end of the line continued talking. Zion shook her head, rolling her eyes.

"Fancy, we're done talking, there is no deal. I don't need your help, so stop sending your little minion here to bother me." She stood shaking her head as the person apparently wasn't convinced.

"Well, if I fail, then I fail and you can come to pick at the remains. Now, I need to go. Goodbye." With that Zion disconnected the call.

Morgan pressed her lips together as she physically held herself back from commenting on the call. Even so, her green eyes widened slightly.

"I'm sorry about that," Zion declared as she put the phone down on the counter.

Morgan shook her head. "No need to apologize, this is your house." She smiled, eyes sparkling with humor.

Zion laughed. "True."

"I really should get out of your way," Morgan said, as she set her empty coffee cup down.

As she made a move to get up, her memory jangled, causing her to wince. "Oh, hell."

"What?" Zion asked, looking concerned.

Morgan sighed loudly. "I forgot," she said, putting her hand to her forehead, rubbing it, "I didn't drive yesterday. I took an Uber, because of the storm. No matter," she added, "I'll just order one…" Her voice trailed off as she looked around. "And I have no idea where my phone is."

Zion chuckled. "Your clothes are in my bathroom, drying out. Maybe there?"

"Aw, yes." Morgan nodding getting up from the table. "Is it okay if I get them?" she asked, since she needed to go back through Zion's bedroom to get to the bathroom.

"Of course." Zion nodded, picking up her coffee and taking a long sip.

Morgan entered the kitchen again after checking the bathroom, shaking her head. "Nope, nothing there. I'm guessing I left my purse with my phone, back at the therapist's office."

"Well, let me get dressed and I can drive you over there," Zion said, standing. "Actually I can give you a ride home if you'd like? I have a light day today."

"I don't want to put you out…" Morgan vacillated, knowing she was already probably being a pain.

"You're not putting me out at all. I'll go get dressed."

A little while later, Zion emerged, dressed in black slacks and a long-sleeved grey shirt. Morgan couldn't help but notice that the woman definitely had style, even down to the black boots she wore and the leather bomber style jacket she pulled out of the closet.

"You should put this on," Zion instructed her, as she handed her the jacket. "The rain has stopped, but it's still pretty chilly out there. I've gathered your clothes; they are in a bag by the door."

"Wow, thank you." Morgan smiled as she pulled the jacket on. It smelled of leather and cologne, it was a wonderful combination.

Next to the bar was a single car garage that Zion led her to. She opened the garage door with a remote on her key ring and Morgan found that she was a bit surprised by the car parked there. It was a blue Mercedes sedan, it looked very sporty and expensive. When she glanced over at Zion, she saw that the woman silently grinning to herself.

Zion noticed Morgan's gaze; she was tempted to ask what kind of vehicle she'd expected her to drive, but decided not to put her on the spot with the teasing question. Walking into the garage, she unlocked the doors, and opened the passenger side door for Morgan.

Inside the vehicle, Morgan was surrounded by the smell of leather and cologne again.

Touching the seat she noted that it was very supple leather, and the dashboard looked more like a jet cockpit to her.

"This is really nice," Morgan commented as Zion got into the driver's seat.

"Thanks." Zion smiled. "It's my biggest indulgence. I save a lot of money living above the bar."

Zion drove them to the therapist's office with Morgans directions. Morgan went inside and spoke to Charlotte's receptionist, Sandy, who handed over her purse.

"She's in session," Sandy told her, "but she said you left this here last night. She was really worried about you, are you okay?"

Morgan nodded. "I am, tell Charlotte not to worry."

Sandy smiled. "I will."

Back in the car, Morgan looked over at Zion. "All ready," she asked. "Are you sure you want to drive me all the way home? I'm down in Pacific Grove."

"Just give me an address," Zion told her.

"It's three hours away," Morgan told her.

Zion smiled. "I'm aware."

Finally, Morgan relented and gave Zion her address. Zion typed the address into her navigation system, and they were on their way.

A few minutes into the drive, Morgan looked over at Zion's very handsome profile. "I really do appreciate this, I just don't want to be a huge inconvenience."

Zion grinned. "I know how to say *no*, Morgan, and I say it when I want to." With that she winked.

Morgan laughed softly. "Well thank you."

They were both silent for a while. Music played from the car speakers, and when the opening notes to Fleetwood Mac's 'The Chain' began to play, Morgan exclaimed in contentment. "I love this song!"

Zion obliged by turning up the volume. They sang the lyrics together. Morgan couldn't help but noticed Zion's look singing the chorus. She seemed quite connected to the lyrics *if the person didn't love them now, they'd never love them again.*

"Is that—" Morgan began, but realized that she shouldn't ask.

"Is that what?" Zion glanced over at Morgan.

Morgan shook her head. "I'm sorry, it's none of my business. Sometimes I let my curiosity get the better of me."

"It's alright. Ask, if I don't want to answer, I won't," Zion told her.

Morgan pressed her lips together, trying to think of a way to ask the question that wouldn't sound too rude. "I was going to ask if that particular song had anything to do with someone." Zion looked puzzled but she continued anyway. "You sang those lyrics, you meant them."

Understanding dawned on Zion then and she nodded. "Yes, you could say it had to do with someone." She chuckled as she said it, but the sound was far from humorous.

Morgan's eyes widened; the question leaped suddenly to the forefront of her mind,

Who would be dumb enough to leave you?

But she forced herself not to ask it, knowing she'd be prying at that point.

"I saw that." Zion grinned.

Morgan pursed her lips, dropping her head and shaking it. "I'm really a hopeless snoop, you'd be wise to stop the car and kick me out now."

Zion chuckled again. "I can take it, go ahead, ask away."

"Well, in all honesty, what I was thinking a minute ago wouldn't be appropriate to ask someone I just met, so I'll keep that one to myself," Morgan intimated.

"Oh, now I really need to know." Zion looked over at her, a wicked smile on her face.

Morgan opened her mouth in mock surprise. In truth she found Zion's smile incredibly endearing. The handsome woman held an endless amount of interest for her. She was very intriguing.

Sighing, Morgan dropped her head again. "I'm caught," she admitted, "I was thinking that someone would have to be incredibly stupid to leave someone like you."

Zion's lips twisted in a disappointed curve. "She's not stupid, she's just not a very good person."

Morgan instantly felt bad that she'd poked at what was obviously a still open wound. "I'm so sorry."

Zion shrugged. "No need to be, she's just a specter that never seems to go away."

"Is that the Fancy that was on the phone this morning?" Morgan blurted before she could stop herself.

Zion murmured derisively, "Yeah, that was her."

Morgan chewed on her lower lip, dying to ask more questions, but knowing that she shouldn't. She decided, instead, to change the subject.

"Your friend was very nice last night," she said with a smile. "I at least remember that. She was very solicitous."

Zion grinned. "Solicitous?"

"Considerate," Morgan clarified.

"I knew what it meant," Zion said. "I just don't actually hear words like that used too often in my profession."

"I'm guilty of using words like that quite frequently," Morgan admitted.

"And why is that?"

"Oh, I'm a writer," Morgan explained.

"Well, that's interesting," Zion commented. "What do you write?"

"Normally I write romance."

"Normally?" Zion asked.

Morgan sighed. "I'm hopelessly blocked lately."

"That sounds bad."

"When it's how you make a living, yeah, it's really bad."

"Yowsa," Zion quipped.

"Yes, definitely, *yowsa*," Morgan emphasized. "So how did you get into owning a bar?"

"I know a lot of alcoholics," Zion deadpanned, causing Morgan's mouth to drop open. Zion laughed, shaking her head. "I'm just kidding. I actually started out buying property. The bar was just the last thing I bought."

"So, you're a real estate mogul," Morgan quizzed.

Zion laughed her familiar laugh. "Not hardly."

"What got you into real estate?"

"I had a CO in the Navy that told me to buy property anywhere I was stationed, but since I ended up assigned to an aircraft carrier, that didn't work. So, I saved a good percentage of my pay for the entire time I was in, and starting buying property when I ended up here in San Francisco."

"Wow!" Morgan exclaimed. "That was really smart."

Zion grinned, nodding. "It's worked out well."

"So the Navy…what led you there? And what did you do in the Navy?"

"Getting away from home led me there," Zion answered. "I did a lot of things, but my final duties were working in avionics as an air-crewman."

"And that entailed…" Morgan prompted.

"I worked with the pilots, in-flight tech, deck crew, basically whatever was needed."

"I see," Morgan said, listening intently. "How long were you in the Navy?"

"I did eight years."

"Well, thank you for your service." Morgan smiled.

"My pleasure, ma'am." Zion inclined her head.

They drove in silence for a while, then Zion's cell phone rang. The view screen in the vehicle read Dax.

"Excuse me," Zion said looking at who was calling, "and I apologize in advance for what you may hear." She emphasized her words with a sardonic smirk.

"Hey D, what's up?"

"Just checking in, how's Jaims?" Dax asked.

"She's good, she's home now."

"That's good. Any word on Rock?"

"Aww, that one's more of a Charlie Foxtrot," Zion commented.

"Geeze, what now?" Dax asked.

"Jaims won't tell me everything, but the upside is that Rock's gone into rehab."

"Yeah…" Dax murmured. "That one has a high drift factor lately, so I'll believe it when I see it."

"Indeed," Zion agreed. "I'll keep you posted."

"Sounds good. How are you doing?" Dax asked.

"I'm good."

"Fancy still up your six about the expansion?"

"Oh yeah, she called again this morning." Zion sighed.

"She seems fairly determined."

"Pain in the…" Zion began, then glancing over at Morgan she said, *"backside."*

"Seriously dude, that one's a major pain in the ass!" Dax corrected.

Zion grimaced, shaking her head as she mouthed to Morgan, *"Sorry."*

"Hey Dax, can I call ya later?"

"Sure, but why the bum's rush?" Dax's voice teased.

Zion's eyes narrowed, her expression turned into a sneer. "Which one of those little shits called you?"

Dax's laugh echoed through the speakers of the car. Zion shook her head, rolling her eyes. "With friends like you…" She let her voice trail off, knowing Dax would get her meaning.

"Hey, CBC bay-bee!" Dax crowed.

"I'll talk to *you* later, and the rest of the crew is paying for their drinks from now on!"

Dax's laughter was the last thing they heard as Zion hung up.

There was silence in the car for a long moment as Zion pressed her lips together. "I really am sorry about that."

"I have questions," Morgan commented, a smile forming on her lips.

"Bring them on." Zion chuckled.

"Jaims?"

"She's a friend of ours that was in the hospital."

"Rock?"

"Her actual name is Raquel; she's having issues with substances."

"Charlie Foxtrot?"

"Uhh." Zion grimaced, looking embarrassed. "It stands for Cluster Fuck."

"High drift...um...something," Morgan stammered, not recalling the whole phrase Dax had used.

"High drift factor, it means she's highly unreliable."

"Aw." Morgan nodded. "I got the Fancy being up your, um, six, thing, I've seen *Top Gun* enough times to understand that one."

Zion laughed at the reference.

"And then there's...wait, I'll remember it...oh, yes, CBC?"

Zion drew in a breath, smiling. "That's what we call ourselves, our little group of friends."

"What does it stand for?"

"Castro Bois Crew."

"Boys?" Morgan queried.

"Not the boys you're thinking of, it's more B-O-*I*-S, not b-o-y-s. Bois are what we call our more butch, or masculine, friends and lovers."

"I did not know that," Morgan said smiling. "I like it. So, you're a crew?"

"Well, Dax and I were both Navy, stationed on the Carl Vinson. So, we refer to the people we hang out with as 'crew' by habit. We all live in the Castro, and we're all butch leaning, so Castro Bois Crew."

"Aww, I get it now," Morgan uttered. "It's like a gang." Her smile grew wider.

Zion laughed. "We're more of a family."

Morgan nodded. "I like that even better."

It ended up being a very nice drive out to Pacific Grove. When they finally got to Morgan's condo, Zion parked the car, and got out to go around and open Morgan's door for her. She offered her hand to help her out of the vehicle.

"Thank you." Morgan smiled, impressed by Zion's chivalry. "And I really want to thank you for everything, all of this has been so crazy."

"It has been my pleasure," Zion replied sincerely.

"I'd really like to make it up to you, if you'll let me," Morgan said, staring up at Zion.

Zion's cornflower-blue eyes held her gaze for a long moment, then she inclined her head. "It's not necessary, but I'd like that. What do you have in mind?"

"Maybe we could go to dinner? What does your week look like this week?" she asked, feeling desperate suddenly to keep this connection.

Zion pursed her lips. "Well, I was planning to head out to Napa this week. I like to go there to pick up new wines for the bar. If you have time, would you like to come with me?"

"That sounds fantastic!" Morgan exclaimed happily.

Zion reached into her back pocket, pulling out her wallet and withdrawing a business card which she handed to Morgan. "Call me and we'll make a plan."

"I absolutely will." Morgan nodded. Taking the card, their hands brushed. Morgan took Zion's hand in hers, and looked up at her. "Thank you again for being so kind, not everyone would have gone out of their way like you did. I'd dare say most people wouldn't have."

Zion placed her other hand over Morgan's. *Those oh so blue eyes* bore into hers.

"Things go the way they're meant to; people are put in our path for a reason. I sincerely believe that." Morgan felt her breath catch in her throat as she felt Zion squeeze her hand gently.

"I'll wait for you to get inside," Zion told her.

Morgan smiled, feeling very much like the damsel in a romance novel, with the gallant suitor escorting her home from the ball. Taking a chance, she leaned up and kissed Zion on the cheek, then walked away as quickly as she could, wincing a little to herself, wondering if she'd just been far too impulsive. When she approached her door, she looked back over her shoulder. Zion was leaning against her car, watching intently with a smile on her face.

Morgan unlocked her door and walked inside. She shut the door and leaned against it, feeling like she'd just been on the best date of her life.

Chapter 9

"So, this is my room." Raquel pushed open the door to the rehabilitation clinic. There were papers, ashtrays, empty bottles of water and soda scattered across the surfaces. "It's kind of a mess."

"Yeah, you're kind of a slob, I've been meaning to say something…" Jaims winked at her friend, and Raquel chuckled.

"Whatever!" Raquel shook her head.

They'd already toured the center and the grounds outside; this was their last stop. Jaims moved to sit on the only chair in the room, looking up at Raquel.

"So how are you?" Jaims asked, her tone sincere.

Raquel took a deep breath in through her nose, and blowing it out slowly, she nodded.

"I'm getting there, they make us talk so much in here, it's hard for me to talk anymore, you know?"

Jaims nodded, her brows furrowed in sincere concern. "I understand."

Raquel chewed on the inside of her cheek, moving to sit down on the bed across from the chair where Jaims sat. "I need to apologize to you, though."

Jaims started to shake her head, which prompted Raquel to get off the bed, and kneel down in front of Jaims, taking her hands.

"Don't shake your head, J, I know I hurt you, and I'm so, so sorry about that." She squeezed Jaims' hands gently. "I don't just mean that last stupid thing I did, I mean, all the times I yelled and threw shit, and all of it."

"That was the drugs, not you," Jaims said.

"But it was me, I mean yeah, the drugs made me do stupid shit, but it was still my fault. I don't get a pass because I was taking drugs."

Jaims drew in a deep breath. "I understand what you mean. And yeah, you really scared me a lot of the time, but mostly I just missed you."

Raquel bowed her head. When she raised it again, Jaims was stunned to see tears in her eyes. "You wanna know something crazy?"

"What?" Jaims asked, her voice barely audible because of the tears clogging her throat.

"I could not wait to get back to the States to see you again...and then I fuck it all up this way." Raquel's eyes searched Jaims', looking for understanding.

"You didn't fuck it up," Jaims told her. "I'm still here, I'm still your friend."

Raquel looked mournful. "You've always been the best friend I ever had, Jaims, always." Tears spilled from Raquel's eyes as she looked down at their gripped hands. "I wanted to come back to...to you, and to our family, the crew and all..." Her voice trailed off as she swallowed convulsively. "But now, now everyone hates me, and it's my own damned fault."

"Hates you?" Jaims repeated. "Who hates you?"

Raquel gestured toward the outside. "The crew, your family, they've all gotta hate me now, because of what I did…to you."

Understanding suddenly dawned, and Jaims let out her pent-up breath, shaking her head as she did. "Oh that," she said, "I didn't tell them about that."

The shock on Raquel's face surprised Jaims.

"You assumed I did?" she deduced, nodding.

Raquel shrugged grimacing as she did. For Jaims, it was heart-breaking to think about what Raquel had probably been putting herself through, because of her own assumptions.

Jaims was afraid Raquel was going to collapse in surprise. She reached out taking Raquel by the shoulders and stood up, guiding her to sit on the bed.

Raquel sat looking completely shell-shocked for a long moment. Finally she looked at Jaims.

"Why didn't you tell them?" It was a simple question, but Jaims could see that the answer would mean the world to Raquel.

"Honestly?" Jaims said, running a hand through her hair. "I didn't want them to be mad at you or hate you."

"Why not?"

Jaims looked back at her ultra-tough cop, soldier friend and couldn't believe how vulnerable she looked right now. "Because I love you, you idiot and because they're your family too, and I didn't want to mess that up for you."

"But I hurt you," Raquel reminded her.

"Yeah, but you weren't you at that point."

"I was me."

"It was you on drugs and in pain, not you," Jaims corrected.

Raquel stared back at Jaims for a long moment. Jaims could tell that Raquel wanted to accept what she'd said, but it was as if she was afraid to do so.

"What are you afraid of?" Jaims finally asked.

Raquel pressed her lips together in a grimace. "That later you'll realize I'm just really a monster."

Jaims grinned. "There's a difference between being an asshole, and being a monster, Rock." Leaning in, she hugged her friend. "And you're an asshole that I love, so you just better get used to it."

Raquel wrapped her arms around Jaims, with her face against the hollow of Jaims' shoulder. "Thank you," came Raquel's simple reply.

Later that afternoon Jaims sat next to Raquel as the clinic held a group therapy session. They listened as others talked about their experiences. When it was Raquel's turn, she began hesitantly.

"The beginning of my addiction was when I was shot…" she started.

"Tell us more about that," the group leader prompted.

"I was stationed in Iraq, we were out on patrol, and it was hot and gross as usual." Raquel curled her lips recalling the uncomfortable memory. "My chin strap to my helmet was making my neck itch, so I loosened it up. Getting the signal that all was clear was taking forever, but then we were told we were clear, that's when the assholes took their shots!" Her face curled in annoyance at the memory. "So when I hit the deck again, my damned helmet fell off. My shitty luck. I couldn't see anything, so I checked through my weapon sights and saw movement. I was warned off." Raquel took a deep breath, blowing it out slowly. "Of course, the minute I decided I better grab my helmet, that's when I heard gunfire. I don't know what happened after that, but I woke up in a hospital in frigging Germany with my brothers looking scared shitless."

"How did you feel about that?" the counselor asked pointedly.

Raquel sighed again, her face scrunched up in anguish. "I felt so bad for them, they told me that they thought I was dead, or that I'd die before they got there." She shook her head mournfully. "And believe me, there were times when I wanted to die, I really did. There were so many fucking tests and scans, I guess it had been really touch and go for a while with me. They'd been through a lot by the time I woke up. Then to find out that my friends, my adopted family, had gotten them there, paid for it and all…" Her voice trailed off as she forced back tears.

As Raquel spoke, Jaims listened intently, realizing how scary it must have been. "Since I've been back," Raquel added, "I've been so caught up in my addiction, I really lost sight of my friends, my family, the people that were there for me and my brothers when I needed them most."

"So how do you think you got to this point?" the counselor asked.

Raquel looked pensive, then shrugged. "Now I know that I was chasing the pain I was in, instead of being responsible about getting help for my pain management, I just stuck with what made me feel good." She looked over at Jaims, with a pained expression. "But it was taking more and more to get that feeling again, and I started stealing and lashing out at the people I love, when I couldn't get enough to make me feel better."

Jaims winced at Raquel's words. Knowing that her friend had been in so much pain bothered her.

"Taking responsibility for your addiction is the first step, admitting that you have a problem, and be willing to address is it very important," the counselor confirmed.

Jaims placed her hand on Raquel's shoulder, squeezing it gently, seeing Raquel nod in response to the counselor's words.

***

"So…the blue-eyed stranger is definitely sexy, huh?" Jessie asked as they carried their purchases into Morgan's condo.

"She's very definitely sexy," Morgan confirmed, "but she's also this very gallant, kind person too."

"When do you leave for Napa?" Jessie asked.

"Tomorrow," Morgan sighed, as she set down the bags she'd been carrying, starting to pull out some of the blouses she bought. "I wonder if this one would be good?" She held up the blouse to herself. It was a beautiful flowered pleasant-style blouse. It had a curved neckline that wasn't too low. "I could wear it with my new sandals and my navy capris," she continued, looking over her shoulder at Jessie. "That's a very Napa, wine country style, right?"

Jessie nodded, sitting herself down in one of Morgan's chairs. "It's beautiful, I'm sure your gal will be pleased."

Morgan gave Jessie a dirty look. "She's not *my* gal."

Jessie grinned unrepentantly. "But you want her to be…" she lulled in a sing-song voice.

Giving Jessie an exasperated look, Morgan pulled out her new sandals and put them up against the blouse assessing.

"I think she has a complicated dating life."

"Meaning?" Jessie quizzed.

"Meaning," Morgan sighed, "I don't think she's looking for a new romance right now."

"Seriously?" Jessie gave her friend an eyeroll. "She invited you to go with her to Napa on an overnight trip, you don't think that means something?"

"I don't know," Morgan replied. "It could just mean that she wants company."

"It could mean she wants more than that…"

Morgan threw a sandal at her friend, who dodged it laughing.

The following morning, Zion rang Morgan's doorbell promptly at 7 a.m. Morgan answered the door with a huge smile.

"Good morning!" Morgan said.

"It is." Zion grinned. "You look great," she announced, gesturing to Morgan's outfit.

"So do you," Mogan admired. Zion wore charcoal grey slacks and a white long sleeved oxford style shirt.

"Thank you." Zion inclined her head. "Do you have a bag?"

"Yes." Morgan nodded, looking back over her shoulder at the overnight bag sitting just inside the door.

Zion immediately walked inside and collected the bag. "Are you ready to go?"

"Sure."

Zion opened the passenger door of the car for Morgan. "I took the liberty of picking you up a coffee; cream, two sugars, right?"

Morgan's mouth dropped open in surprise. "That was so nice of you."

"I'm dragging you out of your house early in the morning, that's the least I can do," Zion said with a smile that lit up her blue eyes.

As Zion put her bag in the trunk, Morgan picked up the cup and took a sip of the coffee.

"Oh, this is wonderful!" Morgan said appreciatively, as she got into the car.

"Is it? I've never been to this place, it's down in town here."

"You didn't get yourself any?" Morgan wondered as she didn't see a second cup.

"Nah, I needed caffeine much sooner than that, plus I love my coffee from a little café around the corner from the bar."

"Is it Orphan Andy's?" Morgan asked with an odd look Zion couldn't quite place.

"Yes...why?"

Morgan blushed a little. "I saw you there."

Zion gave her a quizzical look, as she started the car and put it in drive.

"When?"

"A couple of weeks ago. I'd gone there after one of my sessions. You probably don't remember…"

Zion nodded slightly. "I actually do, that explains why you look familiar to me."

Morgan bit her lip. "I remember thinking that I'd seen your eyes before."

Zion chuckled. "Well, it sounds like you had."

Morgan laughed.

They drove in silence for a while, listening to music and getting lost in their own thoughts.

"So, tell me what we're doing in Napa," Morgan asked.

"Well," Zion began, as she turned the radio down, "we're going to visit a couple of wineries, to check out this year's wines. I like to keep the bar stocked with the latest and best ones."

"That's pretty smart," Morgan commented. "In my experience, wines at bars are…well, less than phenomenal."

Zion shrugged. "I try to stay a cut above."

"That's a good way to do it."

"I have us scheduled for three wineries today, and two tomorrow," Zion informed her, "but if you get tired or bored…" She grinned. "Then I can just drop you off at the B and B I reserved for the night. They have a nice spa and in room massages."

"Wow," Morgan said, her eyes widening, "it sounds nice, but I don't mind touring wineries."

Zion smile matched Morgan's. "Great!"

"I am so bored; do we have to do all this?" Jane complained. "My feet hurt!"

Zion looked back at her. "I told you that we were touring wineries, why didn't you wear more comfortable shoes?"

"I don't get why we need to do all this," Jane grouched. "Your customers wouldn't know a good glass of wine if it bit them in the ass."

"I don't have the same view of my customers as you apparently do," Zion said with a scowl.

Jane snorted in derision. "You've probably screwed most of them, so I'm sure your view is definitely distorted."

Zion's mouth dropped open, as she looked over at the owner of the winery, Jon Louis, who was giving them a tour personally.

"I'm sorry," she told Jon.

"It's okay," he told Zion. "Perhaps the lady would like to sit out on our terrace and sample wines…"

"The lady," Jane replied haughtily, "would like to go back to the hotel and have a massage."

Zion clenched her teeth, feeling completely embarrassed by the way Jane was acting. "Excuse us," she said to the owner. He nodded understandingly. After he stepped away, Zion turned to Jane. "Why don't you just get an Uber back to the hotel."

Jane's eyes widened. "You're going to send me back in an Uber? When I came here to be with you?"

Zion took a deep breath, expelling it slowly to calm herself before she spoke again. "I told you what I was doing here this weekend…"

Jane pouted. "Well, yes, but I thought that you'd at least have some time for me."

"We are spending time together, here at the winery," Zion answered.

Jane blew her breath out in a deep sigh. "Fine, I'll just go back to the hotel."

"Great. I'll see you there later."

"I really can't believe this…" Jane muttered to herself as she stalked away.

By the time Zion made it to the hotel four hours later, Jane was in quite a snit. They fought half the night. It wasn't a great day.

"Just let me know if you get bored," Zion told Morgan with a smile.

"I'll do that," Morgan reassured, sensing that there was a background story to this somewhere. But not wanting to be a pest, she decided to change the subject. "How is your friend…Rock?"

"From what we're hearing from Jaims, her roommate and our friend, she's apparently doing great."

"That's good to hear, I know addiction can be a really hard thing for people to overcome. Has she had substance abuse issues before?" Morgan asked, approaching the subject gently.

Zion shook her head and let out a little snort. "No, she's a cop for San Francisco PD, so no, never before. This is a rather bad time for her. She was sent over to Iraq with her Army Reserve unit, and she was shot."

"Oh, my lord, that's awful." Morgan held her hand over her heart in surprise. "But she recovered from it?"

"Well, it wasn't a short recovery, she was shot in the head." Zion grimaced. "We were really afraid we were going to lose her."

"Does she have family?" Morgan asked, barely able to fathom what that would be like.

"Well, she has two brothers, both younger than her. They lost their parents in a car crash when the boys were in their early teens. Rock assumed legal guardianship of them."

"That was really brave of her to do, that takes a lot of support," Morgan marveled.

"Well, she has us, the crew, we did what we could to help out."

Morgan smiled softly. "Like your own little family."

"That's kind of what we are to each other, the family a lot of us don't have."

"Where is your family?" Morgan asked.

"Back in New York, I imagine," Zion mused. "I don't know really, I haven't seen any of them since I turned eighteen and joined the Navy."

"You've never been back?" Morgan asked, shock laced in her voice.

Zion shook her head, smiling sadly. "I didn't figure they'd want me back."

"Why on earth not?"

Zion canted her head, looking like she remembered. "My dad was never really the kind of guy to understand things, like his only daughter being gay."

"Do they know? I mean, have you told them?" Morgan queried.

Zion's mouth twisted sardonically. "Yeah, I sent my family a letter telling them."

"And did they respond?"

"Not one word," Zion said sadly.

"Oh my God, Zion, I'm so sorry." Morgan reached out, touching Zion's arm.

Zion shrugged. "It is what it is, right?"

"I will never understand parents who can simply abandon their child because of who they love." Morgan shook her head, then she squeezed Zion's arm, realizing belatedly that she was still touching this woman. "I'm sorry if I just brought up a sore subject."

Zion shook her head, giving Morgan a rueful smile. "If I didn't want to answer, I wouldn't have."

Morgan nodded, thinking Zion was a very straightforward person. She liked that about her. "I have another question..." she warned, causing Zion to laugh again. "How exactly did you end up with the group, the crew, you have?"

Zion inclined her head; she gazed in front of her, which told Morgan she was recollecting the memory. "Well, Dax was the one to talk me into coming back to San Francisco with her family. A couple of years later we met Jaims and Steel but separately, at Pride back in 2014. Steel was underage and trying to get us to buy her beer."

"Did you do it?" Morgan asked.

Zion pressed her lips together. "Well, you need to realize that having been in the Navy, Dax and I got to drink really early on, so we did kind of contribute to Steel's delinquency. But we also made sure she was safe about it, and didn't drive home on her own."

Morgan gave her an appraising look. "Okay I guess I'll accept that," she teased.

"We also met Jaims that year at Pride, she was working at her parents' tent for the bakery they run." Zion grinned. "Dax got really hung up on their cannoli…Jaims kept giving her deals."

"How many did she eat?"

"Oh, about two dozen."

"Oh lord!" Morgan laughed.

"I kept telling her she was gonna get fat." Zion shook her head. "But that one has the metabolism of a kid, it's revolting."

Morgan snorted, agreeing with the sentiment.

"I opened the bar in 2015, it was called Z-Bar then and it was aimed at over eighteens. Basically, so Jaims and Steel could be there. Case wandered in one night a couple of years in—she was a refugee from England—and she hit it off with Jaims and Steel."

"That's the one that took care of me that night, right?"

"Yes, Case was the one that took you upstairs for me."

"And a *refugee* from England?" Morgan asked.

"She'd gotten herself in some trouble back home."

"Oh, wait, she told me about this, she said she's a…" Morgan struggled to remember the conversation. "It was something to do with a hat…"

Zion laughed. "She always says she's a white hat, not a black hat."

Morgan snapped her fingers. "Yes! That was it! What is that?"

"The way she explains it, is that black hats are the hackers that will steal all your money. White hats are the good guys, that get it back for you."

"Interesting…" Morgan mused. "Go on."

162

"Let's see, next are Shayne and Flynn, I met them when they needed to rent an apartment, but were honestly too young to do so."

"How old were they?"

"They were both seventeen at the time. No one would rent to them. I guess they heard about me from a friend of a friend." Zion shrugged.

"What did they hear?" Morgan asked.

"That I had apartments for rent at a reasonable price. Hard to come by in San Francisco. Plus, they heard that I was always willing to work with family."

"You mean in terms of members of the LGBTQ community?" Morgan clarified.

"Right." Zion nodded. "Too many landlords are either all about money, or they don't like our kind, or both. I figure I have the properties, so I might as well do some good with them."

"That's really nice of you." Morgan was really starting to get a picture of who Zion was, just through learning about her friends.

"And the last one that joined our crew was Jayden, she was definitely the biggest save for us."

"What do you mean?"

"One of the crew found her in the alley outside of Fancy's." Zion grimaced at the memory. "She'd been kicked out of her home because her family was religious. She was a kid. She'd already been stabbed once and had barely recovered when she found us. We kind of brought her into the fold, gave her a place to live and all that," Zion said it so casually that Morgan found herself gaping at her.

"Like that's not a really huge thing you did?" Morgan questioned.

Zion considered the question, then shrugged. "It's what we do."

"Wow," Morgan uttered, she couldn't think of another kind way to put it.

"Like I said, we're our own little family."

Morgan smiled softly; she was forever amazed at this person taking her to Napa. She hadn't realized there were people left in this world anymore that were this *selfless*.

***

"Whose car is that?" Raquel asked when she and Jaims walked out of the rehab facility.

"It's a rental," Jaims said as she opened the trunk to put Raquel's bag in.

Raquel grimaced. "How bad is your car?"

Jaims bunched her eyebrows. "Bad, they said it might be totaled."

"Aw damn." Raquel felt a spike of guilt. "I'm sorry."

"It's not your fault I was dumb enough to drive with a migraine," Jaims told her, getting into the driver's seat as Raquel got in the other side.

"Yeah but…" Raquel began.

"Dude!" Jaims cried, putting her hand on Raquel's arm to soften her exclamation. "It wasn't your fault, okay? It wasn't."

Raquel seemed to want to argue more, but didn't. Finally she sighed. "Okay, but let's turn this in and you use my Jeep until you figure out the plan with your car, deal?"

Jaims chuckled as she drove away from the rehab facility. "Deal."

A couple hours later, Raquel walked into the apartment that she shared with Jaims. Looking around she saw that nothing had changed, it was an odd sense of comfort for her. What she did notice that made her smile from ear to ear was the stack of movies on the coffee table.

Glancing back at Jaims who followed her into the apartment, she nodded toward the coffee table.

"I figure we can have a *Marvel* marathon...all the movies in order," Jaims enthused.

"Do we have enough supplies?" Raquel asked, as she headed toward the kitchen.

"Yup, stocked up on popcorn, cheese curls, barbecue chips and chocolate. I also got that beer you like, and extra Pepsi!"

Raquel shook her head, putting her hand on Jaims' shoulder. "You take good care of me."

Jaims grinned lopsidedly. "I try."

Raquel's lips twitched; she looked pained.

"Don't do that," Jaims warned. "We're starting with a clean slate, okay?"

Raquel blew her breath out noisily, nodding. "Got it. Just got a boatload of guilt I can't seem to put down."

"Well, drop the pile that pertains to me, okay? We're good," Jaims announced.

"I guess I just need some time to believe that, you know?" Raquel's eyes begged Jaims to understand.

"I know. Go get unpacked, I'll order us some lunch. Want pizza?"

"Pizza! Yes!" Raquel smiled brightly.

An hour and a half later the pizza had arrived, they'd had beverages and were beginning their marathon with Jaims' favorite: *Iron Man*.

They were sat on the couch, enjoying the movie.

"I am Iron Man!" Jaims crowed at the end of the movie. It was her favorite line, and she said it every time they watched it.

As usual, they sat and waited for the credits, to get to the end credit scene.

"I wanna be cool like Nick Fury..." Raquel commented wistfully.

Jaims glanced over at her friend. "You're cool, just not Nick Fury cool."

"Rude," Raquel quipped.

"Right?" Jaims countered laughing.

"What if you could be like Tony?" Raquel offered.

"With the money, or just the Iron Man suit?"

"All of it."

"Oh hell yes!" Jaims agreed.

"Then I can be Fury."

"Deal!" Jaims nodded emphatically.

"Alright, Hulk time," Raquel said, getting up to start the next movie.

"Aww, Ed Norton," Jaims enthused, "better than Bana."

Raquel shook her head. "I kinda liked Bana's Hulk."

"Really?" Jaims said, eyes shocked.

"Yeah." Raquel shrugged. "Sue me."

"I don't know…we may not be able to stay friends this way…"

"Yeah, yeah," Raquel joked. "What's important is that we both like Mark Ruffalo as Hulk in the Avenger's movies."

"Definitely!"

As the movie menu came up, Raquel sat down next to Jaims, bumping her shoulder into hers. "This is really great," she said, gesturing to the pile of movies and the food and drinks piled on the coffee table. "Thank you for this." Her smile was sincere.

Jaims leaned her head on Raquel's shoulder. "It's great to have you back."

Raquel felt tears sting the backs of her eyes. "Thank you for letting me make it back."

It was a very sweet moment, and Jaims felt her heart ache from the joy of it. She also knew that Raquel wouldn't want her to say anything like that, so she just pressed play on the remote.

Chapter 10

"This is so fascinating," Morgan observed as she stood next to Zion.

Zion glanced over, expecting to see an eyeroll or a sneering look, but Morgan only smiled at her. The vineyard owner had offered them a tour of the grounds, and of his latest area of harvest. He was showing them how they harvested the grapes, and how they cared and maintained them, so they didn't get damaged.

A previous memory made Zion wary of seemingly benign comments. Jane had been completely bored and quite vocal about the vineyard. Morgan indeed seemed fascinated by the wine-making process. It was a great relief to Zion. She'd almost said no to the tour, for fear that her companion would embarrass her with an obvious disinterest. She was pleasantly surprised.

"I'm thinking we might want to head back soon," the vintner commented as the gathering clouds looked more and more ominous in the distance.

The three began walking back through the vines toward the parked golf cart, but no sooner had they stepped in that direction, the clouds broke and it started to rain. By the time they made it back to the golf cart they were all soaked. Once again, Zion anticipated an acrid comment from Morgan, but quite the opposite happened.

"And they say it never rains in California..." Morgan grinned brightly, as she wrung out her hair dripping with rain.

Zion chuckled, draping her jacket, that had mercifully been thrown across the seat of the cart, *and was therefore dry*, around Morgan's shoulders. "I'm so sorry."

"Nothing to apologize for." Morgan smiled. "I had no idea it was going to rain either."

"We will get straight over to the B&B when we leave here, it's not too far away."

"Perfect." Morgan nodded.

Morgan wiggled her toes in delight. The bath was warm and the bubbles she soaked in smelled wonderful! She felt the warmth envelop her and sighed happily. The inn they'd checked into was a beautiful place; they had their own private cabin. The bathroom boasted a claw foot bathtub. Zion had suggested a bath so Morgan could warm up and she had readily accepted.

There was a light knock on the bathroom door. Morgan hurriedly checked to ensure that she was covered in bubbles in all her appropriate places.

"Come in," she called softly, noting that Zion had waited until she'd given permission. It was another thing that separated Zion from so many others she noted.

Zion opened the door partially, not looking fully into the bathroom. "Are you decent?"

Morgan smiled to herself; Zion really was the utmost gentle-woman.

"Yes, you can come in."

Stepping inside, Zion peered over at the tub, tilting her head slightly. She'd noted that Morgan was covered in bubbles. Internally she felt something shift toward this woman. Finding someone demure in this day and age was nearly impossible, especially one that looked like Morgan.

"Feeling better?" Zion queried, smiling.

"Much!" Morgan enthused.

Zion grimaced. "I apologize again for not checking the weather."

Morgan shook her head. "It's not your fault, I was so busy trying to look pretty that I didn't think about the possibility it would get cold."

Zion canted her head, narrowing her eyes a little, a smile spread across her lips. "I'm not sure."

Morgan pressed her lips together, a rosy color bloomed on her cheeks and her bright green eyes shone. "That's very sweet of you to say."

Zion shrugged. "Just how I see it." Morgan continued to blush as she playfully patted at the bubbles around her, her eyes did not meet Zion's. Zion found the gesture endearing. "So...we have a few options for dinner."

"Yes?" Morgan now looked at Zion. Her gaze was almost wonderous in curiosity. It was nothing like the expectant, almost challenging look Zion was used to receiving from Jane.

Zion took a deep breath, blowing it out slowly.

"Well, there's a fairly fancy French restaurant in town; there's also a chop house that's pretty nice too." Morgan nodded, looking pensive. "Then again there's some good restaurants nearby, like Grace's Table or Eiko's…" Zion's voice trailed off as Morgan began to nod.

"What kind of food does Grace's Table have? Eiko's sounds like Japanese."

"Right you are," Zion affirmed. "Grace's is kind a mix of Italian, French, and American."

Morgan ran her hand through her hair, then peered up at Zion. "Which one do you like?"

Zion did her best to suppress her smile, so much so that her eyes sparkled with the effort. She was so pleased with being asked what she liked for a change, it was almost painful. "I like Grace's actually."

Morgan nodded, then canted her head. "Any chance we can order in from Grace's?"

"You mean stay in the room?"

Morgan caught her lower lip between her teeth. "It's such a beautiful room, I'd hate to waste it. We do have a little dinner table."

It was difficult for Zion not to reach down and hug the other woman, the idea of just relaxing in the room was a tantalizing thought.

"I think I can arrange that," Zion told Morgan with a bright smile as she took out her phone. She pulled Grace's Table's menu up and handed the phone to Morgan. "Just tell me what you'd like to order."

"You pick," Morgan told her. "I trust you."

Zion took her phone back. "As you wish, madame."

Zion sat down on the small porch, looking over the menu on her phone, and making decisions about what she'd order for her and Morgan. It felt so good having Morgan tell her that she trusted her, it made her feel validated again. Jane had always been so impossible to please when they'd come to Napa.

"I'm not eating at that shit hole!" Jane snapped, when Zion suggested Grace's Table.

"The food is really good there," Zion replied.

"We're eating at La Toque."

Zion did her best not to scowl, she really didn't like French food. Jane knew it, but didn't seem to care. Instead, Zion sighed. "It's been a long day, and we need to get dressed up to go there."

"So?" was Jane's retort. "Why are you trying to ruin my time this weekend? You know I've been stressed, but I guess you just don't care."

Zion blew her breath out through her nose, feeling instantly guilty. "You're right, I know you love that place. Okay, we'll go there."

Jane smiled a brilliant, wide smile, her blue eyes lit up. "Aww, see? You do love me!"

Later at the restaurant, Jane made a big deal about where they sat. "We don't want to be at a loser table," she told Zion, as she snapped her fingers at the hapless hostess who'd been ready to show them to a table located near the kitchen. "The kitchen is far too noisy! Find us something better!" Jane insisted.

The hostesses' eyes widened at Jane's imperious tone. She glanced at Zion, who gave the girl an embarrassed smile. "I'll see what I can do," The hostess said and rushed away.

"We don't have a reservation, and this place is packed," Zion murmured to Jane.

Jane waved away the comment, tapping a scarlet red nail impatiently on the hostess desk. When the news wasn't good, Jane flew into a rage, causing a scene and demanding to see the manager. Zion took a step back, recoiling from her girlfriend, unwilling to be associated with someone acting the way she was.

"I thought I could count on you…" Jane hissed at Zion later when they were seated by the manager himself.

"To what?" Zion queried holding up her hand plaintively. "To scream at the staff like you were?"

Jane's lips twitched, a sign that she couldn't decide whether to blast Zion or not. It always drove her crazy when Zion didn't pander to her needs. Finally, she gave a long-suffering sigh, and nodded. "I get it," she stated, although Zion was fairly sure she didn't. "You're so used to being used as a doormat that you don't know any other way to act." She flipped her hair back from her shoulders, with a smug smile. "Don't worry, I'll take care of you. Someone has to wear the pants in this relationship."

Later, back at the hotel, the sex could almost be described as violent.

Jane had continued to push every one of Zion's buttons. Zion lost some of her iron clad control and Jane enjoyed it thoroughly. Afterwards, Zion retreated to the bathroom to take a long hot shower, doing her best to wash away her shame and anger. Meanwhile, Jane *smoked in the non-smoking room, and smiled like a satisfied cheshire cat.*

"Oh, this is so good!" Morgan exclaimed, holding her hand in front of her mouth as she chewed. "Have you tried this?"

"No, that's new on the menu, is it good?"

"You have to try it!" Morgan told her, taking a forkful of the halibut and leaned forward to offer it to Zion.

Smiling, Zion took the proffered bite, and nodded in agreement as she chewed. "That is definitely a keeper."

Morgan glanced around her at the room, smiling, and took a sip of her wine.

"This is a really beautiful place."

Zion returned her smile, unaccountably pleased. "I really like it; I've been coming here for years now."

"I can certainly see why," Morgan observed. A thought struck Morgan, but she knew it wasn't something she should ask. She was unable to disguise her quizzical look before it piqued Zion's curiosity.

"Ask," Zion instructed her gently.

Morgan shook her head. "It's not my place and it's none of my business."

Zion's eyes narrowed slightly, as if wanting to coax the question from Morgan. "You want to know if I brought Fancy here."

Morgan closed her eyes, and opening one eye she inclined her head. "I'm sorry, I told you, I'm naturally curious about everything."

Zion chuckled. "I did bring her here, yes."

Morgan pursed her lips, she refused to let her mouth get her into more trouble.

"And no," Zion continued, sensing the next question, "she didn't have the same impression of the place you have."

Morgan looked shocked. "She didn't like it here?"

Zion curled her lips in recollection. "She said it was too *low end* for her."

"Well, *la dee da*…" Morgan replied rolling her eyes, already hating Fancy.

Zion chuckled. "She was more of a five-star resort, Michelin rated restaurant kind of girl."

"Sounds like a snob to me," Morgan uttered before she could stop herself.

Zion laughed out loud at Morgan's quick remark. "You can definitely say that."

Morgan canted her head. "What was someone like you doing with her?"

"I'm curious as to what you mean by someone like me."

Morgan bit her lip, unsure she should be *this direct*, but she figured Zion had been upfront and honest with her, so she could return the same favor.

"You strike me as a very gallant, salt of the earth, knight in shining armor type," Morgan intimated, "and she strikes me as the wicked, dragon queen."

Zion chuckled, putting her tongue to her upper lip, her blue eyes sparkled in delight at the description. "She was definitely not who I thought she was."

Zion noticed her friends gathered in a group as she approached them, catching the furtive glances as she joined. She noticed Dax put her phone away immediately.

"What's the haps, kids?" Zion asked.

"Nothing." Dax shrugged. "Why?"

Zion pursed her lips at her best friend, knowing the woman well enough to know she was lying.

"Give."

Dax grimaced. "It's nothing, just a video."

"Okay…" Zion said, eyes perplexed.

"Z, it's…" Jaims began, knowing this wasn't going to go well, her voice trailing off as she shook her head. "You really don't want to see this."

"Dude!" Shayne exclaimed. "She needs to know what's the what here."

"Yeah, I agree with L word," Errol put in.

Dax looked pained, glancing at the other members of the crew, who all ended up nodding in unison. She sighed, and hesitatingly handed Zion the phone, then pressed play on the video.

Zion took the phone, surprised to see Jane in the video. Jane was dressed in a white sequined gown, her hair was tied up, jewels glistened at her throat and her ears. Zion all but fell over when she put her arm through the crook of a dark-haired man's arm.

"Representative Winston Farro just arrived with his wife, Jane. Representative Farro just announced that he was running for governor."

Zion handed the phone back to Dax, feeling sick suddenly. Turning, she strode to the bar, and poured herself a shot, instantly followed *by another and another. Doing her best to drown her disbelief and doing anything she could to forget what she'd just learned.*

"How did you meet her?" Morgan asked.

"She came into the bar," Zion told her, her tone becoming more vacant.

Morgan nodded, and hearing the caution in Zion's voice, she quickly changed the subject. She knew she'd touched a nerve and didn't want to continue to poke at it.

"This wine is really lovely." Morgan took another sip. "It's got a very nice woodsy finish."

Zion noted the change in subject. She appreciated it as she picked up her glass. "Yeah, it's one I'm definitely going to get for the bar."

"I think it's really great that you feature good-quality wines at the bar," Morgan enthused. "I know when I order wine at most bars I'm getting a lower shelf wine. That's why I usually don't even bother." She smirked warmly.

"I figured if I'm going to set myself apart from other bars, I should do things a bit differently," Zion replied.

"I think it's a great business model." Morgan grinned.

"It's been working for me so far."

They continued to chat about random things. Morgan avoided initiating a conversation about Jane, even if her curiosity was killing her.

"I have a question for you," Zion said.

"What's that?"

Zion looked back at her for a long moment, obviously debating asking the question.

"What is it?" Morgan repeated.

"I'm wondering if…well, if you have ever been with another woman."

Morgan's look was both pensive and thoughtful. "I have," she said, "it was very casual, and nothing really came out of it."

"Why?" Zion asked. Her reply piquing her interest.

Morgan shrugged. "I think that neither of us were interested in a long-term relationship. I'd just come out of a dismal relationship with a man, and she'd broken up with her girlfriend recently as well. It just wasn't the time for either of us."

Zion looked satisfied with the answer.

Later that evening, they moved to the couch in the living room area of the small cabin. Morgan caught herself yawning, covering her mouth with her hand. "I'm so sorry. I promise it's not the company."

Zion glanced at her watch. "It is getting pretty late, we should probably talk about sleeping arrangements."

"Aw, yes, I guess we should," Morgan commented, having observed the king-sized bed in the room, but not wanting to assume anything.

"This couch pulls out," Zion said. "I can sleep here, so you can have the bed."

"We can't share that big old bed?" Morgan queried, an auburn eyebrow raised. "I promise I'll stay on my side; your virtue is safe with me." She winked.

Zion laughed. "I didn't want to be presumptuous."

"And I very much appreciate that, but I'm betting the mattress on this pull out is lumpy and uncomfortable."

Zion studied the couch. "Probably." She reached out a hand and touched Morgan's cheek, taking Morgan by surprise. Zion looked serious. "You should know that I'm very interested in you, but I really want to take things slow. I hope that's okay."

Morgan felt her heart skip a beat. "I understand, and of course it's okay." She nodded. Getting up from the couch, she looked at Zion. "I'm going to go change." She picked up her overnight bag and walked into the bathroom.

Zion stared after her for a long moment, a thread of worry wriggling through her. When Morgan walked out of the bathroom a few minutes later, she was clean faced, and wore a pair of silky pajamas. The relief on Zion's face was quite evident.

Morgan canted her head. "I'm guessing you were worried about what I'd be wearing…"

Zion opened her mouth in surprise, but then closed it, nodding.

Morgan laughed softly, reaching out to touch Zion on the chin. "I told you that your virtue was safe with me." She winked. "I meant that."

Zion stood up, acknowledging the close proximity to Morgan. She looked down into Morgan's face, eyes searching. "I trust you." With that, Zion leaned in, kissing Morgan's lips softly, then stepped back. "I'm going to take a quick shower. Pick your side," she said, pointing to the bed. It made Morgan laugh. Zion grabbed her overnight, slung it over her shoulder, and went into the bathroom.

When Zion emerged twenty minutes later Morgan could have been bowled over with a feather. Zion was wearing sweatpants and a tank top. What shocked Morgan to her core was the colorful sleeve tattoos that were on display.

Zion quirked her lips in a grin. "I'm guessing you weren't expecting this," she said, gesturing to her arms, even as she sat down on the edge of the bed.

Morgan moved closer, running her hand down one of Zion's arms. "No, no I was not." Her voice was full of awe.

One of the more prominent parts of the sleeve on Zion's left shoulder was a coat of arms in red, yellow and black. The symbol consisted of a knight's helmet atop a shield, featuring English crosses in red and white, as well as yellow and black diamond shapes. The shield was balanced by a leopard on each side. The name *Calvert* featured in a banner, and she could make out the words *Fatti maschii parole femine* scrolled across a banner at the bottom of the crest.

"What does this mean?" Morgan asked, touching the banner at the bottom of the crest.

Zion offered a small smile. "It means manly deeds, womanly words, or strong deeds, gentle words, depending on who you ask."

Morgan sat back, looking up at Zion. "What language is it?"

"Italian." Zion grinned. "Apparently the phrase was all the rage in seventeenth-century England."

Morgan nodded. "Well it definitely fits you, from what I've seen."

Zion laughed softly. "I can't take credit, it's apparently my family crest, but I like it."

"I understand that." Morgan smiled. "So you're English?"

"English, Scottish, and Northern Irish," Zion told her.

Morgan ran her hand over the other designs on Zion's left arm. "This is really beautiful work. Let's see the right arm now."

Zion chuckled, and obliged her by shifting to show her the other arm. "This is my Navy side," she said, with a proud smile.

"Wow..." Morgan muttered in awe.

Zion's right arm featured a beautifully detailed aircraft carrier moving through the sea, with an American flag waving behind it, and a banner across the bow with the name *USS Carl Vinson CVN 70*. There were also five birds flying around the ship.

"Okay, I assume the Carl Vinson is the name of the ship you served on, but what does CVN stand for?"

"Basically, it denotes it as a Nuclear-powered carrier. C stands for carrier, V stands for volplane, which is French for glide, and the N is for nuclear."

Morgan continued to examine the tattoo and touched one of the birds. "And what does this stand for?"

Zion smiled indulgently. "Swallows represent five thousand nautical miles sailed, in the career of a sailor."

"And you have five..."

"I've gone around the world once, and then some."

"Holy cow! That's a lot."

Zion laughed. "It felt like a lot."

Morgan ran her hand down Zion's arm, shaking her head in amazement. "You've lived a full life, haven't you?"

Zion looked thoughtful. "I suppose I have." She gave Morgan a direct look. "What about you?"

"Me?" Morgan replied sounding surprised.

"Yes, you," Zion countered, moving to join her, sitting back against the headboard. Her blue eyes met Morgan's. "We seem to talk about me all the time, but I never hear much about you."

Morgan pressed her lips together, looking apologetic. "It's a habit of mine to ask a lot of questions, I'm really not trying to be evasive."

"Okay," Zion said, motioning for Morgan to get comfortable, and was pleased when Morgan moved to sit very close to her. It seemed natural for Zion to put her arm around Morgan's shoulder. "Tell me about you."

"Uhhh," Morgan stammered. "I grew up in the Midwest, it was deathly boring. Just dust and crops as far as the eye could see."

"Is that why you began writing? Or did that come later?"

Morgan looked thoughtful. "I guess that is when I started making up stories, but it started with reading voraciously, anything I could get my hands on." She smiled wistfully. "My school was small, and had a tiny library but I think I read every book in it that was fiction. I got to visit other places, other worlds even."

Zion nodded. "What kind of stories would you make up?"

Morgan laughed softly. "Oh, you know, kids' stuff. I read the *Black Stallion* series and always imagined myself being a jockey, or I would read the *Dragonriders of Pern* series and imagined that I could fly in the sky on a beautiful, powerful dragon."

"I read that series too," Zion admitted.

"You did?" Morgan was surprised.

"Oh yeah, I read everything that Anne McCaffrey wrote. There wasn't a lot to do on the carrier when I wasn't working, and someone had brought her book on board."

"So, you *are* a reader." Morgan widened her eyes dramatically.

"I never said I wasn't. I just don't usually read romance books," Zion admitted. "I like science fiction more. Other worlds, other beings, fantastical stories."

Morgan nodded, her eyes remaining thoughtful under her auburn lashes. "What if the romance was sapphic?"

Zion looked intrigued. "I don't know, I've never read any of that either."

"Hmm," Morgan murmured. "Maybe I'll write a sapphic romance one day and I'll get you to read it."

Zion chuckled. "If you write one, I'll read it."

"That sounds like a challenge." Morgan smiled.

"Indeed." Zion returned Morgan's smile. "So, your parents are farmers?"

"My father and brothers are. My mom is the quintessential homemaker."

"Mine was too," Zion commented.

"Was?" Morgan questioned.

"Yes, she died when I was seventeen."

"I'm so sorry." Morgan rubbed Zion's shoulder.

"We're not talking about me, though." Zion's eyes narrowed. "So, when did you start writing down the stories?"

Morgan gave Zion a sour look, not liking the subject to be about her, but she knew it wasn't fair if she didn't share like Zion had.

"Oh, I was a young teen with my very first crush." Morgan sighed dreamily.

"And who was he?"

"His name was Brad Pickford, he was two grades above me, and so handsome. At least I thought so then."

"Did Brad like you too?"

"Ha!" Morgan scoffed. "Brad didn't know I was alive. But that didn't stop me from making up a whole story about the two of us dating and getting married."

Zion glanced at Morgan. "And what ever became of Brad?"

"I killed him off in the next story I wrote." Morgan grinned ruefully.

"Wow!" Zion exclaimed. "Woman scorned and all that?"

"Pfft," Morgan snorted, "more like woman never even existing for him. He turned out to be a real jerk, who got himself a reputation for claiming he'd slept with girls he hadn't. So, my sequel included a plot by all those girls to kill him. It was very satisfying."

"Duly noted," Zion quipped.

Morgan laughed. "You don't have to worry; you strike me as the exact opposite."

"That's true, I'm not a kiss and tell kind of boi."

"Have I mentioned how much I admire your very gallant ways?"

The corner of Zion's lips tugged into a smile. "I learned from old movies."

"Really now? Like which movies?"

"Oh, the classics, *Casablanca*, *Gone with the Wind*, *Twelve O'Clock High*, *Waterloo Bridge*."

"Interesting," Morgan said. "Men weren't always gallant in those movies though."

"Well, if you ignore a lot of the obvious misogyny, and focus on the part where men opened doors, and protect their women, then it's there."

"So…Scarlett or Melanie?" Morgan queried.

"Melanie," Zion answered quickly.

Morgan looked shocked. "Really?"

Zion pressed her lips together. "I'll admit, Vivien Leigh was absolutely gorgeous, but I liked Melanie's character better. She was demure, gentle and genuinely sweet."

"And that's what you prefer?"

Zion blew her breath out in a sigh. "I know, it's hopelessly old fashioned, and probably why I've failed in the big romance department, but yeah, it is what I like."

Morgan tilted her head, giving Zion a measured look. "Would you say you're more like Rhett or Ashley?"

"Ohh…" Zion murmured. "I'd say a bit of both. I try to be even tempered, gentile and loyal, but I'm also no doormat, and given a situation where someone I love is in danger, I can be a door-kicking, fist-wielding Rhett."

Morgan sighed contently. "I like that."

"And would you say you usually date Rhetts or Ashleys?"

Morgan scrunched her face in disgust. "Lately I've been dating a lot of Frank Kennedys or worse, one of the Yankee carpetbaggers. Either they're doormats, or opportunistic parasites."

Zion blinked a couple of times. "Well, that's oddly specific."

"Writer, remember?" Morgan winked.

Zion chuckled. "You certainly are."

They talked some more about Morgan's childhood, and Iowa, where she was from. Morgan leaned against Zion, feeling comfortable and happy. Zion enjoyed the feel of Morgan against her, feeling like they fit together well. Eventually they got under the covers, continuing to discuss things long into the night. It was a lovely evening.

Chapter 11

Doing her best to be quiet, Jaims walked into the kitchen to get a glass of water. Standing at the sink she drank half the glass, then set it down on the counter, thinking to rummage for a snack. Unfortunately, she set the glass too close to the edge of the sink and it fell into it and shattered. Cussing under her breath, Jaims suddenly heard a scream come from Raquel's room.

Moving quickly to the door of Raquel's room, Jaims threw it open and saw her roommate sitting stock straight. Her eyes looked huge and terrified.

"I'm sorry," Jaims said, moving to the side of the bed. Raquel was panting in fear. Recognizing Raquel's terror as a flashback, Jaims did the only thing she could think of, she climbed into bed, and took her best friend in her arms, hugging her.

"It's okay, it's okay, you're here, you're safe." Raquel held onto her as if she were drowning, and Jaims was her life raft. "It's okay, you're safe, it's okay." Jaims repeated the words over and over, and eventually Raquel calmed.

Jaims moved to sit back, but Raquel's hands held her in place.

"Can you stay for a bit?" Raquel pleaded.

"Of course," Jaims agreed. Jaims sat back against the headboard, with Raquel still next to her. After a few moments, Jaims glanced down. Seeing that Raquel's eyes were open, she gently asked, "Can you tell me what you're seeing? Feeling?"

Raquel drew a deep breath in through her nose, blowing it out slowly through her mouth. "It's dark, but so frigging hot…" she began hesitantly. "I can smell sweat, it's almost impossible to stay clean and dry there…and boy do those guys smell. I do everything I can to not smell like BO, but you know guys, they don't care." She chuckled, as did Jaims. "I didn't even realize. I remembered the window above me breaking." Raquel shook her head. "But that sound brought it right back."

"So, we're going out and getting nothing but plastic and paper dishes tomorrow," Jaims teased gently.

Raquel laughed softly. "They tell me that the reactions will fade with time."

"Till then, we'll get through one issue at a time," Jaims told her.

Raquel looked sad. "You shouldn't have to deal with this shit, J, it's my problem."

"Hey, your shit is my shit, got it?"

Raquel curled her lips, wanting to argue, but realizing something at the same time. "I guess me trying to *deal* with my problem on my own is what got me into trouble in the first place, huh?"

"See?" Jaims grinned, squeezing her shoulder. "I didn't want to be the one to say that, but…"

"Uh-huh." Raquel chuckled, feeling better already. "Shaddup you."

Jaims hugged Raquel tighter. "I want to be here for you, okay? So just let me."

Raquel held up a hand in surrender. "I'm letting you; I'm letting you, sheesh!"

They both laughed together. Half sitting, half laying on the bed, they stayed that way for a while. Jaims felt herself getting sleepy.

"You gonna tell me when to leave you alone?" Jaims asked.

"Yeah, when I'm ready for you to leave me alone, I'll let ya know," Raquel said, snuggling closer to Jaims.

Jaims felt a tug at her heart, it made her happy that Raquel was finally allowing herself to be vulnerable. She knew it's what her friend needed in order to stay away from the allure of drugs to dull her feelings and memories.

The next morning as Jaims got up, Raquel opened one eye. "Where are you going?"

"Uh, to make coffee? Maybe go to the bathroom?" Jaims grinned.

"Accepted," Raquel quipped.

"So needy…" Jaims replied jokingly. "Want me to bring you back some coffee?"

"Actually, it's Sunday," Raquel said, "can we meet up with the crew?"

"Absolutely! I'll go shower first, so you can wake up."

"Yeah, and give the crew a heads-up," Raquel murmured.

Jaims glanced back over her shoulder, trying to decide if Raquel was irritated about the thought, but Raquel grinned at her, giving her a wink.

An hour passed. Standing in front of Orphan Andy's, Jaims glanced over at Raquel, who looked a bit nervous. "You okay?"

"Do you think they're pissed at me?" Raquel asked.

"Rock, they are our family, they love you."

"That doesn't mean they won't be pissed…" Raquel murmured.

"We can leave if you're not ready," Jaims offered.

"Move it or lose it bois…" Zion commented from behind them.

Jaims and Raquel turned to see that both Zion and Dax stood there.

"Hey…" Raquel began hesitantly, as Dax extended her hand to her.

"How you doin'?" Dax asked, her look direct, concern laced her eyes.

Raquel took Dax's outstretched hand, nodding as she did. "Embracing the suck."

Dax laughed, nodding her head. "Got your six on that." She clapped her on the shoulder.

Zion smiled at them. "Let's go eat, I'm starving."

As the four headed inside, Jaims peered over at Raquel. Seeing the glazed tears in her friend's eyes, Jaims bumped her shoulder into Raquel's. "Told you." Raquel simply nodded, reaching up to brush away her tears.

Inside, the crew were at their usual table in the front. Seeing Raquel many of them stood to greet her in varied ways.

"Rock!" Shayne called, extending her hand.

"Buddy!" Flynne hugged Raquel.

"Rockin' roll." Case grinned from her spot in the corner of the booth.

"How's it goin'!" Steel added.

Jayden smiled. "Heya Rock."

Raquel accepted the greetings with a hesitant smile. Everyone took their spot at the table, talking amongst themselves.

Their usual waiter, Jerry, came up to take their order, seeing Raquel at the table.

"How are you, boo?" Jerry asked, leaning in to give Raquel a kiss on the cheek.

Raquel nodded. "I'm okay."

"Spacky-tacky," Jerry replied, his version of *spectacular*, and then proceeded to take everyone's order. He poured everyone coffee as he did.

After Jerry sauntered away with everyone's orders, Raquel looked around the table at her friends, her family, and she found that she was so grateful for them.

"Hey guys," Raquel began, her voice a bit tremulous. "I just...I wanted to say that I'm sorry for all the shit lately...I just..." Her voice trailed off as she shook her head.

"We got you," Jayden said, who was sitting to Raquel's left, putting her head on Raquel's shoulder.

"BB's right," Steel said, reaching her hand across the table to rest it on Raquel's arm. "We're here for you, no matter what you need, okay?"

"As long as it's not drugs." Case winked with a pirate's smile on her face.

Raquel laughed. "Cheeky bastard."

The rest of the crew laughed too.

"So, what did happen with that hot red head?" Shayne asked Zion later in the conversation.

Zion narrowed her eyes at Shane's description. "Morgan is her name."

"Wait. Redhead?" Dax queried. "The one you drove home after that storm? There's more?"

"Oh, no one's caught D up?" Case asked, looking far too happy about it. "Oh, let me…"

"No." Zion made a cutting gesture toward Case, knowing the Englishwoman's propensity for exaggeration.

"Morgan," she repeated pointedly, "the very nice writer, who had a bit of an episode in the bar last week…"

"Episode?" Case repeated, her eyes dancing in amusement. "Try breakdown."

"Do I have to come over there?" Zion threatened.

Case held up both hands in surrender, laughing.

"Yeah, I think I need to hear the whole story," Dax said, looking between the two.

Zion proceeded to tell Dax what had occurred.

"So, did she ever figure out if the Davis guy was shot?" Dax asked at the end of the explanation.

"I don't think she's been back to the therapist yet," Zion told her.

"Well, she needs to get to it, we need to know what happened to the bloke."

"Yeah, is Davis dead or not?" Steel asked.

"And did the ex go to jail, or what?" Shayne added.

Jayden's eyes narrowed quizzically. "Is that why the bookstore closed?"

"Yeah, 'cause the guy killed someone?" Flynne interjected.

"A mystery indeed!" Case exclaimed, making everyone laugh.

It was a good morning for them all.

"That went way better than I expected," Raquel commented to Jaims as they got back to their apartment later that morning.

"I told you, you're part of our family," Jaims assured her.

Raquel drew a breath in through her nose, still amazed at how easily the group had forgiven her. Part of her knew that it was because they loved Jaims, and Jaims would be upset if they were mean to her.

"It's because of you," Raquel stated.

"It's not because of me," Jaims replied, turning to look at her best friend. "You just can't believe that people love you and accept you, can you?"

Raquel screwed her lips up in a grimace. "I guess not."

Jaims dropped her keys on the kitchen counter, turning to lean her hip against the counter. "We all fuck up, Rock," she said. "I mean, look at Z when Fancy comes to town, we have to keep an eye on her all the time. You missed the bust up with Dax's girl and the ex, but the crew was together on that too. Everyone has issues, and as a family we deal with it."

Raquel dropped her head. "Shit, you mean like paying to fly my brothers to Landstuhl?"

Jaims inclined her head slightly. "Yeah, stuff like that."

"I can't believe I forgot about that," Raquel commented. "I haven't even thanked Dax and Z for that."

"They don't expect thanks," Jaims told her. "You know that too."

"Doesn't mean I shouldn't do it though."

Jaims shrugged. "Ya still can."

"Yeah." Raquel nodded. "Yeah, I will. Definitely."

Jaims straightened from the counter, putting her hands on Raquel's shoulders. "You've been dealing with a lot since you got back. You have all the time you need to set things straight again. No one is keeping score."

"Except me." Raquel rolled her eyes. "Got it."

Jaims laughed. "You've always been a little slow…"

"Shaddup!" Raquel jostled with a smile, feeling a weight lift from her shoulders.

Jaims smiled inwardly, realizing that the *ever-cocky, ever-confident* 'Rock' needed just as much reassurance as everyone else, maybe more than this point. She was glad, though, that her friend was coming back from the darkness.

***

"Morgan, this is Dax, and this is her girl, Kenzi," Zion introduced.

Morgan offered a warm smile at both women. "It's really nice to meet you. Zion has told me a lot about you, Dax."

"Uh oh." Dax grinned mischievously.

"Nah." Zion winked. "I didn't tell her about that," she said as she held Morgan's chair for her.

"Which that?" Kenzi's eyes sparked with humor.

"You know." Dax nudged her girlfriend. "That that."

"Is this a kind of *that that* which should never be spoken of?" Morgan queried with a raised eyebrow.

Dax and Kenzi both laughed, liking Zion's new lady already. Zion smiled proudly, happy that Morgan already seemed to be getting along great with her best friend. Jane had never gotten along with any of her friends.

The restaurant, Boulevard, was a very busy place, and they seemed to be understaffed, so it took the waitress a few minutes to get over to them.

"I'm so sorry!" she exclaimed, as she filled their water glasses. "Can I get you anything other than water to drink?"

"I'll have a beer, whatever you have on tap is fine," Dax said to the waitress with a smile.

"Babe? Did you want wine, or...?" she asked Kenzi.

"Yes, whatever your house white is, will be fine."

"Morgan?" Zion queried, looking over at her date.

Morgan glanced up from the wine list, smiling brightly at the waitress. "I'd like a glass of the Vielles Vignes."

Zion grinned, glancing over at Dax. "She knows her wines."

Dax rolled her eyes. "Mine's a pilot."

"Yada, yada," Zion countered, then looked over at the waitress. "I'd like a glass of that too, thank you."

As the waitress walked away, Morgan smiled at Kenzi. "Do you fly for Cal Fire like Dax?"

Kenzi shook her head. "At this point, I'm acting as a consultant, but I finally got my license reinstated a couple of months ago, so I'll probably be flying soon."

"Reinstated?" Morgan asked.

"I had a medical issue," Kenzi replied, her look circumspect.

Morgan noticed Dax squeeze Kenzi's hand.

"I'm sorry," Morgan sighed. "In case Zion didn't tell you, I'm a terrible snoop. I apologize if I just made you uncomfortable."

Kenzi shook her head. "It's okay, I had an abusive ex, she caused the issue, but it's cleared up now."

Without hesitation, Morgan reached across the table, putting her hand on Kenzi's. "I'm so sorry." Her eyes reflected her kind words.

Kenzi bowed her head slightly. "Thank you, but I'm in a much better place now." She smiled at Dax, and Morgan could see the love there.

Glancing over at Zion, Morgan noticed that Zion was watching the couple as well. It was obvious to her that Zion liked the two of them together. She'd gotten the distinct impression that Zion watched over her pseudo family like a father would.

When the drinks arrived, the waitress took their dinner order. Zion noticed that Morgan spoke to the waitress kindly and with a great deal of patience, especially when she needed to repeat her order, because the girl hadn't heard correctly the first time.

It was very nice to note that Morgan never seemed to get irritated or angry with the girl. Zion couldn't help but compare that to Jane's behavior with wait-staff. Jane was always impatient, and her words were often critical and snide when dealing with someone she perceived as *bad* at their job. It was endlessly embarrassing to be around her.

At one point during dinner, Kenzi and Morgan excused themselves to go to the restroom. As they stood at the mirror touching up their lipstick, Kenzi smiled over at Morgan. "I'm really glad that Zion has found someone nice this time."

"Compared to?" Morgan queried.

"Oh, the last one," Kenzi intimated. "From what I understand, she was a nightmare."

"You never met her?" Morgan asked.

"No, but Dax has told me a lot about her, and it sounds like the woman was a complete narcissist."

"I've kind of gotten that impression too, from what little Zion has told me about her." Morgan nodded. "I have to say, the writer in me really wants to know more."

"Dax knows the whole story; you could talk to her," Kenzi suggested.

Morgan bit her lip, vacillating. "I don't want to invade Zion's privacy, though, if she wants to tell me about her, she will."

Kenzi considered her response and nodded. "You're probably right. Hang in there though, Zion is definitely worth it. She's got the most generous nature, and I hate that Fancy didn't appreciate her at all."

Morgan smiled, putting her lipstick back in her purse. "I think she's amazing."

"Me too," Kenzi said, "and she deserves to be loved by someone who feels that way about her."

Morgan nodded agreement.

"I really like them," Morgan told Zion in the car on the way back to her house.

"I'm sure they like you." Zion grinned. "Dax doesn't usually joke with anyone until she gets to know them better."

"She does seem very serious at times," Morgan commented.

"Yeah…I think Kenzi is mellowing her out a bit."

"Kenzi is really nice. They seem to be a pretty good pair."

"Well, they didn't start out that way, Dax had just gotten out of a relationship and Kenzi was still dealing with a lot from that bad relationship."

"I can't even imagine being in an abusive relationship." Morgan sighed. "She's very strong to have gotten through it."

"It sounded like it was pretty bad, and Kenzi had no backup for herself then. But we took care of that."

Morgan canted her head. "What do you mean?"

"Her ex showed up here, the crew handled her."

"Wow, that's brave! This ex had the nerve to take all of you on?"

"She didn't know about all of us." Zion grinned. "She thought she was just taking on Dax, and of course brought her own backup."

"Sounds like a big coward to me."

"Anyone who hits a woman is a coward," Zion hissed.

"Absolutely!" Morgan agreed. "I really love that about you, you know?"

Zion looked at her. "What about me?" she asked, clearly confused.

"That you're so valiant, so old-school gentility."

"Gentility…" Zion mused. "Now that is something I've never been accused of."

Morgan laughed softly. "I just mean that you have the manners of classic Rhett Butler, Ashley Wilkes kind of men. It's very rare in this day and age."

"Maybe for men," Zion quipped.

Morgan bit her lip. "Definitely for men."

Zion gave her a lopsided grin. "I guess I watched too many old movies when I was a kid. I grew up thinking that women should be treated gently and with respect."

"And that's amazing, and it's something you shouldn't ever lose!"

Zion shrugged. "I'm pretty much built this way now."

"I like the way you're built." Morgan winked seductively.

"Well now…" Zion smiled warmly as she pulled up in front of Morgan's house. Getting out of the car, Zion walked around to open the door for Morgan, holding her hand out to help her out.

"Even this," Morgan observed the action, squeezing Zion's hand as she got out of the car, "so lovely."

Zion pulled Morgan to her as they stood next to the car, staring down into Morgan's eyes. "I have to agree," she murmured, "so very lovely." With that she leaned in kissing Morgan's lips.

Morgan wrapped her arms around Zion's neck, giving in to the kiss, sighing contently as she did. After much more kissing, Zion took Morgan's hand, escorting her to her front door.

"Thank you for dinner," Morgan announced, "and it was great meeting your friends."

"Thank you for being so gracious and kind to them," Zion replied.

Morgan bit her lip again. "Do you want to come in for a glass of wine? Or a cup of coffee?"

Zion smiled. "I would," she said, sounding truly regretful, "but I'm getting early deliveries tomorrow, and I don't want to sleep through them."

Morgan nodded, doing her best to hide her disappointment. "I understand."

Zion put her hand to Morgan's cheek. "I really do have deliveries, I'm not just telling you that."

Morgan opened her mouth to inform her that it was okay, but she changed her mind. "I just want to spend more time with you, I think I might be a bit addicted."

Zion chuckled. "Well, I appreciate your candor, and I assure you if I didn't have deliveries in the morning, I'd take you up on the offer. I promise we'll get together again really soon, okay?"

"Yes please." Morgan smiled.

They kissed again, and Zion finally walked to her car. Morgan went to bed that night, feeling very lucky to have found such an incredible woman. She only hoped that their next encounter would arrive sooner rather than later.

* * *

Jaims woke to the sound of yelling. It took her a few moments to realize it was Raquel. Jumping up, Jaims rushed to Raquel's door. She flung the door open to see Raquel sitting up in her bed, her head in her hands. Her yelling stopped but she was rocking back and forth. Stepping closer, Jaims reached her hand out touching Raquel's head.

"You okay?" she asked softly.

Raquel drew in a deep breath, shaking her head.

Jaims climbed onto the bed, sitting down perching next to Raquel. Without a word, Raquel moved to lay her head in Jaim's lap. Jaims put one hand on her roommate's shoulder, the other smoothed Raquel's long braid.

They sat in silence for a long time. At one point, Raquel reached up, touching Jaims' hand on her hair, moving it to a specific spot on the side of her head.

"If you feel real close, you can feel the scar…" Raquel told her quietly.

Jaims slid her fingers under Raquel's hair, feeling the inch-long scar there. "Does it hurt when you touch it?"

"No, it's actually kind of numb, it just feels weird. I can tell you're touching it, but I can't really feel it…does that make sense?"

"Yeah." Jaims nodded. "It's like the scar on my ankle from my bike crash."

They were both quiet for a long moment.

"I'm never getting past this, am I?" Raquel whispered, her tone devastated.

"Yes, you will," Jaims told her, "because we're all going to be here to help you. I'll be here, I'll always be here."

The conviction in her friend's voice made Raquel angle her head to look up at Jaims. She saw the kind look in her eyes; the sadness was there too. It was obvious to Raquel that Jaims was worried about her, and it touched her heart.

"You really are always here," Raquel commented. "Even when I don't deserve it."

Jaims grunted. "Okay, new rule, you're not allowed to say you don't deserve things, got it?" Her look was pointed as she stared down at her best friend.

Raquel looked back at her long and hard, it was obvious she was trying to justify her statement, but finally she sighed defeatedly. "Fine."

"Good." Jaims grinned. "Now that we've got this settled, do you want to talk about what woke you up in the first place?"

Raquel moved to sit up, her look haunted. "It was a nightmare, I don't remember it all…I do remember that it wasn't me getting hit this time, it was everyone else on my team though."

"Oh geeze." Jaims grimaced. "That sucks."

Raquel blew her breath out. "Yeah, they said it might be like this for a while."

Jaims nodded. "Is there anything I can do?"

Raquel gave her a lopsided grin. "You're doing it. Being here with me, talking to me about it."

"Well, I guess that's what we'll do then."

They ended up sitting and talking for a long time, each sitting against the headboard of Raquel's bed. Eventually, Raquel was stifling a yawn.

Jaims took that as a signal to leave, and she moved to stand up, telling Raquel to get some more sleep. Raquel's hand on her arm stopped her. "Will you stay here with me?" Raquel requested.

"Of course," Jaims answered immediately, sitting back down on the bed, moving to lay down.

She was surprised when Raquel lay down next to her, with her back to her, but snuggling back against her. It was a rare show of vulnerability for the normally tough ex-soldier, and Jaims knew not to comment. She simply put her hand on Raquel's waist, and did her best to go back to sleep. The problem was that she'd always had a crush on her roommate, and the close proximity was not helping in the slightest.

Raquel lay on her side staring into the darkness, she suddenly realized that she wanted more from Jaims than she'd ever wanted before. In Jaims she'd found the one person that would stand by her no matter what. She just didn't know if that was something that she was brave enough to explore, but laying with her now, being close, she wanted to find out.

Neither of them got much sleep that night.

The next afternoon, Raquel queried, "Think we could go out to dinner, before we go to Fancy's?"

"I, uh, okay," Jaims stammered, glancing over at her roommate who stood in her doorway. "What are you feeling? Are you thinking Andy's?"

"Uh," Raquel vacillated, "what about, um...Maestro's?"

Jaims snorted, the restaurant her friend had named was an upscale steakhouse, so she assumed she was joking. "Sure, are we going to take the limo or the Jag?" She laughed, then turned to look back at Raquel who bit her lip in uncertainty. Jaims turned fully around to look at Raquel. "Were you serious?"

Raquel looked chagrinned and shrugged, averting her eyes. "I just thought it might be nice..."

"Yeah." Jaims nodded, her face showing concern, she didn't want to hurt her friend's feelings. "I don't think either of us can afford that, ya know?"

Raquel chewed on the inside of her cheek. "I just, I um, well, I do have the money, if you want to go. I know you like steak."

Jaims opened her mouth to deliver another remark, but decided against it. Instead she curled her lips in a grin. "I really do love me some steak."

"Cool." Raquel smiled. "Then let me go get dressed."

Jaims chuckled, glancing down at her clothes. She was wearing tattered jeans and a T-shirt. "I guess I better change too, huh?"

Raquel glanced back at her. "I mean, unless you want to totally embarrass me..." She laughed as Jaims chucked a comb at her and headed back to her room.

Twenty minutes later, Jaims walked out to see Raquel standing the kitchen. "Dayum," Jaims commented. "You look nice."

Raquel wore black slacks, black dress boots, and a burgundy silk button-up shirt. Her long black hair hung down her back; she almost never wore her hair down. She even looked like she'd put on the lightest bit of make-up.

"Maybe I should go change," Jaims commented.

"Nah, you look good too." Raquel smiled.

Jaims wore navy blue pants, a white collared shirt open at the throat, and a navy jacket. She also wore black leather loafers. Her short dark hair was a bit more styled, smoothed over to one side, rather than the spikey look she usually wore.

"Let's go." Jaims grinned. "We're going to shock everybody at Fancy's later."

"A little surprise is good for them." Raquel laughed.

"Holy crap this is good," Jaims murmured through a mouthful of steak.

"I know, this is crazy," Raquel responded widening her eyes to emphasize her point. "Who knew the better half lived this good?"

Jaims looked across the small table at her best friend. "Thank you for this, it's really amazing."

Raquel smiled. "I wish I could do this with you more often."

"It wouldn't be as special if we did it all the time, right?" Jaims grinned.

"Exactly!"

Raquel surprised her by putting her hand across the table, covering Jaims' free hand with hers. "But I'm really glad you agreed to come."

Jaims looked back at her longtime friend, sensing that this was not the time to joke about passing up a free meal. She could sense that Raquel meant it sincerely, and she wanted Raquel to know that she understood.

"It was really nice of you to invite me," Jaims announced, turning her hand over and taking Raquel's hand in hers, squeezing gently. "Thank you again."

Raquel smiled softly; she was glad that Jaims understood her gesture. Yes, the meal was expensive, and yes it was going to take her a few months to pay off the credit card bill, but it was worth it, if Jaims liked it.

"Are you tired yet?" Jaims asked, stifling a yawn as she did her best to hold onto to phone.

"Getting there," Raquel replied from her bunk on base, her cell phone cradled between her pillow and her ear. "Tell me another crazy story from your job."

"Well." Jaims settled against the headboard, grinning to herself in the darkness. "Did I tell you about the three-paragraph email I got about how the toilet paper in the bathrooms should be loaded in the over configuration, instead of the under configuration?"

Raquel snorted. "Seriously!" she whispered, laughing quietly. Her bunkmates were asleep, and she didn't want to wake them.

"Yeah! I kid you not, it was three paragraphs about health issues, convenience, and get this, there was even a diagram at the bottom!"

Raquel laughed again. "I'm telling you, these state employees have absolutely nothing to do with their time! What was your response to the email?"

"Honestly, I wanted to write back and ask who their manager was, so I could suggest that he or she start giving them more work to do!"

"Did you?"

"No. My bitch of a boss would have written me up for being nasty to customers."

"That bitch should be written up for being a horrible manager," Raquel growled.

"Yeah, I know." Jaims sighed. "I miss my old manager."

"I miss you," Raquel commented unexpectedly.

"Awww," Jaims replied, amusement in her voice.

"Shaddup," Raquel snapped. "I shouldn't have said that, okay?"

Jaims was caught the undercurrent of sadness in Raquel's voice and knew she'd hurt her feelings.

"I miss you too," Jaims answered honestly.

They were both silent for a long moment, before Raquel changed the subject.

Later that evening when they arrived at Fancy's the crew was indeed bowled over by their more formal attire, but they took all the joking in stride.

"Yo, don't be jealous just because we got to eat at the best steak place in town," Raquel said.

"Did one of you rob a bank?" Flynn asked.

"Or get some crazy inheritance you're going to share with the rest of us?" Shayne asked.

"If we did, we aren't sharing." Jaims winked over at Raquel, who smiled, nodding her head.

"Hey, what's the haps over here, you two look awfully snazzy," Zion commented with a smile.

"They went out to dinner," Steel commented.

"And spent a lot of money," Case added.

"Was it your money?" Zion asked smoothly.

"Uh, no bloody way," Case replied.

"Then pipe down." Zion winked to take the sting out of her words. "You two look great. Ya class the joint up."

"I agree," Jayden enthused.

Jaims and Raquel both laughed, appreciating Zion's input and the closure of the ribbing party that was about to get into full swing.

The night was fun, there was lots of drinking, and since Jaims and Raquel had traveled to the restaurant and the bar by Uber, they were both able to drink for a change.

On the way home in the Uber vehicle, Jaims felt a bit woozy, as the chilly night air hit her.

"You okay?" Raquel asked, glancing over at her friend.

Jaims was doing her best not to look as bad as she felt, but finally shook her head.

"Come here," Raquel told her, reaching over to touch Jaims' arm.

Jaims leaned over, but ended up putting her head in Raquel's lap. Raquel ran her fingers through Jaims' hair and rubbed her scalp soothingly.

"That's nice…" Jaims uttered.

They stayed that way until the driver pulled up in front of their apartment. Raquel helped Jaims to her feet and then helped her to get out of the car. Jaims stood up unsteadily, wavering a little as the driver pulled away.

"Lean on me," Raquel told her, draping Jaims' arm around her shoulders.

They made it to the elevator slowly, but Jaims felt very thankful that Raquel was there to aid her. Once inside, they both leaned against the rail that ran along the back of the elevator. It was so late that they were the only ones in the elevator car.

"I guess I over did it a bit," Jaims lulled lazily, with a look of chagrin on her face.

Raquel glanced over at her as the elevator took them to their floor. "Like you haven't had to help me ever."

"I know, but…" Jaims continued mournfully. "This was such a nice night."

"Still is," Raquel told her firmly, squeezing her shoulder and leaning in to kiss Jaims on the side of the head.

Jaims turned her head to look at Raquel, her eyes were soft. It was in that moment, Raquel leaned back in and kissed Jaims' lips. The action shocked both of them, and the loud ding of the elevator reaching their floor and the doors opening seemed to bring them back to reality.

Raquel stood from the rail, securing Jaims' arm around her shoulder again. She led them out of the elevator and down the hall toward their apartment. When they reached the door, Raquel unlocked it and helped Jaims inside.

Raquel took Jaims to her room, sitting her down on the bed. Kneeling down, she unzipped the boots that Jaims wore and pulled them off, setting them aside. Standing up, she looked at Jaims who was watching her closely.

"I'm guessing you can do the rest." Raquel smiled, then turned to leave the room.

Jaims' hand grabbed hers. Without a word, Jaims pulled Raquel back to her, and kissed her firmly on the lips, her hands roamed the side of Raquel's face. At first it seemed like Raquel wanted to pull away, but instead she gave in and gave herself over to returning Jaims' kiss.

Suddenly, a fire between them ignited. Raquel reached up pulling Jaims' jacket off, and pushed Jaims down onto her back, deepening the kiss with a hunger that both surprised and thrilled Jaims.

There was no discussion about what was happening; they were both just allowing things to ignite. Clothes were removed hastily and cast aside, and once naked, Raquel moved over Jaims, kissing and exploring her lips, her neck, and then moving lower. Jaims' hands slid through Raquel's long, thick black hair, reveling in the feel of Raquel's lips on her skin.

Jaims moaned as Raquel moved lower to capture an already achingly hard nipple with her mouth, her hand caressing the other, making Jaims writhe with pleasure. Allowing her hands to roam over Raquel's shoulders, Jaims felt the strength there, the muscles that rippled as Raquel moved. It only served to excite her more.

Within minutes Jaims felt like she was going to burst, the yearning for release was so exquisite and primal. She found herself arching back, her body silently begging Raquel for what she needed. She uttered a growl, "Please…"

Raquel heard the plea and moved her hand down, sliding it over Jaims skin, slowly, wishing to savor the moment. When she finally let her fingers slide between Jaims legs, touching heat and wetness, Jaims came immediately. She cried out, hands grasping Raquel's shoulders. She bucked her body against Raquel's fingers, as the orgasm took over and seemed to last forever.

As she floated back down to Earth, Jaims started to think about what had just happened, she wasn't sure how this was going to go. She and Raquel had been friends for a long time, and she wasn't sure what this meant for them.

"Stop overthinking it," Raquel murmured against her neck.

Jaims looked at Raquel, she was laying on her side, her hand now laying on Jaims' stomach. She appeared completely comfortable, so Jaims did her best to stop thinking for a moment. They lay next to each other, not talking, but their fingers ended up intertwined on Jaims' stomach. Raquel slid her arm under Jaims' neck, and they fell asleep that way.

The next morning Jaims was woken by the sun streaming through her bedroom window. She squeezed her eyes shut, silently cursing that she hadn't shut her blinds before bed. It took her a minute to piece together the events of the night before. She remembered going to dinner, having drinks at the bar with Raquel. There was a definite memory of feeling really drunk, and appreciative of her best friend, who got them both home. Raquel had even helped her take off her boots...Her eyes flew open as she remembered what had happened afterwards. That's when she remembered Raquel laying there, next to her on her side, asleep.

Holy shit! her brain screamed. She'd had a crush on Raquel forever, and now they had actually become intimate. She delighted in that for a long few moments, but then the doubt seeped in. They'd both been drunk. Was it because of the alcohol? Would Raquel wake up and be horrified at what they'd done? Doubt was a corrosive thing, it started chewing at a person, making them question everything.

"What's going on?" Raquel's voice broke through Jaims' thoughts. Jaims looked at her longtime friend, Raquel's dark eyes searching hers.

"I, um," Jaims stammered.

Raquel canted her head slightly. "You...um," she began, a quizzically amused look in her eyes, "you are lying there freaking the fuck out."

Jaims winced, closing her eyes, then opening one to look back at Raquel. "A little bit."

Raquel's lips curled into a grin. "You're lying there thinking that we got drunk last night, and that's why we're lying here together, naked."

Jaims looked immediately guilty, which elicited a laugh from Raquel. Reaching up between them, Raquel put her finger to Jaims' lips. "First of all, I wasn't that drunk."

"You weren't?" Jaims queried.

"No," Raquel said, "and second, I let what happened, happen."

"But I started it," Jaims countered.

"Right," Raquel nodded, "but that's 'cause I let you."

"Let me?" Jaims' pride asserted itself for a moment.

Raquel laughed again. It was a happy sound, not an angry one. Not a sound Jaims was ordinarily worried about. "Yes, dummy." The finger on Jaims' lips was back. "I'm a trained killer, you think I couldn't have smacked the shit out of you if I'd wanted to?"

Jaims couldn't help but laugh at the remark, nodding her head. "True."

"Very true," Raquel confirmed. "So," she lulled, her look serious, "the question is, do we want to leave it there?"

"Where?" Jaims asked, her somewhat hungover brain making it hard for her to follow the direction of Raquel's words.

Raquel pursed her lips, her look at Jaims assessing. "Do we leave it at *I gave you the best orgasm of your life*, or—"

Jaims' laugh interrupted her. "The best orgasm of my life, huh?"

"Dude, you know it was." Raquel grinned proudly, her eyes sparkling mischievously.

Jaims laughed again, shaking her head. "You're too much."

"I am, huh?" Raquel smiled. "Am I too much for you?" The question was serious.

Jaims caught the tone, and her expression became serious. "You are never too much for me." She reached up touching Raquel's face. "You're the best friend I've ever had."

213

"But not girlfriend material?" Raquel added, her look appeared fragile in the moment.

"You are…" Jaims began, "but I'd hate to lose my best friend…"

Raquel looked thoughtful for a long moment. "Are you willing to try it?"

Jaims had never seen Raquel look so unsure of herself, and it was an arrow straight through her heart. How could she ever say no to that?

"Yeah," Jaims said nodding, as she leaned in to kiss Raquel's lips. "I'm willing to try anything with you."

Raquel's smile deepened. "Careful what you say there, I just might test that statement."

Jaims laughed, feeling happy in the moment. Things were certainly going to be different!

Chapter 12

In Zion's apartment Jane did her best to dry off. She'd been caught in the rain, and white silk and rain meant her dress had become see-through, and without a bra, it was rather X-rated. She grinned at herself in the mirror as she reapplied her red lipstick and touched up her hair. Jane knew she looked hot. She felt her pulse quicken when she heard the door to the apartment open and close.

"Jane?" Zion queried.

Jane stepped out of the small bathroom, the white sheath of her dress touching the floor as she did; the dress outlined her best assets, since she wore no undergarments whatsoever. She heard Zion suck in her breath sharply.

"I…" Zion began, her eyes roaming all over Jane's body, the lust showing in her eyes.

Jane's lips parted in a seductive smile. "Do you see something you want?"

Zion nodded, taking long strides to her, her lips capturing Jane's in a passionate kiss. As Zion's mouth roamed down her neck, Jane gasped in pleasure.

"Are you strapped?" Jane asked breathlessly.

Zion made a sound in her throat, something between a moan and a growl. "What do you know about that?"

"I know I want you to fuck me with it," Jane told her brazenly.

Zion pulled back, looking down at her. A lascivious leer appeared on her face.

"And I want you on your knees in front of me." With the command, Zion took Jane's shoulders and pressed her down to her knees.

Jane moaned loudly, excited beyond reason at the tableau playing out. "What else do you want?" Jane asked, staring up at Zion with her dark eyes.

Zion unzipped her pants, and pulled out the strap on, holding it in her hand. "I want to see those red, red lips wrapped around this."

Jane opened her mouth to respond, but Zion shoved the tip of the phallus into her mouth. Surprised and excited, Jane began to orally service Zion. Zion's hand clutched a handful of blonde hair in her fist, guiding her. It only excited her more.

"Yeah, you like that, don't you?" Zion goaded. "You want me to fuck that hot mouth of yours, don't you?"

"Mmmhmm…" Jane mumbled, with her mouth around the dildo, her nipples hard and straining against the white satin material of her dress.

"Yeah, you do," Zion reached down to touch her hard nipples, her fingertips brushing back and forth, exciting Jane even more. "Now get up, and turn around," Zion ordered, using a handful of hair to pull her up.

"I…" Jane began.

"Shut up, turn around!" Zion growled.

Jane did as she was told and felt Zion pulling up the back of her dress. Then she felt the tip of the dildo at her ass. Zion's hands were pulling her ass cheeks apart, the tip slipped between them.

"I don't…" Jane began again.

"You'll do what I tell you," Zion snapped, the tip pushing farther in.

"Oh my God!" Jane screamed, coming loudly as she opened her eyes. She looked around the empty bathroom. The bubbles from her bath were scattered and there was water everywhere. Not that she cared, she didn't have to clean it up.

She had just given herself one hell of an orgasm.

The idea of Zion not being the gentleman for once, and taking her almost savagely was too exciting not to use, at least in her fantasies. Jane sighed, laying back in the tub; maybe it was time to get Zion to be a little more aggressive…Yes, it was time that Zion start doing her job.

***

It was mid-week and Morgan was surprised to get a call from Zion. Surprised but very happy.

"Hello." She smiled warmly, as she answered the call.

"Good morning," Zion replied smoothly. "I was calling to see if you were possibly free today."

"I absolutely am," Morgan agreed readily.

"How about a wander through Cannery Row?" Zion suggested.

"Sounds wonderful!"

Two hours later, Zion arrived to pick her up. Morgan was pleasantly surprised to see Zion in jeans and a navy-blue henley thermal shirt, she even wore tennis shoes on her feet.

"I think this is the first time I've seen you truly casual." Morgan smiled brightly.

"Gotta take a day off now and again, right?" Zion winked.

Morgan agreed. "Indeed!"

"You look beautiful, I love that color on you."

Morgan was wearing a plum-colored cashmere sweater with dark jeans and black knee-high boots. As always, she was wearing very little makeup, just enough to enhance her features. Zion found that she very much liked Morgan's style, she wasn't overly flashy, but always looked classy.

Morgan bit her lip; she loved that Zion complimented her. It always made her feel very special to have this handsome woman admire her.

"Thank you," she replied.

As always Zion escorted her to the car and opened the passenger door for her, holding out her hand to help Morgan inside. Morgan also noticed that Zion never slammed the door, she always closed it gently. As gentle as the woman herself.

They spent a couple of hours wandering in and out of shops. Zion proved to be a great shopping companion as well, noticing the types of items Morgan tended to look at and proceeding to point out things she thought she'd like. Morgan also noticed that Zion never commented on how much things cost, or made derogatory remarks about how much she thought things should cost. Quite the opposite.

In a shop that featured local artists' jewelry, pottery and paintings, Zion stood looking at a painting of Cannery Row itself. Morgan walked over, standing next to Zion to join her looking at the painting.

"I really like this," Morgan declared.

"The use of color here and there is fantastic, the artist really sees things with a great eye, don't you think?" Zion observed.

"Absolutely." Morgan was enchanted. She reached up to flip over the price tag, and saw that the artist was asking $750 for the painting.

"It's an original work," the shop owner commented hurriedly, as if to justify the price tag. "The artist is a local woman, who tries to capture the essence of our little area here."

"She does an excellent job." Zion glanced back at the shop owner. "It's beautiful. It's obvious this work took many hours. The detail alone is incredible."

The dark-haired woman smiled. She was happy that these people actually seemed to appreciate the hard work the artist, who was a close friend of hers, had invested into the painting.

"I'd like to buy it," Morgan told the lady, "but we've just begun our walk and I'm afraid I will damage it trying to carry it around. If I pay for it now, can you reserve it for a few hours?"

"Of course," the owner said, smiling brightly. "I'll get it wrapped up, so it's protected and keep it in the back for you."

"Wonderful!" Morgan enthused, following the woman over to the cash register.

When the purchase was complete, Morgan and Zion left the store.

"I think you got a great deal for that," Zion told her.

"Me too!" Morgan beamed.

The truth was, Morgan was both pleased with the purchase, as well as the way her companion had interacted with the store owner. Far too often, Morgan found that men she dated liked to comment about how items weren't worth what a shop owner was charging. It was embarrassing to Morgan, and always made her feel foolish for liking something. *As if she didn't know what things were worth.*

"Ready for some lunch?" Zion asked, reaching down to take Morgan's hand in hers.

Morgan found herself biting her lip, always thrilled when Zion held her hand. "Absolutely!"

"Are you okay with seafood?"

"I love seafood!"

A few minutes later they stood at the kiosk to wait for a table at the restaurant.

"I'm sorry," the younger woman told them, looking flustered, "we're super busy right now, it could be as long as thirty minutes. Do you want me to put your name on the list?"

Zion glanced at Morgan to see how she was taking the news, but was happy to note that Morgan smiled at the young woman.

Morgan turned to Zion. "I'm good with that, are you okay with waiting?"

"I am." Zion nodded, looking back over at the hostess. "Please put us down, the name is Calvert."

"Great!" The hostess smiled, happy these people weren't going to yell at her for the wait. "If you like, you can wait at the bar until your table is ready."

"Sounds great!" Zion led Morgan to the bar. "They have a really good wine selection here."

At the bar, a woman with blonde hair and fuchsia lips smiled brightly at Zion.

"Hey Z! How are ya?"

Zion put her hand out to the woman, accepting the friendly pat. "I'm good Becca, how are you doing?"

"Can't complain but you know I will." Becca laughed.

"Becca," Zion said. "This is Morgan Collins."

Becca's eyes widened. "Wait, are you *the* Morgan Collins? The one who wrote *Ten Minutes to Midnight*?"

Morgan smiled warmly, nodding her head. "You've read it?" she asked, sounding beyond pleased.

"Read it? Only like a million times! I love that book! I actually love all of your books!"

"Wow, thank you, that really means a lot." Morgan nodded.

"No problem! So, Z, are you lucky enough to be dating this woman?" Becca chuckled.

Zion gave her friend a lopsided grin. "I do believe so."

"Dayum…" Becca exclaimed. "I didn't even know you swung our way," she told Morgan.

The interest made Morgan blush.

"Wine menu?" Zion asked, to deter the focus away from Morgan.

"Well, duh." Becca said, handing Zion the large menu. Becca sauntered off to help other customers, getting the hint that Morgan might need a minute to recover from being called out.

"You okay?" Zion asked solicitously.

"Yes." Morgan nodded. "I just wasn't sure how to answer a direct statement."

Zion chuckled. "I'm guessing I'm a first for you?" she asked, looking somewhat surprised.

"Well, no...I mean, I have dabbled a bit but you are definitely the first serious woman I've dated."

"Meaning I'm serious, or the date is?" Zion asked with a sly grin.

"Oh!" Morgan put her hand to her mouth, her eyes wide with embarrassment.

"I'm just kidding," Zion teased.

Morgan blew her breath out in a huff and pretended to be mad at Zion. "See how you are?"

"I do," Zion murmured as she moved closer, kissing Morgan's lips softly. "And I like the idea of being the first," she whispered.

Morgan felt her entire body light up in response, so much so she couldn't form a reply.

Becca returned to their place at the bar to take their order for drinks, interrupting the moment. Zion ordered them both a glass of her favorite, and Morgan was grateful to not have to speak.

Half an hour passed and they had engaged in a great deal of small talk. They were then seated at their table out on the covered patio, and after ordering their lunch Morgan looked out at the ocean. They were eating at a restaurant called The Fish Hopper, which was located right on the Monterey Bay. It featured beautiful views of the ocean and there were sea lions playing in the slight swells of the bay.

"This place is lovely," Morgan observed, her red hair blowing in the soft breeze.

"The food is really good, much like the view," Zion commented. Zion's blue eyes were staring directly at Morgan over the rim of her wine glass.

Morgan noticed Zion's gaze and blushed again. "You keep doing that to me today..."

Zion chuckled. "I'm sorry. I'll stop embarrassing you."

Morgan toyed with her own wine glass stem. "Thank you for this," she said seriously.

Zion blinked. "This?"

"For today, the company, everything. It's so nice to just wander and enjoy a beautiful day with great company." Morgan smiled, taking another sip of her wine. Zion looked back at her for a long moment with an odd smile on her face. "What?" Morgan found herself asking.

Zion shook her head. "I just..." Her voice trailed off as she canted her head. "It's nice to be with someone that enjoys simple pleasures."

An instant question popped into Morgans head. She pressed her lips together to keep herself from blurting it out.

Zion spotted the gesture and laughed. "I know you just wanted to ask me something, go ahead and ask."

Morgan bit her lip and sighed. "Am I getting that predictable?"

"Not predictable, just a little obvious when you want to ask a question," Zion told her, a smile still etched on her face.

"I was just wondering if you were thinking of Fancy when you said that," Morgan admitted.

"I was," Zion answered simply. "She always needed things to be more…more." Zion gestured to indicate a larger size.

"Can you tell me about her? And what happened?" Morgan asked gently.

Zion regarded her wine glass, lifted it to her lips, and drained it. She set it down and waved over to Becca for a refill.

"I met her at the bar," she began, proceeding to tell Morgan the entire story, even through lunch.

They were still sitting at the table twenty minutes after they'd eaten, when Zion finished.

"Wow," Morgan exclaimed, looking shell-shocked. "That's crazy."

Zion nodded. "You can see why my friends don't really like her."

"If I were them, I'd have strung her up by now," Morgan said acerbically.

Zion gave a snorted. "Tell me how you really feel."

The rest of their day was spent shopping and enjoying the sunshine. Morgan kept mulling over what Zion had said about Jane. She didn't know how someone could be so evil. It really astounded her.

On their drive back to Morgan's house, Zion held Morgan's hand. Morgan wasn't ready for the day to end.

"Is the bar open tonight?" Morgan asked.

"Nope, closed tonight and tomorrow night." Zion grinned. "My weekend."

Morgan laughed softly. "Well, how about we stop at one of my favorite restaurants and grab dinner to go and eat at my house? My treat."

Zion nodded. "I'd like that."

"How do you feel about Italian food?"

"Love it."

"Wonderful! They make the best lobster ravioli I've ever had," Morgan delighted.

"Sounds like a winner to me."

Some time later, they were settled on Morgan's small veranda, having dinner and chatting.

"So, what is it like to be a famous author?" Zion asked.

Morgan winced. "I'm far from famous."

"A bartender in Monterey knew who you were," Zion told her, "that sounds pretty famous to me."

"She's read a book I wrote, that doesn't make me famous," Morgan chided.

"Okay." Zion held her hands up in surrender. "Let's say that makes you *well-known*."

Morgan sighed. "At the rate I'm going, I'm going to be out of my contract soon."

"Why? Because you're blocked? Don't all writers get writer's block sometimes?"

Morgan huffed. "Yes, but I doubt it's been as long for most of them as it has for me."

Zion looked at her, assessing. "What does it feel like?"

"Being blocked?" Morgan raised her eyebrows.

Zion nodded.

"It feels like part of me is gone," Morgan said, looking forlorn.

"Every day I wake up and think maybe today I can get back into writing, and I sit down at my computer and nothing."

"What do you mean nothing?"

"I mean I can't seem to write anything; nothing comes out right, it all sounds like drivel or too cliché." Morgan covered her face with her hands. "I feel like a failure."

Zion extended her arm, taking one of Morgan's hands, squeezing it gently. "You're not a failure. If you're still trying, you're not a failure."

"How do you figure?" Morgan asked sadly.

"Because you haven't given up."

Morgan smiled a little. "It's still a horrible feeling."

"I'm sorry," Zion said, lifting Morgan's hand, kissing her knuckles. "Is there anything I can do?"

Morgan felt her body tingle at the feel of Zion's lips pressed to her hand. Using her other hand, Morgan reached out and touched Zion's lips with her fingertips. "You could use those on my lips, instead of my hand." She smiled sweetly.

Removing her napkin from her lap and setting it on the table, Zion moved to stand. Still holding Morgan's hand, she pulled her gently up from her chair. Leaning down, Zion kissed Morgan's lips, softly at first, then again deepening the kiss. Morgan let out a soft moan.

Morgan felt her body come alive, feeling like she'd been touched by a live wire. She slid her hands through Zion's hair, eliciting a shudder from Zion. The kiss lasted much longer than any kiss they'd shared before. Morgan pressed closer, feeling her body beg for more than just a kiss.

"Please…" Morgan pleaded against Zion's lips. She wasn't sure what she was asking for, but knew she needed more of everything.

Zion's hands hooked around her waist, and they dragged her closer. Zion peppered kisses down Morgans neck. Morgan clenched a handful of her hair in response. Zion groaned, then to Morgan's surprise tore her lips away from Morgan's neck, staring into her eyes intently.

"I want you," Zion told her simply, "but we said we'd take this slow."

Morgan panting a little said, "I know, but I don't care, please Zion…please…"

With that, Zion took Morgan's hand and led her inside, turning her head to look quizzically at Morgan. "Bedroom?"

Morgan bit her lip and lead Zion to her bedroom.

Zion began to kiss her again. Morgan wasn't sure she could take anymore. She felt Zion's hands tug at the bottom of her sweater. Doing her best to contain herself, Morgan waited patiently for Zion to take the lead.

Zion could feel Morgan trembling, it only added to her excitement, but she was determined to take things slow. Sliding her hands under Morgan's sweater, Zion roamed over silky soft skin. She slid her hands further up toward Morgans lacy bra. She could feel Morgan's breath catch in her throat. Moving her lips back down to Morgan's neck, Zion kissed and nuzzled as her hands continued to explore Morgan's body.

Morgan felt her insides screaming for release, the sensation of Zion's hands on her skin was too much to bear. She wanted to throw off her clothes and beg Zion to take her right there. Instead, she gave herself over to the pleasure of Zion's caress and the feel of her lips on her skin.

When Zion's hands halted at the sides of her bra again. Morgan hoped she wasn't changing her mind. Without warning, Zion's teeth grazed her neck. Her thumbs smoothed Morgan's taught nipples. Gasping, Morgan orgasmed. She clung to Zion's shoulders as waves of pleasure washed over her.

No one had ever brought her to climax while she was still wearing her clothes; nor had she ever had an orgasm that strong. As the waves subsided, Morgan rested her head in the crook of Zion's neck, panting softly. Her heartbeat finally started to slow. Zion's hands continued to touch her skin, but only the non-sensitive parts. It felt incredible and romantic at the same time.

"That was…" Morgan began, unable to find the words to describe the experience.

Zion kissed her lips softly, telling her without words that she didn't need to say anything. Morgan was grateful, because she knew she couldn't adequately describe how she felt at that moment.

When their lips parted, Morgan felt awkward.

"So, anything good on TV tonight?" Zion asked with a grin.

Morgan chuckled and, taking Zion's hand, led her back out to the living room. They ended up watching TV for a while, until Morgan observed Zion stifling a yawn.

"Getting tired?" Morgan asked.

"Mmm, yes, a bit," Zion told her.

"Do you want to stay here tonight?"

Zion looked pensive for a moment. "I don't really have anything suitable to sleep in."

Morgan resisted the urge to tell her she could sleep naked, knowing that Zion's gallant ways would probably preclude that option, and she didn't want to put her on the spot.

"I have a pair of men's sweatpants, if that would work for you?" Morgan offered.

Zion gave her a surprised look, but nodded. "Sure, that'll work. Would you mind if I take a shower?"

"Absolutely not." Morgan smiled, thinking she'd love to join her, but she quashed the thought. "There are towels and toiletries in the guest bathroom right down the hall there."

Zion leaned over, kissing her softly on the mouth. She got up and headed for the bathroom.

An hour later they finally settled in Morgan's bed. Zion wore the sweatpants and a T-shirt that Morgan had found. They each lay on their sides, facing each other.

"So, you have men's clothes, men's body wash and cologne in your guest bathroom…" Zion began.

Morgan pressed her lips together. "My overnight guests are rarely women."

Zion nodded. "So the women you've dated, they've never stayed over?"

Morgan bit her lip. "I've never really gone so far as to sleep with a woman."

Zion bowed her head, and gave her a quizzical look. "And by sleep you mean…"

"I've never had sex with a woman before," Morgan admitted hurriedly. "In college I kissed and made out with women, but it never went further."

"Interesting…" Zion commented.

"In a bad way?" Morgan said worryingly.

Zion moved closer, sliding her hand over Morgan's waist. She leaned in and kissed Morgan's neck, and whispered, "Like I said, I like being the first."

Morgan shivered. "Well you certainly are."

Zion moved to lay on her back, and she slid her arm under Morgan's neck. Morgan snuggled closer, her head in the hollow of Zion's shoulder. They lay that way, talking into the night.

***

"So, it's going well with your handsome blue-eyed stranger." Jessie grinned lasciviously.

"Yes, I think it is," Morgan enthused.

"And even after you told her about all the crazy reincarnations?"

"Yes, even after that." Morgan rolled her eyes. "They aren't crazy, they just are."

"And you think it's normal that you had the same blue eyes following you through your life?" Jessie asked as she took a sip of her cocktail.

Morgan shrugged, sipping from her own drink. "It's believed that people are the same in every life, and are involved with the same people in multiple lives."

Jessie looked skeptical. "You never found out what happened with Sam and Davis, maybe you should find out before things with your new love go too far."

Morgan looked surprised. "What is that supposed to mean?"

"I mean, you should probably know how things end up with them, right? Did they have a long happy life together, or what?"

Morgan didn't like the insinuation, but it got her thinking about what had happened with her previous life. With the thought in mind, Morgan called to get another appointment with the therapist. Charlotte was on vacation for the next two weeks, so it had to wait until she was back.

"Just give me whatever you've got available after she gets back," Morgan informed the receptionist.

***

"Why haven't you been returning my calls?" Jane asked, incensed. She'd swept into the bar half an hour ago, acting every bit the fiery dragon. Zion had managed to avoid her, up until she'd come to stand directly in Zion's path as the bar owner brought up a case of beer.

"Can you move?" Zion asked in a clipped tone, far from being in the mood to have a confrontation with the woman.

Jane's eyes narrowed dangerously; her fists placed firmly on slim hips. "Not until you tell me why you haven't called me back!"

"Then I'm about to drop this case of beer on your foot," Zion countered, as she shifted the heavy load.

Jane blew her breath out in a huff and stepped back out of Zion's way. Zion proceeded to carry the case to behind the bar, setting it down. She bent down and began filling the cooler with its contents. She could feel Jane's ire like a physical presence. Grinning to herself, she continued her task.

"Z!" Zip called from the other end of the bar. "I need an override!"

Zion straightened taking a step toward Zip.

"Don't you dare!" Jane raged.

"I have a bar to run," Zion said, glancing over her shoulder at the blonde. "Why don't you come back later, or don't, I really don't care." With that she walked toward the waiting bartender.

Zion spent another hour moving from task to task to avoid Jane. Every time she glanced in Jane's direction, she could have sworn the woman was turning to stone on the barstool on which she perched.

When Zion moved back to where Jane was still waiting, she turned and began checking liquor levels in the bottles on the shelves, her back to Jane. She was stunned when a glass hit her from behind, and splashed red wine all over her white long-sleeved shirt.

"What the ever-loving fuck!" Zion exclaimed. She pivoted to see that Jane was giving her a 'that's what you get' look.

"Are you insane!" Zion continued, moving to grab a towel, wiping at what little she could reach on the back of her shirt.

"I cannot believe…Zip, I gotta go change!" she called as she turned to walked toward the back stairs up to her apartment, throwing Jane a dirty look.

"You are not invited," she snapped, "get out of my bar!"

Despite Zion's order, Jane followed her up the stairs.

"I think you forget that I'm your partner in this bar," Jane snapped, "so you can't tell me to leave!"

"I can damned well remove you myself!" Zion yelled back, continuing into her apartment, unbuttoning her shirt in angry jerks.

"You can try!" Jane screamed back.

Taking off the stained shirt, Zion scrunched it up into a ball, throwing it in the hamper. She strode to her closet for another. Jane got in her way to stop her, putting her long-nailed hands on Zion's shoulders.

"What is wrong with you!" Jane snapped, her face suffused with color in her anger.

Zion stopped her from edging any further forward, giving Jane a warning look. It was rare that Zion lost her temper, but she knew she was about to do so. "Take your damned hands off me and get out of my way," she growled.

"Not until you tell me what's going on!" Jane retorted hotly.

Taking a slow deep breath, doing her best to stave off her fury, Zion slowly reached up her hands. She took Jane's wrists and moved them away from her.

Jane flexed her fingers and yanked her restrained wrists away from Zion. Jane raked her blood red nails down Zion's chest. Zion snapped, and raised her right hand, ready to backhand Jane. The widening of Jane's eyes and her gasp of sincere shock brought Zion to *her senses. Zion walked away from Jane, and marched into the kitchen. She pulled a bottle of Jack Daniel's out of the cupboard and took a long drink. When she slammed the bottle down, amber liquid splashed on the counter. Glancing to her right, she could see that Jane was standing in the doorway to the kitchen, her arms crossed in front of her chest.*

"Fancy..." Zion began, her voice low and dangerous. "I'm warning you; you need to get away from me right now."

"I don't understand..." Jane began, tears suddenly glazing her eyes. "Why are you doing this to me?"

Zion didn't fall for it this time. Slowly turning her head to look at her, her blue eyes ablaze, she said, "Go ask your husband."

Jane drew her breath in sharply, obviously shocked that Zion knew about Winston. Zion could see her mentally regrouping and didn't wait to see what lies would come out of her mouth next. Instead, Zion strode toward her, taking her by the shoulders and turning her around, and marched Jane to the apartment door, pushing her out of it. She slammed the door after her, locking the bolt into place. Moments later, Jane pounded on the door, screaming that Zion 'didn't understand' and needed to 'let her explain!'

Zion walked away from the door, going back into the kitchen and picking up the bottle of Jack Daniels. She went into her bedroom and sat on the bed. She spent the next hour polishing the bottle. An hour later, Dax came up to tell Zion that Jane had finally stormed out of the bar, but not before causing a huge scene with the crew trying to claim that Zion had become violent with her.

"We knew she was full of shit," Dax told Zion, who was fairly drunk at this point of Dax retelling the incident. "We all told her to leave."

Zion nodded, blowing her breath out. "Thanks."

"You okay?" Dax asked, already knowing the answer. Zion shrugged, her mouth curved in discontent. "Okay, well we got staff downstairs, you just take the night, okay?"

"Thanks," Zion said, as she got up to go into the kitchen for another bottle. This time she picked up some Kraken dark spiced rum.

Dax shook her head, knowing Zion was headed for a bender. It was the first of many for the next few months and periodically whenever Jane would turn up to 'explain.'

A week later at the bar, Jane made an unexpected appearance.

"She won't see you," Dax announced, as Jane swept by her and Kenzi's table.

Jane whirled on Dax. "Leave me alone!" she snapped. Dax grinned, putting her hands up in surrender. Jane narrowed her eyes; she didn't trust that Dax had given up so easily. "Where is she?"

Dax canted her head, an evil glint in her eyes. "That's for me to know, and for you to find out."

Jane's face suffused with color as she glared at the ex-fighter pilot. She looked over at Kenzi who was watching with an amused look on her face.

"Your girlfriend is an asshole," Jane told Kenzi.

"Look who's talking," Kenzi replied flatly.

Jane's hands scrunched into fists. Dax looked pointedly at them, then back up to Jane's eyes. "That'd be about the very last thing you'd do in this life."

"Oh, so tough," Jane said mockingly, but her hands immediately unclenched.

"Roger that," Dax said.

Jane gave the couple a haughty look, then turned and continued toward the bar.

"So that's her, huh?" Kenzi asked Dax.

"Oh yeah," Dax sighed. "Likely to be a long night."

At the bar, Jane demanded to see Zion.

Zip, the bartender, knew exactly who she was dealing with. "She's not in yet," she told Jane, a triumphant look on her face, "but I'm sure she and her new girlfriend will be here soon."

The statement had the desired effect as Jane's mouth dropped open.

"Girlfriend!" Jane exclaimed.

"You heard it here first." Zip smiled, turning and walking away to help another customer.

Jane stood staring into space; it had never occurred to her that Zion would move on from her. Sure, she knew Zion had sex with other women, but Jane had always figured those were one-night stands. Maybe Zip was lying, just to make her mad. The thought made Jane smile, sure that had to be it.

When Zip was near her again, Jane snapped her fingers. "Can you at least do your job and get me some wine?"

Zip chewed on her gum, wanting to punch the blonde bitch in the mouth, but she knew that wouldn't be acceptable to Zion.

Finally, she picked up a wine glass and filled it with white wine, sliding it in front of Jane without a word. She then turned and walked away from the woman before she said anything she would regret.

Everyone knew about Jane, and what she'd done to Zion; no one liked the woman, not even the slightest bit.

An hour later, Jane was fit to be tied, that's when Zion and Morgan walked into the bar. Jane heard Zion's friends greet her and turned around on the barstool where she sat. She observed the redhead that Zion held hands with; she looked very wholesome and that had Jane rolling her eyes. Someone must have told Zion she was there because suddenly the blonde bar owner looked straight at her. Jane moved to stand, as Zion uttered something to the redhead.

The other woman looked over at Jane for a long moment. The redhead then took Dax's proffered hand and let her lead her over to the table where Kenzi sat. Zion marched over toward Jane.

"Why are you here?" was the first question out of Zion's mouth.

"You know why I'm here," Jane told her, moving to kiss Zion on the cheek. Zion pulled her head back, giving Jane a pointed look.

"You need to leave," Zion ordered.

"I'm not going anywhere." Jane folded her arms in front of her chest. "You and I are going to talk."

"There's nothing to talk about." Zion stared down at Jane, her blue eyes as cold as ice. "I've paid you back every penny of your original loan. We are done with our business arrangement." With that, Zion turned her back and began to walk away.

"What if I leave him?" Jane almost shouted.

Zion turned around, giving Jane an appraising look. "That's your business." Zion continued to walk away, leaving Jane standing at the bar.

Jane could not believe that Zion had just walked away from her. Her offer to leave Winston had been her ace in the hole. She really hadn't meant to lead with that, but seeing that Zion had a new woman in her life had made her feel a bit desperate. Getting ahold of herself, Jane realized that Zion having a new girlfriend didn't necessarily mean anything. Women came and went, especially when it came to the handsome bar owner.

Sitting back down on the barstool, Jane ordered another drink and decided to wait and see.

"That was quick," Dax commented when Zion joined them at the table.

"I've got nothing to say to her." Zion shrugged, leaning in to kiss Morgan on the lips. "I'm sorry, I should have asked if you wanted a drink."

Morgan smiled. "You kind of had your hands full there." She waved in Jane's direction.

"No matter." Zion grinned, holding her hand up to one of the passing waitresses, who immediately noticed and walked over to their table.

"Heya boss." The waitress, a cute brunette, smiled at them. She winked at Morgan. "What can I get you?"

"Beer for me," Zion said, looking over at Morgan, "and white wine?" Zion queried, waiting for Morgan's nod. "I'm thinking that new Pride Mountain batch."

"You got it." The waitress nodded. "Do you two need refills?" she asked Kenzi and Dax.

"Yes please!" Kenzi nodded. "Let me try that new white wine too. Thanks!"

"Beer for me too," Dax added.

The waitress hurried away and Morgan glanced over to see that Jane was indeed watching the four of them.

"So, she's just going to sit there?" Morgan asked, surprised by the woman's tenacity.

Dax smirked as she looked over in Jane's direction. "Like a fuckin' vulture."

"Dax…" Zion murmured.

"Sorry, like a *frigging* vulture," Dax amended.

"Just try to ignore her," Zion told Morgan.

Morgan looked doubtful, but nodded her head. As the night wore on, Jane made it impossible to ignore her. She flirted with every butch in the bar, hanging over them, dancing with them, all in an effort to make Zion jealous.

"We don't have to stay here," Morgan told Zion, as Jane walked by with yet another woman who was grabbing her ass.

Zion's lips curved in a grin. "Morgan, she's only making a fool out of herself."

Morgan bit her lip, but didn't comment any further. In truth it had been a nice evening. Zion and Dax had regaled them with tales from the aircraft carrier they'd both been stationed on. The stories were hilarious, and entertaining.

"Has she seen the scars yet?" Dax asked Zion with a raised eyebrow.

Zion shook her head. "No."

"I'm sorry, scars?" Morgan asked, eyebrows raised.

Dax looked at Zion for a long moment. "Is it okay if I tell?"

Zion sighed, nodding her head.

"Zion was on the deck crew, the head of the deck crew actually, so when one of the jets came limping in with one of its engines out, naturally Z was on the deck. It looked like it was going to make it in fine, so the fire crew had started to stand down." Dax looked over at Zion who nodded slowly.

Morgan squeezed Zion's hand in hers, already knowing she wasn't going to like what happened. Zion's lips merely twitched slightly.

"So, the jet just about gets on the deck and at the last minute, the right wing dipped ever so slightly," Dax said, eyes never leaving Zion's.

"Yeah, just enough to have it rolling onto my deck, and catching fire," Zion added as if it had been a personal affront.

"The fire team was too slow in reacting, so Z jumped into action with her crew."

"But one of my men ended up too close, and I knew the engine was going to blow," Zion interjected.

"How?" Kenzi asked. Being a pilot herself, she understood the danger of a flaming plane on an aircraft carrier.

"It was winding up," Zion told her, which had her nodding.

"So, Zion here, being the ridiculous heroic son of a bitch that she is, ran in there to grab him," Dax said proudly.

"Yeah, and almost got out too," Zion commented wryly.

"Almost?" Morgan asked worriedly.

"Hence the scars," Zion said.

"Kenzi grimaced. "Ouch."

Zion shrugged, taking a drink of her beer.

"And she sits there like it was no big deal," Dax commented, shaking her head as if in disbelief.

"It was a long time ago."

"Still heroic," Dax countered.

"Zip it," Zion replied with a knowing grin.

At one point, Zion had stepped away to handle a bar matter, and Kenzi had gone off to the bathroom. Dax looked over at Morgan, smiling.

"What?" Morgan asked, catching the observation.

"I'm glad Z found you," Dax told her.

"I feel very lucky, myself," Morgan admitted.

"She's different with you."

"How so?"

"Usually, Fancy blowing into town throws her for a loop, but not this time."

"Throws her for a loop, how?" Morgan asked cautiously.

"Well, we usually have to drag her out of a bottle for about a week afterwards."

Morgan winced. "That bad?"

"Oh yeah." Dax nodded, seeing that Zion was heading back to the table. "You didn't hear it from me," she intimated to Morgan with a wink.

Morgan smiled.

A little while later, there was a loud yell from the bar. Zion looked over in time to see Jane throw a drink at the butch woman she'd recently paraded by with.

"I told you I'm not going anywhere with you!" Jane screeched.

"Fuckin' bitch!" the butch woman yelled, taking a menacing step toward her.

Zion and Dax were on their feet instantly and striding towards the bar; Steel and Case joined them. Shayne, Flynne and Jayden hurried toward the scene too.

Steel, who'd been up at the bar with Case, stepped up to the butch woman. Case stood facing Jane, telling her to back away too.

Zion reached the scene just as the dark-haired butch was raging at Steel.

"She's been hinting all night, man! Now's she's playing the victim and shit!"

"Dude…" Steel began, shaking her head, but Zion intervened.

"No one talks to ladies here like that," Zion warned the woman.

"Yeah, well, you shouldn't let skanks in here then," the butch woman snapped.

"Okay, I'm just gonna need you to back off, now," Zion said, as Steel started stepping toward the butch.

"What the fuck, man! I come in here all the time!" the butch yelled.

"And you're welcome back, some other night, but tonight you gotta go," Zion ordered.

The butch woman looked from Zion to Steel and then to Dax, seeing that they were all serious. "This is bullshit!" she barked, but turned and left.

Zion turned to look toward Jane who had moved to sit on a barstool at Case's suggestion.

"You okay?" Zion asked, her tone neutral.

"Can you believe that!" Jane seethed. Zion simply looked back at her, the look on her face unimpressed. "She was going to strike me!"

"Maybe you should go home too," Zion commented.

"I can't believe this! You're blaming the victim?" Jane cried.

Zion looked at Case who was already hiding a grin. She looked to Dax who didn't bother to hide hers and then glanced at Steel, who held up her hands as if to say, *this is your problem* and walked away.

"You have a good night," Zion said, sounding anything but sincere. She turned and walked back over to where Morgan and Kenzi were standing.

Morgan commented on it later that night. "So, you defended her..." Morgan said, her tone flat.

They were in Zion's apartment, sitting on the couch. Morgan sat close to Zion, her feet curled under her, her head in the hollow of Zion's shoulder.

"I defended a woman in my bar," Zion replied.

Morgan nodded slowly. "So it wasn't that it was her, it was that she was a woman."

"She was a woman who'd gotten herself into trouble."

Morgan glanced up at Zion. "Some people would say she got what she was asking for."

Zion shrugged. "I won't let any woman be abused in my bar, no matter what stupid things they did to get to that point."

Morgan smiled. "Very gallant." She put her hand on Zion's chest. "So about these scars I haven't seen…"

Zion laughed. Moving forward on the couch, she pulled her shirt tails out and unbuttoned her shirt, taking it off and setting it aside. She wore a white sports bra, but Morgan could see a good expanse of skin. She noticed uneven skin midway down Zion's back and curving along her left down to her waistline.

"Ouch, that looks like it would have been excruciating."

"Oh, it hurt alright," Zion stated.

"I'm sorry that happened," Morgan replied as Zion leaned back against the couch again, "but it sounds like you were very brave."

Zion's lips twitched. "There were people I was responsible for, so I did what I needed to do."

Morgan leaned forward, hugging Zion tightly. "That is an incredibly noble way to see it."

Zion's hand covered Morgan's; she appreciated Morgan's words, but had no response. Instead, she embraced her, leaning down to kiss her lips. After the kiss, Zion stood, holding her hand out to Morgan to help her up off the couch. She led Morgan into the bedroom, and began kissing her again. As they kissed, they helped each other out of their clothes. Zion gently pushed Morgan down onto the bed.

Zion moved to lay next to Morgan, her hand sliding over soft skin, as she kissed Morgan's lips again and again. The passion intensified between them and Morgan was grasping at Zion's waist, wanting more. She was on the verge of begging. She held Zion close, wanting to feel her body against her.

"Please…" Morgan moaned softly. "I want you over me." She gasped as Zion moaned against her lips.

Giving in to the need she was feeling, Zion shifted her body, sliding it seductively down Morgan. She began moving against Morgan, slowly at first, while Morgan's hands grasped at her back, trying to pull her even closer.

Zion was doing everything she could to hold back, wanting Morgan to orgasm before her, but in the end, they climaxed together, crying out in unison as they did. Morgan had never felt so much pleasure in her life. When Zion maneuvered her body to take her weight off Morgan, Morgan's hands held her tightly.

"No, please, just lay here with me," Morgan whispered breathlessly.

"Mmm, how can I say no?" Zion asked, her voice husky.

They lay together for a long while, enjoying the feel of each other.

Eventually, Zion shifted to the side, and pulled Morgan with her to snuggle against her back. "Can you stay tonight?" Zion asked.

"I'd love to."

"Then do," Zion replied.

Morgan smiled in the darkness, feeling happy in the moment. She wanted it to last.

They fell asleep snuggled together.

Chapter 13

"Are we going to Fancy's tonight?" Jaims asked glancing over at Raquel.

They'd spent a great deal of time alone in the apartment since the week before when they'd begun their *relationship*. When Jaims wasn't at work, they were in the apartment, either having sex, or watching movies, or ordering take out. Now it was Saturday, and they were heading into an evening, on a day where they'd normally go to the club. They hadn't talked about how they would handle their friends knowing they were a couple.

Raquel contemplated the question, they were sitting on the couch, having just concluded yet another disaster movie.

"We can." Raquel finally answered.

Jaims nodded slowly. "Sure we ready for that?"

Raquel considered for a moment and finally nodded. "What the hell?" She shrugged. "Let's do it."

They arrived at Fancy's, it was still a bit early, so it wasn't crowded. Walking over to the table they usually shared with the rest of the crew, they could see only Jayden and Ari were there.

"Hey," Jaims called, as they joined them.

Jayden turned around, smiling, and observed that they were holding hands. Her eyes made their way up to Jaims' face, and she grinned.

"Hi!" she said in a neutral tone, moving to stand and hugging Jaims, and then Raquel.

Jaims and Raquel exchanged a surprised look, but neither of them said anything about Jayden's casual acceptance.

"I'll get beers," Raquel told Jaims. "BB, you and Ari good? Or do you need refills?"

"Another Coke for me, thanks!" Ari smiled.

"I'm good." Jayden nodded, watching Raquel nod and walk away. "So…" Jayden began as she sat down next to where Jaims sat, "this is, um…new."

"Yeah." Jaims gave the youngest member of the crew a lop-sided grin. "It definitely is."

"You look happy." Jayden observed.

Jaims bit her lips, nodding. "I am."

"More importantly." Ari leaned forward, putting her hand on Jaims' knee. "Raquel looks really happy too."

Jaims' eyes widened, blowing her breath out. "I think we're both freaked about what everyone is going to say."

Jayden pressed her lips together in a smirk. "Well, you know Errol and L Word will have shit to say, right?"

"That's a given." Jaims chuckled.

"I think you might be surprised by everyone else," Jayden told her.

"I hope that's a good thing," Jaims sighed.

When Raquel came back to the table, the foursome sat and drank and talked until the rest of the crew arrived.

"New couple alert," Shayne commented as she sat down at the table with her beer in hand.

"Alert, alert!" Flynn said excitedly, as she too sat down, reaching over to pat Raquel on the shoulder. "About fuckin' time!"

"How so?" Raquel canted her head.

"Well, we know Jaims' has been into ya forever," Shayne said.

"And it's a good thing," Steel commented from behind them. Flynn nodded. "Definitely."

"Yup," Shayne agreed.

"Bloody right," Case added as she walked over to the table.

Jaims nodded, looking over at Raquel who simply shrugged. "Not sure why we thought anyone would be weirded out."

"'Cause they're all weird already." Jaims laughed.

"Ha, ha," Zion said, reaching around both Jaims' and Raquel's shoulders to hug them both. "Happy for you two."

"Thank ya." Raquel winked.

Raquel's brothers were pleased for them too. They'd driven up to the college to visit the boys, and let them know about them being together.

"Now we're really going to be a family!" Jackson exuded.

"And it's about damned time!" Garrett laughed.

"So, you're both okay with this?" asked Raquel.

"Why wouldn't we be?" Jackson said. "You two have been our family since we lost Mom and Dad."

Garrett nodded. "I was surprised you two didn't become a couple before now."

"Really?" Raquel asked, looking dumbfounded.

Jackson laughed. "I'm glad you finally got it together."

"Seriously." Garrett rolled his eyes.

"So that was a shocker," Raquel commented in the car as they drove out of the campus.

Jaims laughed. "Yeah I guess we were the only ones that didn't think we should be a couple."

"Well, we're stupid, so…" Raquel chuckled, as she shook her head.

Jaims smiled warmly. "Speak for yourself."

"Ya know…" Raquel concluded, squeezing Jaims' hand that she held as Jaims drove.

They were both quiet for a bit. Jaims glanced over at Raquel, seeing her lost in thought. "You thinking about tomorrow?"

Raquel sighed loudly. "Yeah, not sure I'm ready."

The following day, Raquel had her physical qualifications test to get back onto the force. She'd been working out and was physically ready, but Jaims knew that she was worried.

"Rock, you're ready," Jaims told her. "You know what to expect, and you are totally on it. Okay?"

Raquel screwed up her lips. "Yeah, I know you're right, but I guess I'm just afraid to hope, ya know?"

Jaims nodded. "I know, but I really think you've got this."

"We'll see."

That night, they had Sunday dinner with Jaims' family, and officially announced themselves as a couple.

"Well, it's about fricking time!" Carlo laughed.

Jaims' parents hugged them both, congratulating them.

Teresa canted her head at the two, holding hands and smiling. "You look good together."

"Thanks, sis." Jaims smiled happily.

Over dinner, Jaims mentioned that Raquel was doing her physical agility test the next day.

"So don't harass her about eating dessert or keeping us here late," Jaims said, giving her parents a pointed look.

"So, you're ready to go back?" Daniel asked.

Raquel drew in a deep breath, blowing it out slowly. "I really need to get back to work."

"Then we hope it goes well tomorrow," Celeste offered.

"Thanks." Raquel nodded. "I hope so too."

"It'll go great," Jaims said, bumping her shoulder with Raquel's. "You've been working hard, and it'll show tomorrow."

Raquel hoped Jaims was right.

The following day, Jaims waited impatiently at work to get a call from Raquel. Her test was scheduled for 10 a.m., and by noon, Jaims was going nuts. She hadn't heard from her girlfriend. She'd texted Raquel, called, but with no answer.

Sitting in her small office, Jaims started having thoughts about Raquel falling off the wagon. She was lost in those thoughts when there was a knock on her door.

"Come!" Jaims called, turning her chair around to face the door.

Raquel walked in, smiling at Jaims, as she handed her a red rose. Jaims stood up, taking the rose and leaning in to kiss Raquel. They kissed for a long moment. "I was completely freaking out," Jaims admitted.

"I figured." Raquel grinned. "I passed."

"Of course!" Jaims exclaimed. "But where have you been?"

Raquel canted her head, seeing the worry etched in Jaims' eyes. "I wasn't doing drugs; I can tell you that."

Jaims pressed her lips together, worried that her negative thoughts would piss Raquel off. Memories of the bad times replayed in her head.

Raquel's mouth on hers stopped those thoughts immediately.

"I'm never doing that shit again, okay?" Raquel told her when their lips parted. "I'm with you, and now I'm back on the force. I was just filling out paperwork after I passed the test. That's all, I promise."

Jaims shook her head. "I'm sorry, I guess I'm just still a little gun shy, you know?"

Raquel put her hands on Jaims' shoulders. "I get it. You don't know that you can trust me." Jaims drew in a sharp breath, ready to deny that statement. "Jaims!" Raquel interrupted whatever Jaims was about to say. "I totally understand, okay? I didn't give you a lot of reasons to trust me since I've been back."

"I'm sorry." Jaims shook her head again, feeling miserable for not having more faith.

"You don't need to be sorry," Raquel told her. "I need to prove to you that you can trust me again." She put her finger to Jaims' lips. "And I'm going to do that."

Jaims smiled, relieved that her fears weren't being dismissed, and nor were they making Raquel mad.

"You know," Jaims said, grinning, "this might just work out."

"Oh, it's gonna work out," Raquel told her, a mischievous grin on her lips, "I'll make sure of that!"

Chapter 14

"I don't understand." Winston's dark brows furrowed.

"What don't you understand?" Jane snapped, as she put her heels into her suitcase. "I'm leaving you," she repeated, not for the first time.

"I'm sure I've missed something, but I'm not sure what that is," Winston commented, leaning against the large desk in their master suite.

"Probably the fact that I've been seeing a woman on the side for months now," Jane sneered.

Winston blinked a couple of times, his mouth dropping open in surprise. Shaking his head, he moved to his wife's side. "You don't mean that, you're just trying to shock me, get me to pay attention to you. I know that things have been crazy lately with the campaigning and such." He took her hands in his, staring down into her eyes. "I'm sorry, once this election is over, we can go away for a long vacation. Alright?"

Jane looked up at the man she'd been married to for ten years, and she weighed her options. She could stay with him, and still see Zion on the side. Then she could have her cake and eat it too. But she'd told Zion she would leave him, could she get away with lying for a while longer? Then maybe after taking that long trip to the Mediterranean she'd been dreaming about, maybe she could leave him then. It was something to think about.

Even so, she continued to pack the belongings she wanted with her for this weekend. She intended to get Zion back into bed, come hell or high water, and this time she was going to get things the way she wanted them!

***

They were celebrating! The crew happily converged on Fancy's to congratulate Raquel on her getting back on the force. Things were finally getting back to normal for the group and it made every one of them feel more settled.

"So now that you're back on the force," Case commented drolly, "any chance you can fix a parking ticket for me?" She winked, her lips curving in a wicked grin.

"No chance!" Raquel laughed.

"Bloody Hell!" Case laughed.

"C-boi, you will never learn!" Zion shook her head.

"Yeah, dude, the parking signs ain't a suggestion!" Dax bumped her shoulder into the Englishwoman.

"Yeah, yeah," Case sulked. "I can't help it if I forget to look at what they say!"

"You could try." Jaims winked.

"You could bite me," Case replied, smirking wildly.

"So," Jayden began, looking a bit hesitant. "Are you like on patrol again?"

Raquel looked over at the shyest member of the group, knowing her bad behavior had probably scared Jayden the most. "Yeah, BB," she said making sure to smile at her, "back on the streets, looking for bad guys." She winked, seeing Jayden visibly relax.

"When do you actually start?" Steel asked.

"Well," Raquel began, taking a drink of her beer, "they have to process my paperwork, but HR said it's probably only gonna be a week."

"Then bad guys, beware…" Jaims added.

Raquel smiled but looked pensive. "I'll still have to do random drug testing," she sighed, "but I guess that's fair." The group looked sedate suddenly, some of them nodding. "Guys," Raquel cajoled, "I get that I fucked up, okay? And I get that I'm damned lucky to get another chance to fix things. With work, and with all of you."

"We love ya, Rock," Dax said, looking around at the others who all nodded in agreement. "We just want you to be healthy and happy."

Raquel picked at the label on her beer bottle, then raised her head to look over at Jaims. "That's what I'm working on."

Everyone smiled, it was a good sign of things to come.

Morgan arrived at the bar an hour later, she was directed to Zion's office. When she knocked, she heard Zion's voice call out. "Come!"

Morgan opened the door and found Zion pouring over architectural drawings. Walking over, she leaned in kissing Zion on the cheek, her eyes turning to the plans.

"Is this the expansion?" Morgan asked.

"Mm? Oh, yes, sorry." Zion grinned, leaning over to kiss Morgan on the lips. "I think these might be the final ones; I need to get them signed and back to the contractor in the morning."

Morgan nodded, bending down to look more closely at the plans. "Is that a DJ booth?"

"Yeah." Zion smiled. "Something more substantial than the current spot, new sound system, the audio board, everything."

"Wow," Morgan murmured, "that's a big change."

"That's the idea." Zion chuckled. "Hoping to attract talent that will bring in the bigger crowds."

"Is this an outside patio?" Morgan asked, not sure she was reading the plans correctly.

"Sure is." Zion felt a rush of pleasure at Morgan's level of interest. "You have a good eye."

Morgan glanced back at Zion, her look surprised.

Zion shrugged. "Even when Jane was an investor, she didn't care about the actual plans, it was more about controlling things."

Morgan licked her lips, not wanting to sell the thought that had just popped into her head.

Zion caught the gesture, canting her head. "Just say it."

Morgan pressed her lips together, embarrassed to have been caught again. "I was just thinking that narcissists always tend to want to control things."

Zion rolled her eyes. "You have no idea."

Morgan grimaced. "I'm sorry."

Zion shook her head. "No reason to be sorry, you're right, she's definitely a narcissist."

The two spent the next couple of hours examining the plans. Morgan pointed out anything she saw that, in her opinion, Zion might want to question.

"Yeah, I'm not sure why they're doing a half wall there," Zion answered one of the questions Morgan had asked. "I will definitely ask," she said, as she noted the question on the side of the plans. She smiled over at Morgan. "Thank you, I didn't even see that."

Morgan shrugged. "Always good to have another set of eyes, especially ones that haven't seen the plans before."

"Good point," Zion agreed.

A short time later they were interrupted by a knock on the door.

"Yeah?" Zion called out.

Zip opened the door. "Z, Fancy's here."

Morgan and Zion exchanged a look of dread, then Zion nodded. "Just have her come in here, I don't need another scene in the bar."

"Got it!"

Zion made a point of rolling up the plans, setting them back behind her desk. Her look at Morgan was pointed. "No need to give her anything extra to talk about."

Morgan laughed softly, just as there was another knock on the office door. Zion called for Jane to come in.

Walking in, Jane noted the redhead standing with Zion, and she narrowed her eyes immediately.

"I'll give you two some privacy," Morgan said, responding to the look on Jane's face.

"No need," Zion told Morgan, putting her hand on Morgan's hand resting on the desk.

"I would prefer to speak with you alone," Jane told Zion.

"I really don't care what you'd prefer," Zion replied mildly.

Jane gave a long-suffering sigh.

Playing the victim, was Morgan's immediate thought.

"Say whatever it is you came here to say," Zion prompted impatiently.

"I left him," Jane said in a rush, "for you."

Zion blinked a couple of times, then gave a short, humorless laugh. "Well, that was pointless."

Jane's mouth dropped open in response to Zion's remark. "I left my very successful husband to be with you, why would that be pointless?"

Zion stared back at Jane for a long moment, unable to fathom the level of ego it took for Jane to completely misread her audience. Finally, Zion widened her eyes, blinking them rapidly as she shook her head.

"I'm fairly certain that the last time you came here, I told you that I was no longer interested in pursuing a relationship with you," Zion told Jane in a matter-of-fact tone.

Jane made a frustrated sound in the back of her throat. "Obviously that's because I was still with my husband, but I'm not now."

Morgan couldn't help the look of utter disbelief that crossed her features. She looked over at Zion, seeing a similar look.

"Who *are* you anyway?" Jane snapped, turning her frustration on Morgan now.

Morgan jolted. For some reason surprised that Jane had finally acknowledged her presence.

"I'm Morgan," was the only response Morgan could come up with in the moment.

"Morgan?" Jane repeated, her tone snide. "Why don't you be a dear and leave me and Zion alone?"

The tone of her voice and the sheer look of disgust she was giving Morgan made her seethe, the writer couldn't take anymore.

"Why don't you go have your hearing checked? Because obviously you're not hearing Zion when she says she's not interested."

Zion snorted in subdued laughter, her blue eyes connected with Morgan's. They shone with a light of new respect. Zion looked toward Jane, who looked completely shocked that someone had spoken to her that way. It was the final straw in Zion's controlled composure, and she began to laugh, shaking her head.

"I think you heard that right?" Zion asked Jane, sliding her arm around Morgan and pulling her close into her side, feeling very proud of the fiery redhead she was dating. She kissed the side of Morgan's head affectionately.

Jane took in the scene before her, and felt humiliation suffuse her features. Turning, she stormed out of the office, slamming the door resoundingly.

"Wow," Morgan said in the aftermath.

"And then some," Zion agreed whole heartedly.

Jane seethed all the way to her vehicle, which was parked in a lot across the street from Fancy's. She used the remote to unlock the car doors, and then proceeded to kick the driver's side and scream her head off. Getting in and starting the vehicle she threw it into gear and stepped on the gas, tires screeching as she drove out of the parking lot.

Who the fuck does she think she is! The thought screamed through her head, *and who the hell is this redhead bitch? She needs that smart mouth of hers shut for good!*

***

Jaims was at work when she got the call from Raquel's partner. There'd been a shoot-out that day on their shift.

"Is Rock okay?" Jaims asked immediately, feeling terrified.

"She's fine, well..." Jack vacillated. "She wasn't shot, but she seemed really spooked, so I wanted to let you know."

"Okay, thanks." Jaims nodded. "Did she go home?"

"Left a couple minutes ago."

"Got it." Jaims stood up, reaching for her jacket. "Thanks again."

Half an hour later, she walked into their apartment, but Raquel wasn't home. She waited another hour, then called Raquel's phone; she got no answer. Then she tried using the 'find my phone' app and was able to see that Raquel's phone was pinging at the beach. Jaims drove down to the beach and immediately saw Raquel's Jeep in the parking lot. She parked her car next to Raquel's vehicle. Jaims looked around, seeing Raquel sitting out on the sand.

Walking over to her, Jaims moved to sit down next to her. Raquel jumped slightly, but then turned her head, seeing Jaims.

"What are you doing here?" Raquel asked.

Jaims detected no anger in her tone. "Jack called me," she told her.

Raquel sighed, nodding. "I was trying not to bring it home to you, ya know?"

"It scared you."

"Yeah." Raquel nodded. "More than I expected."

Jaims shrugged. "You were shot, Rock, that's gonna stick with you for a bit."

Raquel huffed, then scoffed. "I guess I was hoping it wouldn't."

"So much for that, huh?" Jaims grinned, bumping her shoulder into Raquel's.

Raquel sighed again, leaning against Jaims' side. Jaims put her arm around Raquel, pulling her closer and kissing the top of her head. "I want you to bring things home to me," she said softly. "I want to share your burdens, that's what couples do."

Raquel snuggled closer to Jaims. "I'm not used to that."

"Well, do me a favor, and get used to it, okay?" Jaims said, her tone only slightly chiding.

"Still learning," Raquel offered.

"I know."

"I heard the shots," Raquel began a moment later, "and I just froze."

Jaims nodded, waiting for her to continue.

"I've never done that before."

"You never almost died before," Jaims pointed out.

"Yeah, but it just scared the shit out of me."

"Were you able to pull out of the fear?" Jaims asked.

Raquel drew in a deep breath, then nodded. "I was, but it took longer than it should have."

"You gotta give yourself a break, babe," Jaims consoled.

Raquel looked resigned. "I'm just glad there wasn't any real ramifications because of my screw up."

"You didn't screw up!" Jaims insisted. "You had a perfectly human reaction to gunfire! You know, normal people are terrified of that sound in real life."

Raquel snorted. "Well, it's really not a good thing for a cop."

"You're just getting back into it," Jaims pointed out. "Give yourself some time."

"That's what Jack said too," Raquel glowered.

"Jack's almost as smart as me." Jaims winked. "But not nearly as cute."

Raquel laughed, nodding. "That's true."

They hugged, sitting and watching the waves roll in and recede, lost in their own thoughts. Finally, Raquel stood up, putting her hand out to Jaims to help her to her feet. They walked back to their vehicles, hand in hand.

"I'll race you home." Raquel beamed.

"The loser makes dinner!" Jaims yelled, getting into her car.

They made it home in record time, even with the evening traffic.

In the end they ordered takeout and stayed up watching movies, calling in sick the next day so they could hang out together.

Their relationship was changing and evolving, but at the same time, they still had the original friendship intact. It was something worth working on, and they both were invested in doing just that.

***

Friday night at Fancy's was crowded as always. Construction on the new space was proceeding nicely. Jane hadn't come back after the last rebuke; Zion was hopeful that Jane had finally given up. It was nearly eleven o'clock when Morgan finally turned up at the bar. She located Zion with her crew at the table near the dance floor. Dax and Kenzi were there as well.

Zion stood to greet Morgan with a wide smile, leaning in to kiss her lips and hugging her.

"I was wondering if you were going to make it," Zion commented.

"I'm sorry, I'm late," Morgan replied. "I was actually writing!"

Zion's eyes widened. "And how is that going?"

"It's going great!" Morgan enthused. "I've started on a whole new book, and you'll never guess what it's about."

"What's that?" Zion queried.

"It's a lesbian romance," Morgan intimated, "it's about reincarnation and past lives."

"Aw." Zion nodded. "You'll be able to write off the sessions with Charlotte."

Morgan laughed. "I never thought of it that way, but yes, I will."

Zion held a chair for Morgan, and signaled to a nearby waitress, ordering some champagne. "We will need to celebrate." She winked at Morgan.

Morgan smiled widely. "We do indeed."

"So, lesbian romance…" Zion murmured as she sat down next to Morgan.

Morgan nodded with a bright smile. "One needs to write what one is excited about."

Zion licked her lips, her eyes sparkling. "Well, I can certainly help with that."

Morgan touched Zion's cheek, tracing Zion's jaw with her nail. "Oh you already have."

Zion grinned mischievously. "Oh, you have no idea…"

Morgan laughed, nodding. "I'm all in to find out!"

The night proceeded with rounds of champagne and congratulations passed all around, with Morgan finally being over her writer's block.

"God knows we need more lesbian writers!" Kenzi put in.

"I may have to take up reading." Flynn winked.

"Can you read?" Raquel joked.

"All the little words." Flynn shot back.

"And the dirty ones," Shayne added.

Flynn, who'd just taken a drink of her beer, held up her finger, nodding and pointing back at Shayne.

"I'll keep that in mind." Morgan smirked at the pair, making both Flynn and Shayne erupt into laugher, the rest of the crew joined them.

Zion smiled to herself, Morgan seemed to fit right in with her friends, unlike Jane, who had either dismissed them as 'children' or, *when drunk*, had flirted outrageously with them to make Zion jealous. It was a marked difference, and Zion couldn't help but appreciate it.

Sliding her arms around Morgan, Zion hugged her close, leaning in to nuzzle Morgan's ear. "Thank you," she whispered into Morgan's ear.

"For what?" Morgan asked, turning her head slightly to look back at Zion.

Zion sighed. "For just being you."

Morgan looked puzzled, but couldn't help but feel warmed by the look in Zion's eyes. She'd never felt more appreciated, nor as enthralled by someone in her life.

The following morning, Morgan woke in Zion's arms, in her bed. Turning over to look up into those cornflower blue eyes that were already looking down at her, Morgan smiled.

"Good morning," she whispered softly.

"Yes, it is," Zion agreed, leaning down to kiss Morgan's lips in a way that left both of them breathless.

"What you do to me..." Morgan murmured as Zion moved her lips to Morgan's neck. Morgan slid her hands through Zion's short hair, holding her head as she delighted in the feel of Zion's lips.

She felt exalted as Zion's lips continued down her body. They made love then, enjoying each other's bodies thoroughly.

Later, they sat drinking coffee at Zion's kitchen table.

"What's on your agenda for today?" Morgan asked.

Zion curled her lips. "I need to do a stock check and get online and order supplies. Exciting stuff."

Morgan smiled. "That does sound enchanting."

"What about you?" Zion asked. "Are you going to work on your book?"

"I am," Morgan replied. "I brought my laptop with me; would you mind if I stay up here and work?"

"As long as I'm allowed to come up and interrupt every so often," Zion teased.

"Oh! I think that would be quite acceptable."

"Then you have a deal."

"I do have an ulterior motive," Morgan admitted, "I have an appointment with Charolotte today."

"She's back from vacation?" Zion asked.

Morgan rolled her eyes. "Yes, finally! I swear she was gone forever!"

Zion chuckled. "The nerve!"

"Honestly!" Morgan laughed. "She's left me hanging with Davis and Sam for over a month now!"

"Oh, I see. You need to see what happened with them, huh?"

"Of course. I don't like cliff-hangers," Morgan told her.

"I understand completely."

After a quick shower, Zion dressed in jeans and a T-shirt, and headed downstairs.

While Morgan, after showering herself, settled into work. As predicted, she was interrupted by Zion every hour or so; there were kisses and snuggles, as well as a lunch break which resulted in a love-making session.

Morgan had never been so happy in her life. The relationship with Zion seemed so natural and easy, it was an amazing feeling. She found herself dumping all of those feelings into her writing. She was truly shocked when she looked up to realize she'd actually written over twelve thousand words on her new book. It was as if the words were just flowing out of her. The feeling of being able to write again was such a blessing.

Glancing at the clock on the wall above Zion's TV, she realized she needed to get ready for her appointment with Charlotte. After getting changed into more professional looking clothes, she made her way downstairs to find Zion. She heard her before she saw her.

"Zip, you just counted those, could you…no, not there, behind you, check your six!"

"I'm sorry, Z!" Came the reply.

"It's cool, just pay attention, okay?" Zion replied calmly. "I don't want another frigging strawberry schnapps debacle."

"There was a strawberry schnapps debacle?" Morgan asked from the stairs. "Sounds serious." Her eyes sparkled with subdued humor.

Zion looked up, smiling widely. "You have no idea! We ended up with four cases of the stuff."

"And I'm guessing strawberry schnapps isn't a big seller?" Morgan grinned.

"I had to come up with a specialty drink just to move all of it." Zion rolled her eyes.

"Would you like to try our Strawberry Slammer?" Zip quipped; it was obvious from her mockingly robotic voice that she had to say that to a lot of people during that time.

Zion chuckled. "Yeah, it was strawberry hell for a bit."

"You're tellin' me!" Zip exclaimed. "I can't even smell strawberries anymore without feeling sick."

"Mistakes can be fatal." Zion winked in her direction.

"I know, I know." Zip held up her hands in surrender. "I'll pay attention."

"Count that back wall, I'll get back with you in a minute," Zion said, walking up the stairs to meet Morgan, kissing her as she reached the stair she was standing on. "Are you headed to your appointment?" she asked as she gestured for Morgan to head back up the stairs.

"Yes, I just wanted to let you know, I didn't mean to interrupt," Morgan apologized as they reached the top of the stairs.

Zion shook her head. "You're fine, I'm glad that you let me know you were leaving."

"Of course." Morgan beamed. "I have a few other errands to run before my appointment, so I'll be out of your hair for a few hours."

Zion escorted her to the doors and unlocked them for her. Turning, she leaned in, to kiss Morgan's lips. "I hope the story between Sam and Davis has a happy ending."

Morgan laughed softly. "You and me both!"

As Morgan left the bar, there was an accident in the street. Zion immediately moved to help; Morgan followed her. Within minutes they discovered that no one was badly injured.

"You're going to miss your appointment, babe, just go. I've got this," Zion instructed Morgan.

"Okay, see you later," Morgan replied.

Shortly after, the police arrived to take over the scene, so Zion headed back into the bar, resuming work on the inventory count.

Two hours later, Zion was sitting at the bar, eating a sandwich and having a beer before the bar opened. Zip was behind the bar getting things set up for all the stations. Music played in the background. Zion's back was to the front doors, so she didn't notice them open.

She was stunned when she heard movement behind her. Turning, she expected to see Morgan.

"So how did it..." she began, but her voice trailed off when she saw Jane standing there. "Jesus, what now?" Zion snapped.

"That's no way to greet your partner," Jane replied mildly, her face composed.

"We aren't partners anymore, or did you forget?" Zion asked, tired of having this conversation already. "Before you go, leave your key on the bar." With that she turned back to the bar and continued to eat her sandwich.

"What makes you think I still have a key?" Jane asked.

"The fact that those doors were locked," Zion replied, without turning back around. "I know, because I locked them. Can't have strays wandering in off the street." The last was said in an acerbic tone.

"Oh," Jane replied, "I'm a stray now, am I?" Zion could hear the venom laced in Jane's voice.

"You don't belong here anymore, Fancy," Zion said simply.

"I belong with you," Jane insisted.

Zion shook her head. "You belong with your husband."

"I'm leaving him."

"I'm sorry to hear that," Zion replied, still refusing to turn back to talk to Jane.

"Why are you sorry?" Jane asked. "We can be together now, all the time."

Zion didn't speak for a long moment, putting her sandwich down and picking up her beer bottle, taking a long sip. "I've moved on, Jane, you should too."

"You've taken a big step down," Jane commented, "but I'm willing to forgive you."

Now, Zion turned around. "Forgive me?" The completely flabbergasted look on her face matched her tone.

"Why would I need your forgiveness? You're the one who lied."

Jane's eyes narrowed. "I was going to tell you about Winston."

Zion snorted. "When?"

"When you were ready to hear it," Jane replied arrogantly.

Zion blew her breath out through her nose. "I see, and you got to decide when that was."

"It's my business, Zion, so of course I get to decide," Jane replied haughtily. "Regardless, it's out in the open now, and I'm leaving him, you should be grateful."

Zion opened her eyes wide, blinking a couple of times in her bafflement. "Grateful?"

"Yes," Jane retorted, giving Zion a look as if she questioned her insanity. "I'm leaving the money and the privilege to be with you, a simple bar owner."

Zion guffawed as she looked over at Zip who was standing behind the bar watching the entire exchange with a look of incredulity on her face. Zip simply shook her head, unable to believe what she was hearing.

"Don't do me any favors, doll," Zion replied.

"You simply don't understand." Jane shook her head. "You are so unworldly. Winston comes from a great family! We have homes in the Hamptons, one here on Knob Hill, as well as a mansion in the Cayman Islands! And what do you have, a bar and an apartment building or two."

"Four actually," Zion replied with a sardonic grin, "but who's counting?"

Jane rolled her eyes. "Inconsequential compared to what Winston has."

"Then go be with Winston, the money bags," Zion retorted.

"I want to be with you," Jane said, looking frustrated at having to state the obvious.

Zion jerked her head. "That's unfortunate."

"What do you mean?"

"You want to be with me, I want to be with Morgan." Zion shrugged.

Jane flattened her lips, shaking her head. "Some no name writer!"

Zion's eyes narrowed. "At least she's not married."

"Who'd marry her?" Jane chided. "Why would you give up such quality, to be with that?"

Zion blew her breath out, shaking her head. "Why would I want to be with a lying, cheating, narcissist like you?"

Jane's mouth dropped open; she could not truly believe what she'd just heard. Clearly, she hadn't heard correctly, there was no way that Zion was going to choose that trashy red head over her!

"What did you just call me?" Jane asked, her tone bordering on rage.

"Which part did you not hear?" Zion asked flatly. "The lying part, the cheating part, or was it me calling you a narcissist that you didn't comprehend?"

"How dare you!" Jane screeched, reaching into her purse and to Zion's utter shock, pulling out a gun and pointing it in her direction. "You take that back, right now!"

Zion took a step back, her hands going out to her sides, as she glanced back at Zip. "Get down," she ordered Zip.

Zip started to duck down behind the bar, and they were both shocked when a shot was fired from the gun.

Morgan walked down the street, carrying the packages she'd purchased before her appointment with Charlotte. A frown creased her brow as she turned the situation over and over in her head. She still couldn't believe what had transpired in her session. What she wanted to do was to hurry back to the bar to see Zion. She had felt the worst sense of dread since leaving the doctor's office.

As she passed what was formerly the book shop, she couldn't help but remember the scene that had occurred there years ago. It

273

looked completely different now—there was scaffolding and plastic up over the façade. The building was being transformed into an extension of Fancy's. Just as she passed what used to be the front door of the bookstore, she heard a shot ring out. At first, she thought it was an echoed memory from the past, but then the sense of dread swelled and almost choked her with fear.

Dropping the packages, she ran the rest of the way to the bar and threw open the front doors, flooding the bar with light.

The scene before her felt far too familiar, and terrifying at the same time. There stood a familiar figure…Jane. She wore a blue silk dress, white high heels, and her hair was perfect, as were her blood red nails, which were curled around the handle of a gun!

"Zion!" Morgan screamed from the doorway, as she started to scurry toward her.

"You stop right there!" Jane screamed at her, as she turned with the gun in hand.

"Morgan, it's okay," Zion told her. "Just go outside, it'll be okay."

"No." Morgan shook her head, tears in her eyes already. "It won't. I heard a gunshot!"

"It's okay, it hit the bar, everyone is fine," Zion told her. "Just go back outside, please."

Morgan started to move toward Zion. Zion held her hands up in a stopping gesture. "Morgan, wait! Please!"

"You just get out of here!" Jane screamed at Morgan, gesturing toward the doors to the bar with the gun. "Go, or I'll fucking kill you!"

"Jane!" Zion yelled. "This is between you and me, leave her out of this!"

Jane's head snapped around to look at Zion. "She's part of this now, isn't she?" Jane snapped. "She's in your head now."

Morgan was watching Zion intensely, feeling a sense of déjà vu. Zion returned her stare, her eyes begging Morgan to listen to her. Those blue, blue eyes, just like Davis's eyes…

"Zion…" Morgan moaned tearfully.

"Get out of here you stupid bitch!" Jane screeched, turning the gun and her attention back to Morgan. "You're getting in the way of our happiness!"

Zion responded immediately to the very real threat to Morgan. She started to run toward Morgan. Jane's attention was caught by the movement. The gun wavered and then turned back toward Zion, tracking her progress. Morgan could see Jane's finger tightening on the trigger. She couldn't let it happen again! Just as Zion reached Morgan and threw her arms around her to shield her, Morgan pivoted, moving Zion away from the line of fire. The gun went off again.

Morgan immediately felt a burning sensation, that same sensation Jack had felt when he'd been shot on Burnside Bridge during the Civil War. It was achingly familiar to her. She could hear screaming, and she saw Zion's face contort into a terrified mask.

She heard Zion call her name, but then she was falling, and the room went dark. Just before she passed out, she murmured Zion's name.

Chapter 15

Morgan woke up in a hospital room. She became aware of machines beeping, and voices over an intercom calling for Doctor somebody or other. She felt very tired, her eyes didn't seem to want to open at all. Instead of fighting her heavy eyelids, she lay still and let her mind navigate her surroundings. Her back ached, and when she flexed her hand, she felt an IV in it. The beeping of the heart monitor was regular, that was a good sign. As she lay there, she started to remember how she'd come to be in a hospital. *Zion!* The thought ricocheted around her head, and then she forced her eyes open, determined to get ahold of someone to find out what had happened after she passed out.

Opening her eyes she looked around the room, she saw beautiful flowers on the table to her right, but there was no one in the room. Feeling around on the bed, she felt the box with the call button, picking it up, she depressed the button to call the nurse.

"Z!" Shayne called, hurrying into the waiting room. "She's awake!"

Shayne had been purposefully hanging around the nurse's station flirting with some of the younger nurses. Her purpose had been waiting to see if they said anything about Morgan or if she had woken up. Since none of them were family, there was no option for them getting updates on Morgan's condition.

Zion looked up from the bed she sat in, a cast on one arm. "Did the nurse say anything?"

"No, but Morgan hit her call button," Shayne related.

Zion nodded, feeling hopeful finally. It had been two days. Morgan had been taken from Fancy's by ambulance to the hospital. She'd been unconscious. They knew she had surgery, and that she'd made it through, but the nicer lesbian doctor had rotated out, and no other doctor or nurse would give them information on her condition.

Ten minutes later the nurse appeared in the waiting room, summoning Zion.

"She's asking for you," the nurse, whose name tag read Janet, told her, smiling.

Zion followed the nurse to Morgan's room. She almost fainted with relief when she saw Morgan was sitting up in bed. Striding to her, Zion reached her hand out, gently touching Morgan's cheek, smiling down at her.

"The doctor should be in soon to talk to you," Janet told them, then she left.

"Your arm…" Morgan gasped, seeing the cast on Zion's arm.

"I'm okay," Zion told her. "I'm more concerned about you."

"I think I'm okay," Morgan said.

"I'll wait to hear that from a professional."

Morgan bit her lip. "What happened after…"

Zion sighed loudly, her eyes widened. "You mean after the deranged lunatic shot you?" Morgan winced at the recollection.

"She started to scream about how it was my fault she had to do that." Zion shrugged. "I ran at her."

"You…ran…at a woman holding a gun who'd already shot someone?" Morgan managed to say in shock.

"I wasn't going to let her hurt anyone else," Zion told her.

"But she could have shot you!" Morgan exclaimed.

"Oh, she did." Zion held up her arm.

Morgan gasped. "My God!"

"It's fine, I'm fine, and as long as you are too, that's all that matters." She gave Morgan a stern assessing look. "But do you want to tell me what the hell you were thinking doing what you did? You could have been killed!"

Morgan looked circumspect. "I was more afraid she'd kill you."

"Morgan…" Zion began, shaking her head.

"It's happened before," Morgan told her, her tone grave. Zion tilted her head, giving Morgan a quizzical look. "I had my appointment with Charolotte, remember? I saw what happened with Davis and Sam."

Zion drew in a deep breath. "Tell me."

"I heard a gunshot!" Sam exclaimed, as he stared at the tableau before him.

Davis stood in the middle of the bookstore, his back to the front door. Jake was standing at the back of the store, his eyes wild, looking at Davis.

"It's okay, Sam, I'm okay," Davis said. He didn't look back, he kept his eyes on Jake. "We're okay, right Jake?"

Jake's eyes shifted to Sam standing in the doorway, and his eyes welled up with tears. He reached up with the back of his hand to wipe the tears away. That's when Sam realized that Jake was holding a gun in his hand.

"Oh my God!" Sam whispered in terror. He started to move toward Davis, but Davis held his hand up to try and stop Sam from edging any further forward.

"It's okay, Sam," Davis repeated, sparing a quick glance over his shoulder at his lover. "Go on home, I'll be there later."

"I can't! You have to come with me now!" Sam insisted, seeing Jake's eyes shift back and forth between them.

"I can't," Davis said, shaking his head, looking back at Jake again. "Jake and I need to talk this out, don't we Jake?"

"No!" Sam said, striding forward toward where Davis stood. "We need to go."

Jake began shaking his head. "Davis?" he uttered, his voice breaking.

Davis turned to take Sam's hands in his. "Please go home," he whispered.

"Please come with me," Sam replied, his eyes glistened with tears.

"I'll be there soon," Davis told him.

Jake had begun pacing, his face suffused with color, his eyes darting back and forth, looking over at Davis and Sam, and then down at the gun in his hand.

"No!" Sam cried softly. "This isn't safe, please just leave with me."

"Baby…" Davis said. "I'll be okay, it'll be okay."

"You won't, he's got a gun, please Davis…" Sam pleaded, as he stepped back, trying to pull Davis with him.

"I love you," Davis uttered softly. "It will be okay, I just—"

"You love him!" Jake cried.

Davis turned around, dropping Sam's hands and holding up his own. "Jake, please calm down, let's talk about this…"

Jake shook his head, still pacing, it was obvious he was becoming more agitated, he was to the left of them, his pacing having shifted his position. "No, no!" Jake yelled. "He needs to go!"

"He's going to go," Davis told Jake, his voice soothing, "he is going to go now." Looking over his shoulder at Sam, he nodded toward the door. "Go."

"Davis…" Sam began.

"No! This isn't right!" Jake screamed. "He's taking you away from me!" With that Jake raised the gun, pointing it directly at Sam. "You need to go!" he shouted, as he squeezed the trigger.

"No!" Davis screeched.

Everything happened at once, the sound of the gun going off sounded like an explosion to Sam. As he realized Jake had fired the gun, the understanding hit him…he was probably going to die. He raised his eyes to Davis, and realized suddenly that Davis had stepped in front of him. The moment the bullet struck Davis in the back, Sam screamed his name. Suddenly Davis was falling forward. Sam did his best to catch him, and they both sunk to the floor, with Davis landing on top of him.

"Davis!" Sam cried, as he struggled to move. He wanted to see Davis's face. "Talk to me!"

Sam could hear Jake crying, and he heard what he was sure was the gun clatter to the floor, but he didn't care about that, he needed

to see Davis's face. He finally managed to shift enough to turn Davis
face up. His breathing was labored, his hand reaching for Sam.

"Davis! Hold on!" Sam pleaded through sobs, but he could already
see blood pooling around them. "No, baby, no...please hold
on...please..."

"I...I...love you..." Davis gasped out, and before Sam could even
respond, Davis took one, final shaky breath and died.

Sam felt dizzy and immediately sick to his stomach, his world
seemed to shatter in that instant.

"So, you thought Jane would kill me, because Jake killed Davis,"
Zion surmised.

"Yes!" Morgan insisted, tears glazing her eyes, just from the
retelling of Davis's murder. "It was so familiar, Zion, and I just
knew that history would repeat itself. I couldn't let that happen."

"You could have been killed," Zion insisted, reaching out a
hand to brush over Morgan's cheek.

"Better me than you," Morgan whispered.

Zion looked back at Morgan for a long moment, sighing
deeply. "I couldn't live with myself if that had happened."

"Thankfully, it didn't." Morgan smiled.

The doctor walked in, looking between the two women.
"Hello, I'm Doctor Morrow."

"Hello." Morgan smiled somberly.

"Doctor." Zion nodded, extending her hand to the doctor.

The doctor shook Zion's hand. "We got really lucky here," he
told them. "The bullet missed all major arteries, and came out

cleanly. You'll probably be with us for another day or two, just so we can make sure there's no infection, then you'll be discharged."

"Thank you," Morgan said.

"Yes, thank you," Zion added.

The doctor smiled, nodding, and then left the room.

"So, what happened to Jane?" Morgan asked.

Zion moved to sit in a chair, reaching out to take Morgan's hand. "Well, after I tackled her, the cops arrived. Apparently, Zip was hiding behind the bar and calling them while everything was going on."

"So, she was arrested?" Morgan asked hopefully.

Zion nodded. "Although, her powerful husband has already bailed her out."

Morgan pressed her lips together. "She shoots two people and gets to bail out that easily?"

Zion shrugged. "Hopefully he'll at least keep her in Sacramento until she's charged."

Morgan sighed; she was too tired to worry about it any further.

Morgan was released from the hospital the following evening. She and Zion had discussed where she would convalesce. They'd decided that Zion's apartment would be easiest, since Morgan would likely have follow-up appointments at the same hospital. Little did she know that she would have a lot more support than she'd ever hoped for.

The morning after she was released, Zion got a call from the police department, they told her she needed to go down to the police station for more questions that the police had.

"Kenzie is on her way over to help you with anything you need, while I'm gone," Zion told Morgan.

"I don't want to put anyone out…" Morgan began, but Zion's lips on hers stopped her.

"They want to help," Zion said, cupping her face tenderly.

Morgan pressed her lips together in consternation, not wanting to seem ungrateful. "Okay, I'm sorry."

"No need to be sorry," Zion soothed, "just let us help you, okay?"

"Okay," Morgan agreed.

An hour later, Zion left the apartment, just as Kenzie arrived.

"How are you feeling?" the redhead asked.

"A bit sore," Morgan commented, "but I guess that's to be expected."

Kenzie nodded. "Definitely. Did Z have time to get you a coffee or tea or anything?"

Morgan shook her head. "She got the call and needed to get ready."

"Okay, so what can I get you?"

Morgan was about to protest, even attempting to get up off the bed, but a searing pain in her back stopped her.

Kenzie rushed to her side. "Easy, easy!" she insisted, as she helped Morgan to settle against her pillows against the headboard. "Don't get me into trouble with my partner's best friend." She winked.

Morgan chuckled softly. "Some tea would be lovely, with cream and sugar, please."

When Kenzie brought back the tea, as well as a cup of coffee for herself, she sat in the lounge chair close to the bed.

"How did you and Dax meet?" Morgan asked. She was ever the inquisitive writer.

Kenzie grinned warmly. "Well, our first meeting was her insulting my footwear."

Morgan blinked a couple of times. "I'm sorry?"

Kenzie chuckled, almost spilling hot coffee on herself but proceeded to describe her first meeting with Dax. "She apologized when she found out I was essentially going to be her boss, but it took a while for us to become friends."

"How did it evolve to where you are today then?" Morgan asked, but she realized as soon as the question left her mouth that she might be overstepping. "I mean, if it's okay that I ask."

"It's okay. I was pretty tough on Dax when we started off, I had a real issue with butch lesbians. But Dax was so patient." Kenzie smiled softly as she remembered how much care her lover had taken with her. "She really put up with a lot from my damaged psyche."

Morgan nodded, knowing she shouldn't ask what she really wanted to ask. Kenzie, who was observant, much like Zion, saw it on her face. "You're wondering why I had a problem with butch lesbians, right?"

Embarrassed that she'd been caught, Morgan grimaced guiltily. She nodded softly, as if in silent answer.

"I'd been in a horribly abusive relationship with a butch woman, and it really skewed my opinion on them as a whole."

"I'm so sorry," Morgan offered.

Kenzie accepted the sympathy. "Dax showed me that it wasn't the type of lesbian that was abusive, but instead it was the type of person."

"Zion is the first lesbian I've ever been truly intimate with," Morgan commented. "But her level of gentility really amazes me."

"Oh, Zion is definitely the epitome of a gentleman," Kenzie agreed. "From what I understand that Fancy creature really destroyed her."

Morgan recoiled. "Almost literally."

"Yeah, she's an extra helping of *narcissist* with a side of *crazy*." Kenzie rolled her eyes.

Morgan chuckled at the description. "Apparently."

"Hopefully Z can open the bar again soon."

"It's been closed?" Morgan asked, surprised.

"Ever since the night of the shooting."

"Are the police keeping it closed?"

"I don't think it's them, I think Z just didn't want to take time away from your recovery." Kenzie shuffled on the spot, wondering if she'd just said too much.

Zion came home later that morning, taking over from Kenzie. She made Morgan lunch and they ate it sitting on the bed.

"It looks like the DA is going to charge Jane with two counts of attempted homicide, and a few other charges, like possessing and concealing an unregistered firearm," Zion told Morgan.

Morgan exhaled, feeling relieved. Then she gave Zion a sideways glance. "Is the bar being closed because of me?"

Zion looked back at her for a long moment, then shrugged slightly. "I had more important things to worry about just then."

Morgan's pointed look made her sigh.

"Not just you, I needed to deal with the clean-up and stuff," Zion added.

Morgan suspected that *stuff* meant her and being shot. "Did you worry about your own injury?"

Zion lifted her casted arm. "How could I not?"

Morgan nodded. "Are you in a lot of pain? Is that why you're keeping the bar closed?"

Zion smiled softly. "No, you don't have to worry about me."

"Hey," Morgan retorted, giving her a narrowed look, "if you get to worry about me and take care of me, it goes both ways."

Regarding her for a long moment, Zion's smile widened fondly. "Okay, I'll let you worry about me."

"And take care of you?"

Zion flattened her lips in a determined line, but Morgan's stern look had her chuckling and holding her hands up in surrender. "Okay, okay."

The next day, they were leaving the bar and were planning to go down to Morgan's condo, so she could get more clothes. Zion was just locking up, when a man approached them both.

"Amy?" the man inquired.

Zion turned to look at the man, her eyes widening significantly. "Bobby?"

The man smiled, nodding emphatically as he stepped forward to embrace a slightly stunned Zion. When they parted, Zion examined and took in one of her eldest brothers.

"How...I mean, what...I mean..." Zion stammered.

"I saw your picture on the news, they said you owned this bar here in the Castro."

Bobby looked over at Morgan his look questioning.

"Oh, sorry." Zion shook her head. "This is Morgan, Morgan this is one of my oldest brothers, Bobby."

Morgan looked surprised, but held out her hand to Bobby. He took it, shaking it gently.

"You were one shot trying to protect my sister, right?"

Morgan lowered her eyes modestly, but she nodded.

"Well, thank you for that." Bobby smiled again, but then looked chagrinned. "I'm sorry, is this a bad time? I figured it was a better time than when you were open for business..." His voice trailed off as he realized that he'd assumed a lot already.

"It's fine," Zion offered. "Let's go back inside, we can talk there."

The trio walked into the bar.

Bobby looked around. "Wow, this place is pretty cool."

Zion grinned, innately pleased that he thought so.

"Thanks." She gestured to one of the larger tables. "We can sit down here. Do you want some coffee, Bobby?"

"No, I'm fine thanks," he replied.

They settled into the chairs; Zion leaned forward on the table between them. "So, what are you doing here?" she asked. "I mean, here in San Francisco," she added hurriedly when she saw the shocked look on his face.

"Oh." He chuckled nervously. "I thought you were worried I was coming to get something from you," he said honestly.

"I live here, well...I mean, in Novato, but here in California."

"Wow!" Zion exclaimed. "How long have you lived here?"

"About two years now, my wife is a California girl." He grinned.

"Wife?" Zion smiled. "How long?"

"Ten years now," Bobby told her. "We've got two kids, a boy, Jasper, he's seven, and a little girl, Amy. She's three."

"Amy huh?" Zion chuckled.

"I guess you didn't need it anymore," Bobby commented wryly.

"Uh, no." Zion grimaced. "I wanted to get away from that."

"And us, and home…" Bobby added.

Zion blew her breath out in a sigh. "I couldn't be myself there, Bobby, you know that."

Bobby nodded slowly. "Doesn't mean we didn't miss you."

Zion curled her lips in disdain. "Did Dad miss me after that second letter?" she asked, referring to the letter where she'd admitted to being gay.

Bobby frowned. "He was pretty set in his ways."

Zion wrinkled her nose. "Yeah, I knew that."

"It doesn't mean the rest of us were," Bobby chided.

"Yeah, but how was I supposed to reach out to all of you, without him interfering?" Zion contested hotly. "And how did I know you guys would be okay with who I am now?"

Bobby pressed his lips together, knowing she was at least partly right; their father would have forbidden any of them, that still lived with him, from communicating with her. He shrugged in futility. "It's moot point now…Dad died about two years ago."

"How?" Zion asked, even as Morgan reached over and took her hand squeezing it gently.

"Heart attack," Bobby stated flatly. It was obvious that their father hadn't become more pleasant.

"You know he never bothered with eating healthy after Mom died. And his latest wife only indulged his bad diet and drinking."

"Latest?" Zion queried.

"Yeah," Bobby commented drily, "he ended up marrying Jenny Slattery about three months after you left. That didn't work out. He got married three other times after that. Each one worse than the last."

"None of them were Mom," Zion stated wryly.

"Nope," Bobby agreed. He reached out his hand to Zion. "But we are still family, and no matter what's happened in the past, it doesn't mean I don't want to get to know you now, okay? We all missed you."

Zion drew in a sharp breath, feeling tears glaze her eyes, she accepted what he was saying. "I'd like that. How is everyone?"

"Carl and Danny are both married, still living in New York," he told her. "Eric was married, but it didn't take, so he's back on his own." He rolled his eyes. "Whoring around Vegas, last time I heard."

"Carl is Bobby's twin," Zion told Morgan. "Danny and Eric are twins too."

"But nothing alike," Bobby added with a laugh.

Zion laughed too. "Eric was always a ladies' man, even when he was a kid."

Morgan smiled; she was enjoying hearing about Zion's family.

"Now Frankie, well he turned out like you." His voice softened at the words.

Zion looked alarmed. "How did Dad take that?"

Bobby scowled at the memory. "About as well as you'd think."

"Damn…" Zion breathed. "Where is he now?"

"Last time I talked to him, he'd broken up with his boyfriend in Rhode Island and was headed here."

"To San Francisco?" Zion asked.

"Yep," Bobby confirmed. "I'd bet he's somewhere in the city as we speak."

Zion shook her head. "Wow, yeah, he might be, we just don't run in the same circles." Bobby raised an eyebrow and Zion laughed. "This is a lesbian bar, genius, we don't get a lot of gay men in here."

Bobby had the temerity to look embarrassed. "I guess I should know better, huh?"

"Nah," Zion conceded, "you wouldn't know any better."

"I'll learn," Bobby told her seriously.

Zion accepted his answer with a kind nod. "So what about Georgie?"

Bobby sighed loudly. "He's been in and out of trouble for years."

"What kind of trouble?"

"Stupid stuff, petty theft, boosted a car or two," Bobby reeled.

"He got out of jail about a year ago. He seems to have cleaned up his act, but he's having trouble finding a job with his record and all. Frankie was trying to talk to him into coming here, that way we could have kept an eye on him."

Zion nodded, looking thoughtful. "If he comes here, I could offer him a job in the bar. I could even get him into affordable housing."

"There's affordable housing here?" Bobby questioned.

"Is Novato affordable?" Zion countered.

"No, but since I'm an architect, I can afford it." Bobby grinned.

"Wow, architect huh?" Zion queried, clearly impressed.

"Yep." He nodded. "Carl's a lawyer, and Danny is a doctor."

"Calvert boys are cleaning up." Zion chuckled.

Bobby laughed at that. "So, affordable housing?"

"Yeah, I have some apartments I rent out for reasonable prices."

"Some apartments?" Bobby asked, suspiciously.

Zion shrugged. "I own a few buildings. A couple of them are apartment buildings, I rent them out to friends and members of the community."

"Community?" Bobby asked.

"The gay community," Zion clarified.

"Very socially conscious of you."

Zion narrowed her eyes at her older brother. "What's that supposed to mean?"

Bobby held up his hands. "Just what I said." He shook his head.

"Leave it to you to take care of everyone," he commented proudly.

"You have no idea," Morgan murmured.

Bobby canted his head at her comment,

"Meaning?"

Morgan pressed her lips together as Zion gave her a glowering look. Zion sighed. "She means that I've kind of formed my only family, and we all take care of each other."

"Your own family?"

"Other lesbians that sometimes have no one else," Zion answered. "Some of them rent from me too."

Bobby nodded and grinned. "I hope I get to meet this other family too."

"I'll make sure of it," Zion told him.

***

"Thanks for picking me up," George commented, his blue eyes, just like his sister's, reflecting his appreciation.

"Of course." Zion smiled over at her younger brother. "How was your flight?"

George widened his eyes dramatically. "I've never flown anywhere, but first class sure seems like the very best way to do it." His grin was an engaging one. "Thank you for that too."

Zion nodded. "New York is a long flight away, figured it would be nice to not be cramped up in coach."

George nodded in agreement. "Being stuck in a confined space is kind of a phobia now."

Zion looked over at her brother, as she drove out of the airport. She could see that the years truly hadn't been kind to him. She hoped this was going to be a good move for his sake.

Reaching over, she took his hand, squeezing it gently.

George put his other hand over hers, squeezing it in response.

"You look really different," he told her after a few minutes.

Zion grinned. "My hair was a bit longer."

"Uh-huh." George nodded, with a wry grin of his own. He canted his head. "You look good, sis."

Zion returned his stare, trying to ascertain if he was teasing her or not. When she realized he was serious, she smiled.

"Thanks."

"I hear you're like a real estate mogul now," he commented, his blue eyes dancing in humor.

"Oh, is that how Bobby put it?" Zion scoffed.

"Yup." George nodded. "He said that big sis owned half of San Francisco!"

Zion erupted in laughter. "Yeah, I wish! I own a bar and some buildings, that's all."

"That's more than I own," he replied.

"Doesn't look like you own a razor," Zion joked, reaching over to rub at the scuff on his jawline.

"Hey, it's been a long day, okay?" George told her, rubbing his chin.

"Uh-huh."

At the bar, Morgan was bustling around, trying to set out dishes and cups for everyone who would be attending. Kenzie worked with her to make the bar feel as homely as it could.

"It's a bar for God's sake!" Kenzie huffed. She laughed when Morgan had fussed at the setting up, trying to give it a warmer feel.

"Yeah, we serve alcohol and appetizers!" Zip had called from the back bar.

Morgan pouted in exasperation. "I just want to help."

"You're helping," Kenzie assured her. "It looks great."

They'd arranged the few rectangular tables in the bar so everyone could eat together.

Zion had ordered food from Orphan Andy's, and they were due any minute to set up. It was the only way to fit the entire crew and the members of Zion's family into one area. Morgan had gotten tablecloths to adorn the tables, to make it feel a little more like home.

A couple of hours later, the room was filled with people, talking and eating. Zion was thrilled to meet her niece and nephew, and also to see her brother Frankie again after so many years apart.

"I can't believe it's been, what, twenty-four years!" Frankie exclaimed, as he hugged Zion again.

"Twenty-three, actually." Zion grinned.

"Damn! You're old!" Frankie teased, garnering a shove from his sister. Then he moved closer, jerking his head toward the serving tables. "Who's the cutie patootie over there?" he asked, pointing to one of the servers from Orphan Andy's.

"That's Jerry." Zion grinned knowingly.

"Is Jerry single?" Frankie asked, his bright eyes begging her to say yes.

"I think so," Zion replied, giving her brother a shove toward the serving table, "why don't you go find out?"

"If you insist!" Frankie winked at his sister and sauntered off.

Zion watched him depart with an amused smile on her face.

"What is he up to now?" Bobby asked as he moved to stand next to her.

"What else?" Zion queried.

Bobby chuckled, then surveyed the room. "Your friends are nice."

"I know," Zion replied.

"You've put together an impressive alternate family," Bobby added.

"Thanks." Zion nodded in agreement, then canted her head up at him, turning her eyes to his wife, Cynthia. "Your wife is way too hot for you."

"Tell me about it!" Bobby smirked warmly.

"And your kids are beautiful." Zion's voice softened. "Probably 'cause they don't look like you."

"And there it is…" Bobby snickered. He sobered then, looking down at Zion. "I've missed you, sis."

Zion assessed her brother's face. "I've missed you too."

They hugged. When they parted, Bobby nodded over toward Morgan. "She seems like a good one."

"She is," Zion agreed.

"Probably too good for you," Bobby added slyly.

"Uh-huh." Zion shook her head with a smile. "But I think I'll try to hold on to her anyway."

"Good plan." Bobby winked.

***

Six months had passed since Zion reconnected with her brothers. Fancy's was having a grand re-opening. Zion had considered changing the name of the bar, but it had been Morgan who had talked her out of it.

"It's not about her," Morgan said, "it's about the ambiance of the bar...it's 'fancy'

"In terms of?" Zion queried.

"You've upgraded the wine list; you've also added a full-time chef to prepare more...appetizing appetizers." Morgan skewed her lips to indicate her fluster at the odd phrase.

Zion chuckled, pressing her lips together. "I'm guessing that wasn't your best writer jargon, huh?"

Morgan opened her mouth in shock, then started to laugh. "I'm out of writer jargon for the moment, thank you!"

Morgan had just completed final edits for her first lesbian romance novel, her first new release in two years. She was already getting critical acclaim for In Time for You, *and her publisher was beside herself with the new avenue Morgan's writing had gone down.*

"Regardless..." Morgan gave Zion a pointed look. "The bar is more 'fancy' now, so it's not about Jane anymore."

"Got it." Zion nodded.

In the end, she'd fully agreed with Morgan and did not change the name.

"Is it crazy that I'm nervous?" Zion asked, as she attempted to tie the rainbow tie she was adjusting.

Morgan reached up, pushing aside Zion's hands so she could do it for her. "It's not crazy, because it's not just the bar opening."

Zion blew out her breath. All of her brothers were going to be in attendance at the celebration. It was a lot to think about.

An hour and a half later, Zion walked through the bar, glancing at the waitresses that were standing ready to serve. She walked over to the new stage and DJ booth, climbing a couple of steps to poke her head into the booth.

"Thanks again for doing this, Memphis," she said to the blonde sitting at the soundboard.

Memphis glanced up at her, smiling. "Always fun to break in a new board."

Zion chuckled. "Just glad I got the right equipment, thanks to your advice."

"Friends don't let friends buy crappy sound equipment," Memphis quipped, her blue eyes sparkling with humor.

"Got it!" Zion laughed.

Making her way through the bar she stepped over to Morgan, leaning down to kiss her on the lips. Morgan could see that Zion was still nervous. Reaching out she took Zion's hand, squeezing it gently.

"Ready?" she asked.

Zion puffed her cheeks out, blowing out her breath, even as she nodded. "As I'll ever be."

She looked over at her brother George, who was standing ready at the front bar. She winked at him, and he grinned and winked back. She then opened the double doors of Fancy's allowing the huge crowd gathered there to enter.

"Welcome back to Fancy's!" Zion called, as a cheer erupted from the crowd.

"We're late!" Jaims observed, looking at her watch as they searched for a parking space.

"We're gonna be lucky to find a place to park," Raquel noted. "We'd have been better off Ubering it tonight."

"Yeah, probably," Jaims agreed anxiously.

"I'm sorry I was late tonight," Raquel said, glancing over at Jaims.

"You said it was important," Jaims replied. "It's okay."

"Ha! Right there!" Raquel crowed, as she pinpointed a car's reversing lights light up.

"Nice!" Jaims exalted, as she pulled up to wait for the car to leave.

A minute later they were parked.

As Jaims went to exit the car, Raquel's hand on hers stopped her. "Hold on a sec."

Jaims sat back in her seat, looking over at Raquel, who seemed suddenly nervous. She couldn't help but think that Raquel was going to tell her she'd slipped up. Things at the department had been busy lately, there'd been a step up in crime, and Raquel seemed to be working all hours of the day and night.

"What is it?" Jaims asked nervously.

Raquel noticed the look on her girlfriend's face, and she knew immediately what Jaims was thinking. Unconsciously, Raquel's hand curled around the package in her jacket pocket. Blowing her breath out, she did her best to understand that Jaims would be worried about drugs for a long time, so she needed to prove to Jaims that she was staying clean.

"I know I've been working a lot lately," Raquel said, taking Jaims' hand, "and I already know what that look is about."

Jaims drew in a sharp breath, worried that it was going to make Raquel mad. Were they about to have a nasty fight?

"I'm sorry." Jaims shook her head.

"It's okay," Raquel told her, "but I need to give you something."

Jaims blinked a couple of times, and her eyes widened when Raquel withdrew a small box out from her the pocket of her jacket. Raquel opened the box, and nestled inside was a black band with two square black diamonds set adjacent to a center square-cut emerald.

"Wow…" Jaims breathed.

Raquel grinned. "You like it?"

"It's fantastic," Jaims said, then looked back at Raquel. "What is it for?"

"Well, I'm hoping it'll suit as an engagement ring." Raquel smiled. "I'm hoping you'll marry me."

Jaims' mouth fell open in shock. She stared wide-eyed at Raquel. "You said you'd never get married."

"Well, I never thought I'd love someone so much." Raquel shrugged with an impish grin. "Go figure." Jaims continued to look shocked as she laughed. "I guess I haven't actually told you that I love you, either, huh?"

"Um, no, no you didn't." Jaims shook her head, her eyes settled back on the ring. "So that's for me?"

"Yeah, it's for you, dummy." Raquel chuckled.

"Oh, very romantic, calling me a dummy." Jaims rolled her eyes.

"I, oh, I um…" Raquel started to retreat, until she saw the grin on Jaims' face.

"Oh, shut up and say yes already!" She leaned forward kissing Jaims resoundingly on the lips.

"If you insist." Jaims laughed, holding up her hand. "Well, put it on me."

"Yes ma'am!" Raquel bit her lip as she slid the ring on Jaims' finger.

"Do I have to get you one?" Jaims asked, as she admired the ring on her finger.

"Probably," Raquel replied.

Jaims looked back at Raquel, her eyes softening, "I love you too."

"Phew!" Raquel huffed.

The night was full of great moments for Zion: hearing the announcement that Jaims and Raquel were engaged; seeing her brothers again, meeting their wives and catching up with them; celebrating with her friends. Even the surprise guests, including Wynter Kincade singing one of her latest hits, while her wife Remi LaRoché stood close by. As always, Memphis Lassiter's DJing brought everyone to the new, larger dance floor. Everyone seemed to be having a great time.

"I think you did alright here," Carl told her, as they stood next to the back bar. "You've done really well for yourself, sis."

Zion looked out over the crowd, watching her friends dance, and seeing the throng of customers at the bars, and sitting at the tables eating and drinking. "Yeah, I think it's gonna do just fine."

"Still adjusting to the whole name-change thing, though," Carl commented with a sly grin.

Zion looked up at him, seeing the grin. Reaching up she rubbed the back of her neck. "Amy just didn't fit anymore."

Carl nodded slowly, his eyes on the dancefloor surveying all the women there. "Where did you come up with Zion?"

Morgan walked up to Zion at that moment, putting her arms around Zion's waist and leaning her head against Zion's shoulder. Zion leaned down to kiss Morgan on the side of the head, hugging her tightly.

Looking back at Carl, Zion shrugged. "I guess I just went from A to Z."

Sherryl D. Hancock is from California and is the bestselling author of the lesbian romance *WeHo* series. Her books regularly touch on important topical issues such as mental health, the Don't Ask, Don't Tell policy and abuse.

You can find more on the author and her books at:
sherrylhancock.com
vulpine-press.com